THE BUSINESS OF LOVE

THE BUSINESS OF LOVE

An Eros & Co. Book

KERRI KEBERLY

Independently published
FIRST EDITION

Cover design by German Creative

For Ryan, the Eros to my Psyche.

ACKNOWLEDGMENTS

When I started this book almost four years ago, I didn't expect to finish. Truth be told, it was a test, to see if I could actually do it. And then I went and fell in love with it and here we are.

True to form, when it's time to thank everyone who has made this book what it is, I cannot for the life of me think of what to say. Here goes:

Ryan, for all the hours you gave up being with me in real life so I could spend them with imaginary people. You have supported me in more ways than one, and there aren't enough words to tell you how grateful I am. But I'll start with these three: I love you.

Mason, for recounting the story of Icarus like a boss one afternoon and making my heart soar. Thank you for being you, and making me the proudest mom ever. Also, please accept my apology for feeding you endless platefuls of pizza rolls for dinner.

Kristen Brockmeyer, my Wonder Twin and EFF, your pep talks kept me from throwing this book into the hell portal more than once. Thank you for not running for the hills when a random weirdo emailed you, strongly suggesting that you be friends with her. Because that random weirdo was me.

My Pitch Wars mentor, Laura Brown, for taking a chance on Eros and I. This book wouldn't be half of what it is today without you. Literally. Jami Nord, your vote of confidence is appreciated more than you know. Carrie Pulkinen, the other best thing I got out of Pitch Wars, for taking me under your wing. I owe you so much.

Friends and family who knew I could do it before I did: Connie, Laura, Aaron, Janell, Rebeca, Aubrey, Michelle, Jennifer, Kimberly, Mom, Dad, Carolyn, Sally, Rob, and everyone who agreed to beta read this crazy story about Cupid having a day job, thank you from the bottom of my heart.

And last, but certainly not least, Alyssa Alexander. Who knew Leos and Scorpios could make such good friends? To say I'm thankful for that fated writing retreat would be an understatement. I mean, I probably could have lived with out the prosthetic leg turned toilet paper holder, but you? Never.

CHAPTER ONE

Eros pushed open the door to Life Industries by its gilded handle and high-tailed it across the polished marble floor. He never claimed to be the promptest god, just the most romantic. But when his notoriously hot-tempered boss scheduled a performance review for 9:00 a.m. sharp, love as a forte meant crap over showing up on time.

His atrophied wings twitched as he hurried through the lobby and over to a wide stone staircase. It would be so much easier to snap his fingers. A flick of the wrist worked, too. But no, commuting to and from work using magic was forbidden. For everyone, even the Olympians. Typical Zeus. He could be a real controlling son of a Titan sometimes.

Eros pushed up the sleeve of his suit coat and checked his watch. 9:17 a.m.

Gods dammit.

Stomach in knots, he sprinted up the steps. With each tap of his shoe against hard marble, a thought popped into his head . . .

Zeus. Is. Going. To. Kill. Me.

He jostled his shoulders, flattening the feathery nubs against his back.

One crisis at a time, please.

There were more pressing things to contend with than a tantrum from his divine but withered appendages—Zeus's penchant to wield lightning, for one.

Eros loved his job—binding the hearts of mortals was a fantastic gig, truly—but it got harder and harder to drag himself into the office with every decade that passed. Because, well, a devastating breakup made it damn near impossible to bring one's A-game. Imagine that. Creating lasting love while saddled with a broken heart.

A lone peacock meandered past the front desk. Well, well, well. Look at the lucky bastard with no place to be. He'd trade places with the showy bird in a heart—scratch that. Zeus didn't need any ideas.

The receptionist quickly hung up the phone and stood. She smoothed the dark hair at her temples before pushing at the pins holding her neatly coiled chignon in place.

"Eros, darling, what are we going to do with you? You've been late every single morning for the past fifty-two years. You did know today was your review, didn't you?" She waved him in before reaching for his briefcase. "Here, give me that."

He veered toward her, handing over the cracked and worn case. "Yes, but apparently, sometimes love has horrible timing."

Her blue eyes sparkled with humor as she held out a notepad with a pen clipped to it. "Only sometimes?"

He smiled and took the proffered items. "Thanks, Leto."

Gods, when had he become such an unorganized mess? Oh right, never mind. The broken heart thing.

"Remember, let him go," she said with a dismissive wave. "You know how he hates being challenged. He'll calm down . . . eventually."

Eros nodded before turning toward the corridor that led to Zeus's office, the string of curses he'd managed to swallow falling like bricks into the pit of his stomach. Gripping the notepad for dear life he continued on, hoping he'd at least done a halfway decent job of showing no fear. Because, in reality, he had a feeling this time would be bad. Years of overtime bad. Possibly even demoted to Assistant Level bad.

There was even a chance Zeus would take away his wings. Not all gods and goddesses were blessed with them, but he had been, and they were two of his biggest defining features besides. Smallest now since, like an idiot, he'd let them waste away.

Nerves sparking like a live wire, Eros pulled in a calming breath before tapping a knuckle on the massive glass door. He'd only ever been in Zeus's office a handful of times. Once when he congratulated him on the promotion to Chief Coordinator of Hearts, and another when he personally thanked Eros for his Valentine's Day contribution to the Advancement of Love project.

Life Industries' CEO frowned at him from behind his desk. The pressed linen suit, starched shirt—both a blinding white—and metallic gold tie complemented his stiff personality to a tee. Phone pressed against his ear, he motioned with his free hand for Eros to enter.

Zeus's deep-set gray eyes narrowed, causing Eros's gut to loop. The space his boss took up was massive, and he was imposing—*intimidating*—even while sitting.

Thankful his sweaty palms didn't slip off the slick chrome handle, Eros pointed at the door, silently asking whether he should leave it opened or closed. Zeus glanced at the clock behind him before mouthing, *"Close it."*

Shit. Shit! Shit! Shit!

Zeus covered the mouthpiece with a large, ring-clad hand

and nodded toward a set of chairs stationed in front of his desk. "Have a seat."

Eros forced his legs to move, and warned his wings to remain still. He sat in one of the chairs as instructed, but instead of leaning back into the soft, supple leather, he remained at attention on the edge.

"I don't mean to cut you off, Hera, but Eros has arrived. I'm going to put you on speaker." Zeus nodded at Eros as if to say, *"get ready"* before pushing the speaker button and setting the receiver in its cradle.

Eros's heart picked up. He hadn't known Hera was going to weigh in on his performance, too.

As expected, her greeting was as warm as frozen steel. "Hello, Eros."

The hairs at the back of his neck prickled, and his response bobbed in his throat before popping out more enthusiastically than he'd intended. "Good morning, Hera."

The sound of her voice alone was enough to make him want to take off like a bat out of Hades' Realm, but the chill in it intensified the urge. Being one of the most powerful deities in the Greek pantheon, not to mention one of the most feared, she just had that effect.

Zeus sighed lightly and leaned back in his chair, no stranger to his wife's frigid demeanor. "Let's get started, shall we? We wanted to talk a little bit about your—"

"I'm sorry, Eros, but we're going to have to let you go." Hera's interruption prompted Zeus to shoot forward and grip the edge of his desk.

And Eros's notepad to fall to the floor.

"What?" He held onto the arms of his chair for support.

"Your performance has been lacking for some time," said Hera. "Your numbers have been low for decades. Divorce rates are skyrocketing."

His wings fluttered, protesting the bit about divorce rates.

"Divorce rates aren't my department. I'm Chief Coordinator of Hearts."

"My point exactly. You're the Coordinator of Hearts, yet your match output is pitiful."

He pressed his lips together to keep what he truly wanted to say from escaping. He'd worked hard to get that promotion. "It's Chief—"

"I know. *Chief* Coordinator. Titles aside, people aren't falling in love like they used to. If you do manage a deep enough connection, it's taking you longer and longer to hit your mark, which means I have less time to do my job."

He tried to get his argument out before Life Industries' Marriage Manager cut him off. "But—"

"Exactly how do you propose I make marriages work without love?" She snapped each word for maximum effect.

It worked.

The pounding in his ears intensified. She'd asked a fair question, but he wasn't sure he could answer it with any amount of satisfaction on her part. Her silence told him he better try. "Helen and Paris? I hooked those two up."

"Don't even go there. I still find it absolutely *absurd* that half-wit mortal awarded your mother the golden apple, deeming her more beautiful than me."

Ah, so that's what this was about. His mother. And the grudge Hera had been holding since losing that asinine contest centuries ago. His mother was the goddess of love—and *beauty*—for Olympus' sake. Hera should have known she wouldn't have been able to compete.

"Hera, leave Aphrodite out of this," warned Zeus.

Hera did nothing to stifle her grunt of disgust.

Eros had made countless perfect matches over the years. Surely his track record wasn't as bad as she was implying. "Cleopatra and Mark Antony. That match was rock solid."

"Need I remind you how that ended?" Zeus clasped his

fingers together and tilted his head, one of his thick, white eyebrows arching. "He stabbed himself with a sword."

Not to be outdone, Hera pointed out the rest of history. "And she let a venomous snake bite her so they could be together in death."

And your point is?

He'd hit his mark. It was Octavian who'd marched his army into Alexandria and messed things up. It wasn't his fault the two lovebirds ended their lives with a suicide pact. He opened his mouth to say as much, but Zeus shook his head. The instruction was clear. Abandon the argument, and fast.

Eros complied, but it didn't stop the anger from sparking at the base of his skull, threatening to ignite. He was being forced to let a perfectly valid point go, and it sat with him about as well as an empty box of donuts. The good kind. The cake ones, with sprinkles.

He had pride, like any other god, and he didn't appreciate it being wounded.

He shifted in his chair, his composure even closer to unraveling. But he couldn't lose it. Not here, not now. His job was on the line and going head-to-head with Hera wasn't on the top of his list of fun things to do. Never mind that it wasn't a very smart hill to die on. "I appreciate your concern, and I admit, my performance has been lacking lately—"

"Lately?"

He could only imagine how far back her head jerked in disdain. Enough to derail the Zen he was trying to keep. "I know my contribution has been low for a while now." Embarrassment warmed his face. Low for a while was an understatement.

Mortal belief and worship were their ambrosia, and Zeus had created Life Industries to ensure they didn't run out. They all had day jobs, to do their part in turning the intangible into the very real—and rather delicious—nectar of the gods that kept them from fading away.

But Hera was right; his heart hadn't been in it for a long time. His job performance had more than slipped over the years, and he couldn't deny it. Fine, maybe he didn't have an argument. Maybe he was pitiful.

The next thing from his mouth tumbled out before his brain got a chance to approve it. "The split with Psyche was really tough on me."

Zeus cleared his throat. "I heard about that. I thought making her immortal would be a good thing. I didn't know it would lead to . . ." He paused before continuing, trying to be sensitive. Failing, he barreled on like a dump truck in a nitroglycerin factory. "Regardless, I think you may be burned out. Perhaps we should lighten your load for a while. Take a few responsibilities off your back—"

"I'm not burned out, I swear! My responsibilities are fine!" Eros's voice climbed an octave with every word at the realization he had no plan B.

On top of beauty, his mother was more than adept at every aspect of love, particularly pleasure. He had no other skill set with which to bargain. Except, perhaps, romance. But he knew Hera would only say romance was dead.

And if he didn't get his act together real quick-like, it truly would be.

Zeus stared, waiting, while Eros regained some semblance of self-control. Perhaps it would be better to appeal to Zeus's sympathetic side, virtually nonexistent as it was. The fact that Eros was still sitting there, intact, gave him hope. Gods knew, it was a miracle he wasn't already wingless by now.

Eros opened his mouth, but Hera didn't give him the chance to speak. "Face it, your passion for love walked out the door with Psyche."

He clamped his lips shut and stiffened, the impact of the low blow somehow much harder through the phone line. He believed in patience and kindness, and had been prepared to take his lumps and agree to a lengthy hiatus, but she was rubbing salt in his wound on purpose now. No, worse than that, she was going for the jugular. His chest tightened, anger pushing against it, begging to be released for one glorious moment of white-hot rage.

He twisted his back once, twice, just far enough to coax the tension there to loosen. He might not be one of the strongest gods, or have been bestowed the longest list of gifts, but he sure as the Underworld didn't want to lose what little he had. He'd keep his cool and promise to put the break up behind him. Swear to give one hundred and ten percent from here on out.

And give Hera zero satisfaction.

Pride shored up his nerve, and he squared his shoulders. His wings trembled in response, asking him, *"Are we really doing this?"* The sharp stabbing in his temples increased, but he ignored the pain. Yes, they were going to do this. His tongue darted out over his bottom lip. "Let's be honest. This isn't really about my performance, is it?"

They might be ganging up on him, but no one said he couldn't fight back by tossing Hera's inability to fix the cracks in her own marriage in her face. The silence that followed his cheap shot was palpable, indicating the goddess of marriage and fidelity understood exactly what he was getting at. Passively aggressive, of course, since assertively aggressive was out of the question.

Per usual, he realized his ill-conceived revilement was a mistake much too late.

Thunder rumbled in the distance and Zeus's office darkened. Nostrils flared, he zapped Eros with a look filled with murderous intention. A painful tingling shot through his limbs, the gathering electricity in the air humming with deadly consequences. He cringed at the thought of being burnt to a crisp, and suddenly his brave-a-second-ago lungs refused to pull in air.

As if the ominous gathering of storm clouds visible from the windows wasn't proof enough of Zeus's power, several bolts of lightning flung themselves down from the sky. His infidelities were not open for debate, let alone to be used as ammunition against Hera. Another round of thunder boomed and echoed, driving the point home.

Eros bowed his head in deference to the king of gods sitting before him. It didn't take a fool to guess Hera knew he'd backed down. The confirmation by way of a snicker from the other end of the phone made his teeth grind.

Gods, she is such a b—He squeezed his eyes shut and forced himself to breathe—*Think about something else. Think about . . .*

Psyche popped into his head. Had it been four and a half decades already? It seemed like only yesterday he'd found that letter.

Dear Eros . . .

Curse that damned letter. It had been the beginning of the end. His end. He used to be a god with purpose. Now look at him, twitchy nubs for wings and begging for his job.

He waited until his breathing slowed, and he had more control over his trembling wings, before opening his eyes. Breath and wings now steady, he fixed his gaze on Zeus while taking a moment to choose his next words carefully. A different approach was in order. Perhaps the confident and irrefutable might work. "Look, I'm the only one who can do this job. I know all the files, inside and out."

"You mean these files?" Zeus passed a hand over the massive heap on his desk. "They're in shambles. When is the last time you've opened some of these things?" He slipped on a pair of reading glasses before flipping through several manila folders stuffed with paperwork.

Eros swallowed hard. He didn't have a clue, but if he had to guess, he'd say sometime before the joy of marital bliss had turned into a daily struggle to do his job with a heart that had gone through a paper shredder. In lieu of an acceptable answer, he asked a question. "Who would you even get to replace me?"

Zeus scrubbed a hand over his chin, smoothing his already neatly trimmed beard. "I'm considering Artemis."

"Absolutely not," snapped Hera.

Eros flinched, fully expecting some sort of poisonous goo to ooze out of the speaker.

Undeterred, Zeus answered with authority. "Then Dionysus."

Eros hadn't expected to hear *that*. "The god of wine? No offense, Dion is a nice guy and everything, but he's a mess. There's no way love will last beyond the next morning." He clamped his lips together to stop any more defiance from escaping. But to his amazement, Zeus agreed.

"Right. Well then, Apollo."

Eros inhaled sharply through his nose, struggling to keep calm as a tsunami of panic crashed over him. "With all due respect, sir, I know he's your most esteemed son, but he doesn't know the first thing about love."

Or humility.

"He's right. Especially with this whole Daphne business still going on. No on Apollo," said Hera, her tone final.

Eros blew out his relief. He regretted his part in how things had turned out between Apollo and Daphne, he would admit that, but even so, he couldn't bear the thought of being replaced by that arrogant ass.

"Hera," Zeus began, but stopped when the phone started to vibrate. This time, something did come out of the speaker.

Steam hissed as it punched through the tiny holes until the phone rattled and screamed like a teapot ready to blow.

Eros held his breath, in case the steam was actually poisoned gas, and ducked out of the way, leaning down and on the edge of his chair. It was the best possible position to dodge shrapnel should the thing explode.

"He's in love with a tree for Olympus' sake!" bellowed Hera, the phone lifting off the desk and wobbling in the air before dropping back down with a *thud*.

Zeus dragged in a breath, so deep it seemed to go on for ages. When he sighed, it took just as long. "Fine, but, whether you want to admit it or not, we both know he's exceptional at everything. There's no doubt in my mind he could take care of this . . . disarray." Zeus pointed to the mountain of paperwork on his desk.

Hera's telephonic instrument of rage sat still. Too still. Calm-before-the-storm still. In the tense silence, a thought Eros had managed to push out of his mind came back, full force, making the throbbing in his head worse. It made sense now, why the punishment didn't seem to fit the crime, and he knew exactly what Hera was angling to do.

Zeus stared at him again, this time with an even more grave expression etched across his face. "I'm assuming, Hera, you're pushing for a demotion to Mortal Status?"

Eros braced himself for the answer he knew she would give.

"I am."

He shook his head. Not in disbelief—her lack of empathy was no shock—but at her utter hatred and dogged determination to destroy his mother's world. Hera wasn't pushing, she was shoving. The best way to get back at his mother was to destroy her beloved son.

His dry, scratchy throat burned as he croaked out the horrible words. "If I become a mortal, I'll eventually die."

Vile and bitter-tasting though they were, he had to say them out loud. His consequence must be clear. There was no room for error, no time for assumptions.

"That is correct."

Eros rubbed his forehead, the stabbing in his temples sharpening. In fact, the tiny daggers were now also piercing his gut. Truth be told, he could handle losing his job. He could even accept living out the rest of his life as a mortal. What terrified him wasn't being forced to forfeit his power to bind hearts. It wasn't even the thought of one day ceasing to exist. Not only would his mother suffer unfathomable loss, so would he. He'd lose the chance to win back the love of his life's heart.

Psyche.

The pressure coiled within his body—fists, in particular—was dangerously close to springing loose. But instead, he took another deep breath, unclenched his teeth and unfurled his hands so he could calmly place them in his lap. No wonder he had a headache.

Powder keg of emotion notwithstanding, exploding in a fit of rage would do him no good. He was no match for Hera, and would definitely lose should her burly husband fire up the old lightning bolts. The only thing he could do now was convince Zeus to give him another chance.

Eros sat straighter in an attempt to appear less rattled than he felt. "You can't do this."

He'd addressed Zeus, but Hera answered, "He can and he will."

"Hera, I'll hear him out."

"I misspoke," said Eros. "*Please* don't do this."

"I don't know that you've left me with much of a choice." Zeus nodded toward the phone.

"You do have a choice. You're the CEO of Life Industries. Ruler of the Gods . . . Destroyer of the Titans." Laying it on thick, Eros played to Zeus's immense ego. "Give me another chance. By your grace, I will not fail. Love is all I know."

Hera scoffed. "I can't stand all this groveling. I'm hanging up now. Zeus, you know where I stand. My vote is for an immediate demotion. I trust you'll make the right decision."

The line disconnected with a *click*.

Eros could do nothing but remain silent as his boss shuffled through the files in front of him. He had made his case. He'd be a fool to risk ruining his chance at redemption, if he even had one, by opening his mouth again while the god of gods mulled over his decision.

Zeus's groan rumbled in his chest. "You've got a target on your back when it comes to Hera. This nonsense has been going on ever since that kerfuffle with her and Aphrodite. She's been biding her time, and today you gave her the excuse she's needed to get rid of you for good. She got you on a technicality, my boy." Zeus pursed his lips before pinning him to the receiving end of a knowing look.

Eros dropped his gaze. Zeus was right. Hera had the patience of a Christian saint, even though she wasn't anything close to one. Even worse, *she* was right. He'd let love slip through the cracks, in more ways than one. He hadn't been pulling his weight, and now he'd be the pawn she would use to finally take her revenge.

A few moments of awkward silence stretched themselves into several agonizing minutes before Zeus pulled out a folder. "But you've always been a good kid," he said, tossing it onto the end of his desk. "Here's the Johnson/Simmons account. Close it, and you can stay."

Eros fought the urge to sink deeper into his chair. He might as well hand over his wings right then and there. Because those two words—Johnson and Simmons—turned any relief he felt into complete and utter despair. Any hope his plight was one of Phobetor's nightmarish practical jokes, meant to scare his time management skills into proper working order, was also gone.

The Johnson/Simmons account was the single worst account on Earth, with the two most stubborn clients ever. He'd been unsuccessful in matching Elizabeth Johnson and Leopold Simmons for over three hundred years, over multiple lifetimes. At this point, neither of them believed in love anymore. It would be a Herculean feat just to get them to *like* each other, let alone fall in love.

The squirming between his shoulder blades pitched him back and forth in his seat. Swallowing another round of panic, he asked a question on their behalf. "You're not going to take away my wings, are you?"

Zeus regarded him carefully as he cupped his bearded chin, trapping some of the long white hairs between his fingers before tugging. "No, but I am suspending your powers." He held up his hand when Eros's eyes widened. "When you're at the top of your game, you contribute a substantial amount to our survival. It would be a shame to see you demoted. However, Hera is going to go apeshit when she finds out I gave you a second chance, so you're not allowed to use your powers for anything except entering and exiting the mortal world. Oh, and before you're ready to strike. Is that clear?"

"Yes, sir." Eros nodded, but his mind had moved on to other, more concerning thoughts. "How long do I have?"

"Six months." Before the words had a chance to sink in, Zeus dealt another blow. "Mortal time. I want this thing wrapped up sooner rather than later."

Stunned, Eros craned his neck forward. "Mortal time?" He'd be lucky if he could close the Johnson/Simmons account in six mortal *years*. Time on Mount Olympus didn't move as fast as it did down on Earth. To the gods, mortal time passed much more quickly. “Sir, there’s no way I can close this account in that amount of time.”

Zeus leaned forward and rested his elbows on the edge of this desk, his fingers steepled with impatience. “Hera’s got one foot on the war path, and we all know what it’s like when she’s halfway down the damned thing.” Zeus dropped back in his chair and folded his arms, confirming there was no other compromise he was willing to offer. “My hands are tied. I love her, but she’s hell on wheels, my boy. Hell. On. Wheels.”

Protest bubbled up and out before Eros could stop it. “So you want to keep the peace, and I’m the sacrificial lamb.”

Zeus drew up his broad, barrel chest and peered at him over the top of his glasses. His office began to darken again. “I can get Dionysus in here as early as tomorrow.”

“No, no.” Eros’s hands flew up in surrender, hoping to abate the electricity crackling and snapping in the air. “I appreciate the second chance, sir. I won’t mess this up. I promise.”

Dear gods on Mount Olympus. If his ability to keep this promise turned out to be anything like his ability to be on time, he’d be doomed.

CHAPTER TWO

Eros clawed at his necktie. Air. He needed more air. He might even need a drink.

The *clack* of hard-soled dress shoes bounced and echoed off the corridor walls. Out of habit, he reached for his cell phone, but caught himself and stopped. The walls were made of ancient stone, fit together and mortared a millennium ago. They did nothing for cell reception. Likewise, the sconces burning at even intervals were mostly for show, since they failed to lend any real warmth.

Who did he think he was going to call, anyway?

He clutched the Johnson/Simmons file for moral support as he scurried down the cavernous hallway. Life Industries' partners—and Zeus's fellow Olympians—glared down at him from their enormous gilded portraits lining the wall. All but his mother and his best friend, Hermes, who'd quit the corporate rat race centuries ago to freelance from home. They smiled at him, but the others, with their stern brows and pursed lips, scrutinized him, as if they already knew how much he had screwed up.

Engrossed in another phone conversation, Leto gave him the perfect opportunity to slip by her and duck down a side hall. He hurried past a half dozen sets of fluted columns before entering the Department of Love. Once safely at his cubicle, he threw the heavy folder onto his desk. What he'd give to rewind this day, the last fifty-two years, in fact, and make more of an effort.

He shrugged out of his suit coat and hung it up before sinking into his office chair with a huff, the low buzz of fluorescent lighting filling the silence. Maybe he could schedule a meeting with Chronos, the god of time.

Who was he kidding? If it hadn't been his punctuality, Hera would have zeroed in on his marksmanship. His aim *had* gotten a little shoddy over the years. More than a little. It would have come to this eventually.

His shriveled wings spasmed at the revelation, prompting him to lean over, rip down one of the inspirational quotes he'd pinned to the gray fabric walls, and throw it into the trash. It would take more than a positive affirmation printed on a piece of paper to pull this off.

Lost in thought, he flinched when Leto stuck her head into his cube and held up his briefcase. "You forgot something."

"Thank you." Eros eyed the Swarovski Crystal-encrusted belt around her waist as he took his case. "Nice belt. Goes great with those strappy heels. Are those new?"

Her belt was quite fashionable for a goddess of her age, but she'd only come fishing for details. There couldn't be a worse time for him to be dealing with the goddess of gossip than right now.

He needed to review that file.

"They are!" Her face flushed with excitement as she lifted up the hem of her simple linen peplos to the middle of her shin. She proceeded to stick out her foot and pivot her ankle so he could take in the full glory of the metallic leather. "Jimmy Choo."

"You know, a Diane von Furstenberg wrap dress would be killer with those."

Leto dropped the skirt of her classic Greek dress and crinkled her nose. "I don't know. I think I prefer my old tried and true."

A smile curled his lips. She'd taken the bait. "Not ready to accept the long list of merits a rayon spandex blend can offer?" He chuckled, dialing up the charm. "Come on, Leto, it's the twenty-first century. You'd look great in a wrap dress."

She grinned and cocked her head to one side. "It's such a shame."

He knew exactly what was coming next.

"You know, it just boggles my mind no one's snapped you up yet."

There it was. *You're too sweet to be single.* A sentiment he wholeheartedly agreed with, naturally, but the truth of the matter was he didn't have the power to control his own love life. If he did, he wouldn't be a bachelor.

His relationship status wasn't a secret among the Mount Olympus crowd, but he didn't care to discuss it. Not now, and especially not after his brush with unemployment that morning. He preferred to keep pretending otherwise, even though his breakup was still a sore spot. And how in Hades' Realm had the subject gone from wrap dresses to his love life so quickly?

Apparently he wasn't as good at distraction as he thought. Great, something else he could add to the growing list of things he was horrible at.

He winked, hoping she'd notice the gesture was forced and take a hint. "Too busy being Mr. Matchmaker, I guess." He followed up with his trademark lopsided grin. At the very least, maybe he could disarm her into silence with his boyish good looks. "Oh, hey, can you please order some more printer paper? We're running low." Desperation to steer the conversation toward a more workplace appropriate and less personal, soul-crushing direction clipped his tone.

"I've already ordered a case, but you'll have to pick it up from receiving yourself. I'll be on vacation all next week."

"Vacation?" asked Eros, a bit confused. Leto never missed work. How else could she keep on top of everyone's business than work 3,650 days a decade?

She rolled her eyes. "Hera is coming in on Thursday for the staff meeting. Heaven *forbid* I'm anywhere near this place when she's around."

"That's right, you and Hera . . . She . . . still hates you, doesn't she?" he stammered before blurting out the obvious.

Hera didn't come in often, thank the fellow gods—she liked to work from her remote office, *Hera & Associates,* most of the time—but it was more than any of them would like. Of course Leto wouldn't want to be reminded of the necessity to be absent whenever Hera came storming into Life Industries.

He cringed when her face blanched. "That was insensitive. I'm sorry, I don't know what came over me."

It's okay, darling," said Leto, the color returning to her face. "It's true, after all. I slept with her husband, and she wants to tear me from limb to limb, even after all these years."

The image of Leto being dismembered by a jealousy-fueled Hera, pupils nothing more than pinpoints of rage, flashed through his mind. He gulped as the image of Hera ripping *him* apart took over.

When it came to revenge, Hera was the worst. Zeus at least heard one's side of the story before exacting punishment. Hera? Not so much. The only thing that kept her from leaving a trail of godly body parts across Mount Olympus was her husband's status as absolute ruler.

He gathered himself and casually rested his arms on the top of his desk, hoping the increased airflow would help with the dampness beginning to form under his arms. He'd come closer to being torn asunder that morning—albeit, with much less bloodshed—than he was ready to admit.

"I mean, I guess I can see her point, but it was, what, over four millennia ago now?" Leto continued, turning up a palm. "Everyone knows my relationship with Zeus is strictly platonic. Well, now it is, anyway. Besides, it's not like it wasn't legit. I was his sixth wife for crying out loud. She should really try and let bygones be bygones, for Artemis and Apollo's sake, you know?"

"Right." Eros pulled his laptop out of his briefcase. He wasn't friendly with either of Leto and Zeus's offspring, but he was nothing if not polite. "How are the twins doing, anyway?"

"Oh, they're good. Apollo is busy as ever."

Eros tried not to roll his eyes as he stifled a groan. "And Artemis?"

The conversation was officially out of his control, and yet he kept throwing wood onto the fire. Sometimes he hated his own politeness.

"Artemis is Artemis. I swear that girl is never going to get married." She arched a brow. "Unless she meets Mr. Right . . ."

"Now, Leto." Eros forced a chuckle. "I'm Mr. Matchmaker, remember? I'm far from being Mr. Right."

Just ask Psyche.

"But you both like archery."

"Artemis likes hardcore outdoorsy stuff, and I'm a stay-in-and-watch-a-rom-com sort of guy."

She nodded her head and sighed. "You're right. I know

Arti's destined to be alone, and it's what she wants, but I'm holding out hope for god babies at *some* point. It doesn't hurt to try."

"I can see about setting her up with someone else if you'd like." He racked his brain for a suitable match for Artemis. No one came to mind.

"That's okay. She'd probably disown me if she knew I was even asking. Besides, it's not like that grudge holder Hera would support a union anyway." Leto paused before tilting an ear forward and leaning farther into his cube. "So, not to change the subject or anything, but how did your performance review go?"

Eros plastered on a smile and stood, counting on his acting chops being better than his diversion skills. "It was a little iffy at the beginning, but I let him go and he sputtered out, just like you said he would. Thanks for the advice."

She eyed him suspiciously as he slipped past her and headed toward the kitchenette. The scent of roasted coffee beans was strong, but his need to end the conversation was stronger. Besides, if he wasn't mistaken, he detected a hint of glazed donuts permeating the air as well.

Once back at his desk, Eros set his cell phone down and removed a donut from the top of his coffee mug. Fragrant steam rose as he pondered his next move. The promise of a sweet coffee buzz coaxed his lips toward the rim of his favorite mug—red with little pink and white hearts—for a sip.

He'd have to work offsite, obviously, but then what?

Eros took a bite of donut before plunking down in his chair. The Johnson/Simmons folder, thick and daunting, taunted him, and the longer he looked at it, the stronger the urge became to swipe it off his desk. It would be satisfying, to see the papers go flying, but he'd have more of a mess to clean up. He'd also have to set down his donut.

He settled for sipping his coffee, the conversation he'd had with Zeus earlier clanging like a cacophony of too-loud bells in his head.

"Hera is going to go apeshit."

"I am suspending your powers."

"Six months . . . Mortal time."

Things were already bad, but this deadline was going to make them so much worse.

He followed up his latest sip of cream, sugar and a splash of coffee with a bite of donut. His mind raced from the caffeine and processed sugar. Everything else twitched from anxiety. There was no time to procrastinate any longer. He set down his mug and opened the file.

ACCOUNT: Johnson/Simmons
MATCH# : 81572101219759107
STATUS: Active/Pending

CLIENT: Elizabeth Johnson
LOCATION: Seattle, WA, U.S.

LIFETIME 1: Match incomplete. Retry granted. Revised by: Clotho

LIFETIME 2: Match incomplete. In order to expedite the closure of this account and decrease inefficiencies displayed by Life Industries, this client's fate has been revised to include a shorter lifespan. The client must be matched before the age of twenty-five from this point forward. Revised by: Lachesis

LIFETIME 3: Match incomplete. Fate revised to include

tragic childhood, ensuring mistrust of men and the avoidance of feelings. What's the deal with your aim, matchmaker? Revised by: Atropos

LIFETIME 4: TBD

Eros took another bite of his donut before thumbing through the papers to find his second client's profile. He swallowed, then forced himself to scan the paper, nervous of what he might find.

ACCOUNT: Johnson/Simmons
MATCH#: 81572101219759107
STATUS: Active/Pending

CLIENT: Leopold Simmons
LOCATION: London, England, UK

LIFETIME 1: Match incomplete. Retry granted. Revised by: Clotho

LIFETIME 2: Match incomplete. As previously stated in corresponding client's file, inefficiencies have occurred that affect this client's fate. Fate revised to include multiple insecurities and an extreme aversion to commitment. Revised by: Lachesis

LIFETIME 3: Match incomplete. Fate revised to now include the loss of a parent, ensuring insecurities and extreme aversion to commitment are heightened. Get it together, matchmaker. This is your final revision. Revised by: Atropos

LIFETIME 4: TBD

Eros cradled his forehead in his hand. That's right. His clients' lives had been revised by the Fates, the all-knowing beings who weaved, measured and cut the threads of destiny —even Zeus's—making them untouchable. They didn't answer to any god or abide by any rules, and those who interfered with their business, or worse, created more work for them like Eros had, could pretty much kiss any hope of getting help saving their job goodbye. They weren't three of the most feared businesswomen on Mount Olympus for nothing.

He dug a thumb into his temple. He hadn't had any illusions it would be easy closing the Johnson/Simmons account, but looking through the hot mess sprawled out in front of him, it was evident he had blocked out the worst of it.

He reached for his phone and double tapped the calendar icon. At least a month to get them in the same city, maybe even two. That would bring him to the end of April. One month to get them to notice each other. May. That left him with three months of dating, which, judging by the revisions the Fates had made, wouldn't be enough time. In order to hit his mark, and make love last, he'd need Liz Johnson's heart free of any and all obstacles. Her defenses had to be down.

All the way down.

He swallowed around the lump forming in his throat. The walls she put up would make his job difficult, yes, but there was an even bigger problem. In her current lifetime, Liz's birthday was in August, right smack in the middle of August, and approaching in less time than he'd been granted.

August 15 was the day she would die, taking his immortality with her.

He put his phone down and selected a pen from the coffee mug that served as a penholder. He twirled it between his fingers while he glanced at the paperwork to check their current locations. The pen skittered across his desk. She was in Seattle, and he was thousands of miles and an ocean away in London. Eros grabbed his phone again and began typing out a text.

Eros: You got time to do me a solid?
Hermes: Sure. What's up?
Eros: Meet me in my mom's office in ten
Hermes: K

Nervous energy propelled his knee up and down. He needed to get to Earth ASAP. This show had to be on the road now or he'd be doomed to wander the mortal world aimlessly until, how did they put it? Until he kicked the bucket.

Stripped of his powers. How embarrassing. Grow old and die. Sad. Never again lay eyes on the love of his life?

Oh, gods.

He shoved the papers back into the file and slid his chair away from his desk. He stuffed the rest of his donut into his mouth and washed it down with the last of his coffee before scooping up the file and heading to the Hall of Olympians.

He flashed his work badge at the Spartan warriors guarding the entrance and hurried down the covered arcade. When he came to an office door painted a deep, rich red brandishing a rose-shaped brass knocker, he shuffled the Johnson/Simmons folder into the crook of an elbow and tapped the small loop of metal against its base. It was more of a courtesy than anything, since the door was already ajar. The Director of Love had an open-door policy.

His mother's office resembled the sitting room of a French chateau, with mahogany paneling, luxurious crimson and gold damask wallpaper, and gilded frames artfully arranged to display paintings of lovers in various states of undress.

"Bonjour, mon chéri." She had started speaking with an accent long ago, when her proposal for French as the official language of love had been approved. She came around her desk to greet him, her hands settling on his shoulders as she leaned in to deliver a quick peck to each cheek.

He raked the fingers of his free hand through his hair before balling it into a fist and sliding it into a pocket of his dress pants. There was no time to mince words. "I'll be working in the field effective immediately."

"Oh?" She took a step back, the smooth skin of her forehead wrinkling. "Why is that?"

"I need to bind two very specific hearts or I lose my job."

His mother let out a small gasp, her mouth dropping open. An instant later her aquamarine eyes narrowed down to slits. "Hera?"

His gaze shot up toward the crystal chandelier, down to the grand fireplace, over to the sixteenth century armoire—anywhere but toward his mother. This was his fault. He couldn't bear to look her in the eyes, afraid of what he might find there. What if he saw anger . . . or worse yet, disappointment?

"That *vache,*" she said under her breath.

He tossed the file down on an end table sporting ornately scrolled legs. "Cow?" His whole body began to tremble, fury filling him like a well.

She shrugged. "Well, if the shoe fits."

His throat burned with anger as the words spewed from his mouth. "Try gods-damned harpy!"

How could he have been so stupid? It had been him who'd given old snake eyes the opportunity to strike. Frustration churned in his belly, but he closed his eyes and drew in a deep breath.

Be the light, man. Don't let your dark side show.

Love was supposed to be kind, not an angsty dick.

His mother ignored his outburst and motioned for him to sit in one of the two large wing-backed chairs upholstered in red crushed velvet. If there was one person who understood his struggle to keep his temper in check, from lashing out at the ones he loved most, it was his mother. She knew who he'd gotten the propensity from well. His father, Ares. The god of war. "How will you get these two hearts together, *chéri*?"

He reeled in his anger, sank into one of the plush chairs and shook his head. "I don't know yet."

His mother also sat, and with a wave of her hand two steaming cups of lavender herbal tea appeared on top of the folder. Her hands shook the tiniest bit as she reached for one of the cups. They both knew Zeus, as fair as he considered himself to be, would turn him mortal on principle, to appease Hera.

He picked up the other cup of tea and took a tentative sip. It did nothing to calm him. Dozens of vases filled with red roses adorned the room, their fragrance infusing the air. He inhaled, but the familiar scent, which was soothing under normal circumstances, also did nothing.

He set his tea down and stood, walking over to a row of large windows, each framed with heavy silk brocade, and peering out at a view of the Paris skyline at night. It was an illusion, of course, but the Eiffel Tower was lit up in the distance and the scene before him was no less breathtaking than the real thing. He tucked an arm under one elbow and crooked a finger over his top lip as he ran through all the different ways to fall in love.

Schoolyard crush . . .

Love at first sight . . .

College roommates . . .

Friends to lovers . . .

Enemies to . . .

He spun on his heels toward his mother. "Forced proximity. That's how I'm going to do it. That's how I'm going to get Liz and Leo together."

"That's certainly one option." She set her teacup down. Her hands no longer trembled, but only because she was now clasping them together in her lap. She was keeping a pretense of calm for his sake. Hera might not have power over Zeus, but she had influence, and lots of it.

Hermes breezed into the room. "What's an option? And who are Liz and Leo?" Unlike Eros, the UPS man of the gods possessed perfect timing.

Eros eased back down into his chair. "The two mortals I need to bind, like yesterday. It's a long story. I'll fill you in later, but I'm going to get them together by orchestrating an office romance."

"How ambitious of you." Hermes shot Eros an inquisitive look as he strolled over to the settee across from the chairs and took a seat. "Who's going to cover for you while you're out?"

Thank the fellow gods Hermes never forgot to read the fine print.

"I will." His mother rose from her chair with her characteristic grace and glided over to Eros. She smoothed an errant curl before patting him on the cheek, the loving gesture finally succeeded in calming him down. "Because the thought of losing you forever, *chéri*, terrifies me. You must close this account, and I must help you in any way I can. If that means working my *derriere* off while you are away, then that is what I'll do."

His heart swelled as he pushed himself to his feet and wrapped his mother in a hug. "Thanks, Mom. But are you sure?"

"Please, *mon chéri*, have you forgotten who I am?" She leaned back and directed her attention to the enormous, yet elegantly curved bow standing of its own accord in a sparkling glass case. "I'm the goddess of love. I have been showering intense feelings of deep affection on this world since before you were flitting around in diapers."

True. She was Aphrodite, one of the most revered goddesses he knew. She could handle anything, with one arm tied behind her back. Well, anything but Hera's insatiable need for revenge, he was afraid. No one could escape that.

Hermes cleared his throat. "This Liz and Leo, they're worlds apart, yes? And I take it that's the reason you require my delivery services?"

"Yep. You in?"

Hermes' sea green eyes, dazzling by all accounts, twinkled with good nature. "Of course I'm in, matchmaker."

Eros smiled. For such a shitty situation, things seemed to be coming together. He hoped they continued along the same trajectory during the next phase of the plan. "Okay, good, because I also need you to come up with my new name. I have a feeling Cupid's not going to cut it."

CHAPTER THREE

If Liz Johnson's eyes could roll any farther back into her head, she would do it in a heartbeat. Thomas, her co-worker in the next cube over, was in the middle of a NSFW conversation, which not only made him sound like a love-struck idiot, but also a total creep.

"What do you say, sweets? Maybe we can try a little whipped cream this time, you know, right down the middle? I know you like it when I . . ."

"Jesus Christ, Thomas. Seriously? Haven't you ever heard of sexting?" Liz yelled over the partition before grabbing the ear buds she wished were noise-cancelling headphones.

No. Just, no. She'd remain single, thank you very much. Especially if it meant no one would call her "sweets" and tell her where she liked her whipped cream. Not that she was opposed to whipped cream. It was the other part she detested. Opening up. Being vulnerable. Giving her heart away for what? To be let down?

Been there. Done that.

The faint rustle of paper sounded right before she nestled her ear buds into place. What was the point of sending her hardcopies of support tickets to file in this day and age of technology? She grumbled as she hooked the cords around her neck and wheeled her chair the short distance to the company-issued implement of torture labeled "INBOX."

It held a single envelope.

She snatched it up and inspected the heavy pound parchment paper, moving a finger over the embossed winged-foot logo. A faint smile pushed her lips upward. Maybe she'd been nominated for some kind of employee of the month thing and had gotten free tickets to some show. She bit her bottom lip, excited by the prospect. She might not be the most approachable employee, but no one could say she wasn't a hard worker.

She dragged herself back toward the small section of desk where she did most of her work and pulled open one of the storage drawers. A ruler, staple remover and paperclips, but no letter opener. Impatient, she tore off the edge of the envelope and squeezed the creased edges, opening a pocket for easier access to her tickets. Except, the envelope didn't contain tickets.

Dear Ms. Johnson,

Due to cutbacks, we regret to inform you that your employment with Star Crossed Records has been terminated effective immediately. Thank you for your service, and the commitment to our IT Department you have shown during your employment with us.

Management

Wait a minute, did she just get fired? She blinked a few times before reading it again, discovering not a single word had changed from the first time she'd read it.

She crumpled the letter and launched it. The ball of parchment paper bounced off her computer monitor, landed on her keyboard and tumbled back down onto her desk. This was not happening. She pushed her dark-framed glasses higher onto the bridge of her nose. This. Was. Not. Happening.

She needed to occupy her hands, or else her keyboard was in real danger of taking up sailing. Through the air. She blew her bangs out of her face and knotted her hair into a messy bun at the top of her head.

Her chest itched, but she ignored the ugly red splotches she knew were creeping up her neck. Hives. Her body's delightful way of announcing to everyone around her that she was embarrassed, nervous, or like right now, super pissed. Scratching only made them worse. She placed a hand on the ball of paper, curled her fingers around it and squeezed.

10 . . . 9 . . . Stay calm . . . 8 . . . This is your place of employment.

Correction. It *used to be* her place of employment. And they were kicking her to the curb, just like everyone else.

7 . . . 6, 5, 4, fuck it.

Her chair flew backward, hitting the padded wall of her tiny cubicle. She marched down the hall—balled up letter in hand—and into her boss's office. She didn't bother to knock, nor did she feel bad about it. Zero effs given was her *modus operandi.*

A real chip off the old block, huh, Dad?

She dropped the mangled piece of paper onto her boss's desk. "What the hell, Doug!"

He picked up the letter and smoothed it out. She watched his gaze move across the page before the color drained from his face. "What? You're the best IT tech we have. I don't know why they'd be letting *you* go." He lowered his voice. "They should be letting Thomas go. He has no clue what he's doing."

"Not to mention he's a creeper." She folded her tattooed arms, let her weight fall to one hip and stared at him from the other side of his desk. "So, you're going to pretend like you didn't know, then?"

"I didn't." He handed the crinkled paper back to her.

She reached over and swiped it out of his hand. "You're telling me a little birdie flew into the office, dropped off a pink slip and then flew back out?" How stupid did he think she was?

"I don't know, maybe. But I'm telling you, I had nothing to do with it. I had no idea this was coming. I swear."

She pinned him to his seat with dagger eyes. After a few moments of uncomfortable silence, she spun toward his bookshelf. Instead of reading material, it was lined with *Star Wars* memorabilia. His office was full of it. Posters, figurines, life-sized cardboard cutouts—if it had anything to do with *Star Wars*, Doug Hamilton owned it.

She wrinkled her nose. There was also the faint smell of Cool Ranch Doritos mixed with gamer sweat. "I moved here for this job, you know." She plucked a collectible drinking glass off the shelf and inspected it with feigned interest. "I've worked my ass off for two years. *Two years*, Doug."

He vacated his chair and hurried over to remove the glass from her hand. Having secured the precious item, he returned it to its place of honor on the shelf. "I don't know, Liz. I really don't. I'm hoping this is a clerical error. You know, like, your name got on the wrong list or something." He wedged himself between her and the bookshelf to deny her any further access to his highly prized, highly breakable possessions.

"Oh, okay. Right. Like Human Resources is going to mess that up." She breezed toward his desk full of bobble-headed figurines. It was only right to make him sweat. There was no way he didn't know about this. "Maybe I need to make a trip down to see them myself. What do you think about that?" He flinched when she spun around to face him.

"I think that m-might be a good idea. M-m-maybe they can help s-sort this out."

Pity tweaked her gut, and the memory of standing before her father, his face contorted with loathing while she stammered out a response, loosened her shoulders. Maybe Doug was telling the truth. She always had been. "Fine."

She was rough around the edges, a fact her mother pointed out all too often, but she didn't do it on purpose. Okay, she did, but she had a good reason. Trust wasn't her strong suit. Her father had taken that ability with him when he left. Her mother of all people should know what that was like.

"I'm sorry. I really am." Doug's gaze flicked to the inked designs on her arms before back to her face. He opened his mouth to say something else but closed it again, resembling a fish out of water. A fish out of water about to jump from the frying pan and into the fire.

She tried to scoot out the door before he could say anything else. She'd never learned how sympathy worked. Though, as foreign as it felt, she thought she might be feeling a little bit of it at the moment, and she didn't want what she'd managed to eke out of her blackened soul to be for nothing. Because honestly? Caring was exhausting.

"Liz, wait." She turned in time to see the rather pronounced Adam's apple on his skinny neck bob up and down. "If it turns out I'm not your boss anymore, would you want to go for a drink sometime?"

Every last bit of desire to turn over a new leaf drained out of her. He'd gone and done it. Used her personal crisis as an opportunity to ask her out. Well, she wasn't that vulnerable, and she sure as hell wasn't that desperate.

Her brows arched with fake flattery, one even tipping

higher than the other. "With you?" She almost felt bad for saying it with just the right amount of inflection so he'd think she was actually considering it. An expressionless look fell into place when she delivered the final blow. "Not in a million years."

She blew out of his office like a hurricane and stomped past the row of cubes lining the wall. Thomas peeked his head over the top of his as she stormed by. "Everything okay?"

"Yeah, sure, Tommy. How about you go back to sexting and not worry about it?"

Liz Johnson was a realist. Life wasn't the romantic comedy other people seemed to think it was. Unless mind games were considered funny, her parents had proven her theory correct years ago. It wasn't a montage of adorable mishaps and silly misunderstandings where boy met girl, girl got fired, boy asked girl out for drinks, they fell in love and lived happily ever after. She didn't think love was a comedy at all. Nope. In fact, she thought it was a goddamned tragedy.

She rounded the corner to the elevator bay and jabbed at the down button three times in rapid succession. It was already lit, but she punched it once more for good measure. When the shiny metal doors slid open, she bolted inside. Her chest heaved as she pressed the button that would take her to the loading dock. She needed to cool off. More important, she needed a box to pack her things as soon as possible. Even if this did turn out to be a simple mix-up, there was no way she could work there now. Not after that.

"Hey, there," someone called out. Liz glanced in the direction of a UPS deliveryman walking up the metal ramp toward her. "Looking for a box?"

She stopped picking through the mound of cardboard and

forced the last of her patience through her nose with a sigh. "No, I was looking for my pet unicorn." She gestured toward the mess next to her. "It jumped into this big pile of boxes. Have you seen it?"

To her surprise, he didn't bristle. Or leave. Instead, he folded his arms and grinned like he was staying a while. She blinked. Did he not get the hint? Scram. She was perfectly capable of—

Oh geez.

Liz gulped down her facetious tone. Could eyes be that green? Or were they blue? His impossibly straight, white teeth were hard to miss. The epitome of tall, dark and handsome to begin with, but toss broad-shouldered and hard-bodied into the mix and the man was nothing short of a god. She snapped her mouth shut.

He's not a god . . . He's just a regular guy with excellent orthodontia.

Hunky UPS Guy continued to smile down at her, irritating her even more. If he wanted to ignore the warning signs of a woman ready to blow like a volcano for the second time in one forty-minute period, then he was asking for whatever he got.

"I just got fired—oh wait, they like to call it 'getting let go' these days." She threw in air quotes for emphasis before waving a hand in the direction of the unruly heap beside her. "I need to pack up my shit, but all these boxes are too big. So, if you'll excuse me."

Hunky disregarded her dismissal. "I'm sorry to hear that. About you getting let go, not that all the boxes are too big."

The last hour hit her like a ton of bricks. She thought she'd made it clear she wasn't in the mood for company. Why would she be in the mood for jokes? "Smart ass," she muttered under her breath.

Hunky folded his arms and leaned forward. "I didn't quite catch that, but by the sound of it, I'd say it wasn't flattery."

She took a step back. Was this guy actually throwing shade at her? Well, let him try. She didn't rise to Expert Level without playing the "I Do Not Give Two Shits" game her whole life. She switched her stare-gun over to death-ray and blasted holes into him.

But he still refused to leave.

Her exasperated sigh came out in a loud huff. Forget it. She had bigger things to worry about. Like finding another job. "Yeah, well, sorry." She didn't feel apologetic, but knowing society frowned upon blurting obscenities at strangers, she figured she should at least throw it out there before walking away. "It was nice talking to you."

"Hey, wait," Hunky called after her. "I think I saw some smaller boxes in the next dock over. Let me go check real quick."

Liz turned around. My, but he was persistent. And she was . . . fried. At this point, all she wanted to do was find a frigging box, pack up her stuff and go. Besides, it wasn't like she didn't have the time to wait a few minutes. "Sure, okay."

Hunky dashed out, and a blast of cold air swirled around her. She rubbed her hands up and down her arms, wishing she'd grabbed her jacket before coming down. March in Seattle wasn't frigid, but it was brisk enough for goose bumps.

Several more minutes ticked by, and when she stuck her head out and around the corner of the loading area doorway to see what was taking Hunky so long, she collided face-first with his chest.

"Oops." Hunky caught her by an elbow as she stumbled backward. Once she was steady, he handed over a box. "So what do you do?"

Um, okay, nosy. Your good deed does not equal my life story.

She took the box from him and inspected it. Damn. It was the perfect size. "This will do. Thanks." She thought about ending the conversation there, but before she could stop herself, she kept talking. "And you mean what *did* I do."

"I'm Robby, by the way. And, yes, what *did* you do?"

"Liz." She tucked the box under one arm and tipped her chin up at him. "I was an IT tech for a small independent record label. I mean, I still am an IT tech. Just not with those guys anymore." She jerked a thumb upward, toward the space in the building her former employer occupied.

Robby leaned on the metal piping that served as railing for the ramp. "You never know, it might be a blessing in disguise that you got let go. What does an IT tech do, exactly?"

"Software installs, server patches, end user support, stuff like that. But I mostly talked label execs off the ledge when the email server went down. They went total Gollum without their precious email access."

"That sounds stressful." Robby straightened. "But I get the feeling if anyone could put a bunch of high-strung, email-less guys in their place, it'd be you."

She shrugged. "Perhaps."

When Robby suppressed a laugh, she opened her mouth to say something sarcastic, but all that ended up coming out was a chuckle. A little one, and she would classify it as more of a snicker. He hadn't made her feel *that* much better.

"You know, I have a buddy who's looking for you—someone like you. He started his own company a few . . . ah . . . well, its right here in Seattle. I think you'd be perfect for it."

That got her attention. Zero job hunting? Yes, please. "Oh really? So you'd vouch for my sunny disposition, then?"

"Sure, you seem nice . . . ish," said Robby. "Seriously, though, I'm warning you. You're going to fall in love. The pay is excellent, and the hours are great, too. Plus, you'll know someone. I'm helping out with deliveries and running errands until my friend can get some people together." A toothy grin almost cracked his face in half. Whatever the joke was that made him so proud of himself, it was over her head. "He needs someone in IT and a marketing director. You wouldn't happen to know of anyone in marketing who's looking, would you?"

"I'm a computer dork. Do I look like I know any cool people? What kind of company is it, anyway?"

"Flower shop."

She snorted. Her? Work at a flower shop? The Man Upstairs sure had a warped sense of humor. "Um, you had me until flowers. I don't think I'm cut out for that. At least the record label was something I liked." She smirked, her mind made up. No thanks. She'd rather job hunt than be surrounded by other people's feelings all day.

"What do you have against flower shops?" Robby tilted his head. "I thought everyone liked getting flowers?"

She shook her head and ignored the warmth pooling in her cheeks. "Not everyone." She assumed she didn't like getting flowers, since she'd never gotten any to know for sure.

"I get it, you're not the feelings kind. But hey, if it pays the bills." He shook his head at her in that annoying older sibling way of his. "Boy, you really are a tough nut to crack, aren't you?"

She pushed up her glasses. "Yes." And it was going to stay that way.

He pulled a business card out of the front pocket of his work shirt. "Okay, well Tough Nut to Crack Liz, here's his name and number. You should give him a call." He glanced at the box she was holding. "It can't hurt."

CHAPTER FOUR

A busker scratched out a tune on his cello as Eros maneuvered office furniture down the ramp of the delivery truck. He tried to block it out. Not that the street performer didn't have talent, but the mournful sounds were about as uplifting as a funeral dirge. The lyre, now there was a stringed instrument that boosted the spirit. Most gods preferred its high, sweet plinking, himself included.

Same with the air. It wasn't as crisp and clean down here as it was on Mount Olympus. It felt thicker and smelled a bit like a locker room, and that was the nice way of putting it.

Once the sidewalk cleared of pedestrians, he wheeled an office chair into the service entrance of Follow Your Heart Flowers & Gifts. "Thanks for doing the legwork on this place, Herm. It's perfect." He grunted as he hoisted the ergonomic contraption up by the arms and carried it over the threshold.

Hermes, balancing a credenza on his back as if it weighed nothing, waited for him to wrestle the spinning piece of furniture into the building. "Not a problem. Leg work is my specialty."

Eros set the chair down as gracefully as his underdeveloped muscles could manage and stretched his back, the armpits of his T-shirt already damp. Hermes wasn't even breathing heavy. Some gods had all the luck. Some, apparently, hated working out.

Eros wiped the sweat from his forehead before heading back to the truck. "So what's the status on Leo?" he called over his shoulder.

"I'm about to deliver an offer he can't refuse," said Hermes, following close behind.

"Perfect." Things were in motion. So far, everything was going according to plan. With the exception of one thing, or should he say one *person*. "Now if Liz would call me already. You gave her my card, right?"

"Of course I did." Hermes set down his side of the desk they were carrying. "You know, I've been meaning to talk to you about something. The whole enemies-to-lovers thing is solid, but can I make one small suggestion?" He used his finger and thumb to emphasize how small.

Eros set his end down, too, and hooked his hands around his hips. Hermes' suggestions were never small. Thing was, they were usually good.

"Give Psyche a call."

"No." Eros gripped the underside of the desk and lifted. Hermes followed suit.

"Why not?"

News of his current predicament had no doubt made the rounds—knowing Leto, before he'd even left Zeus's office—but he wasn't about to use his near-death experience as an excuse to call his estranged wife. "Simple. It's too soon. Besides, the last thing she wants to do is help me."

"You'll never know if you never ask," said Hermes. "That mind thing she does could come in handy. I don't know if you know this, but our little mortal ice queen has got some serious abandonment issues."

"Oh, I know." He'd read her file, half a dozen times.

"Then doesn't it make sense to open her mind as well as her heart? You of all gods should know it takes both for true love."

"I see your point, and I agree, but there's no time," said Eros. "I'll have to shoot her in the heart regardless of whether her mind is ready or not."

Thank the fellow gods the street cellist was drowning out their conversation.

They set the desk in his office. He'd always had a cube, and he couldn't resist the lure of having a walled in space of his own. It was on the cozy side, with just enough room to fit a desk, the credenza and a small love seat, but it was his. He sat in his new office chair and tested it out.

Likewise, Hermes tried out the love seat. He swung an arm up over the back and crossed an ankle over one knee. "That's what I'm saying. Her heart will never fully be open unless her mind is, too."

Eros fiddled with one of the levers under the seat of his chair. He was about to offer up another excuse when he caught a glimpse of movement out of the corner of his eye. When a large Monarch butterfly fluttered into the office, he froze, any argument he may have had lodging in his throat. One hand still gripped the lever, and the other clutched the arm of the chair. He lifted his head to glare at Hermes. "You didn't."

"Hey, don't look at me. She either heard about it at the staff meeting or from Leto. What did you want me to do? Lie when she asked me if it was true? I'm the patron of thieves, not liars."

Eros sat up, both hands on the arms of the chair now. His gaze followed the delicate black and copper wings as they propelled their owner along its bouncing journey toward him.

"I mean, I may have *accidentally* told her you were working off site . . . in Seattle . . . in Belltown at a flower shop between First and Vine."

"Accidentally on purpose, you jackass." Eros's thoughts collided with each other as they raced around his brain at break-neck speed. What was the protocol for seeing the love of one's life for the first time in decades? Be polite and stand? Play it cool and remain seated?

Psyche stepped through the office door. Her hoop earrings and butterfly pendant glinted in the track lighting overhead. Amber eyes held his gaze captive, and her long chestnut waves squeezed his heart into action. He sucked in his stomach and rose from his chair. While he had the face of a Greek god, he no longer had the hard, sculpted body of one. The separation had been tough, and the donuts had gone down much too easy. Nervous, he shoved his hands into the pockets of his slim-fit jeans.

Slim-fit. Oh, dear gods, enough with the irony.

The jangle of her ever-present bangles tinkled, and the Monarch flitted its way toward her, nestling itself into the soft waves of her hair. The flattened wings under his cotton tee trembled with restraint, as did every fiber of his being. They wanted to take her into his arms as much as he did. But he refrained. They'd barely spoken since the split.

Her gaze slid over to Hermes. "Nice to see you." She directed it back toward Eros. Honey. They were the color of the sweetest honey. Her lips were full and luscious and perfect. Her vocal chords issued a melodious sound that felt like home. "Hello, Eros."

"Hi."

Hi? She's talking to you again and all you can say is hi?

His wings twitched. With the way they were goading him, it was a wonder they didn't convulse right off his back. He squeezed his shoulder blades together to quiet them.

"You look disappointed. Shall I leave?"

He shook his head. Of course he didn't want her to leave. He'd never wanted her to leave. "No, no. Please stay. It's not disappointment. It's just been a while. You look great." He sucked his gut in even harder.

A smile pushed her lips upward. "Thanks. So do you."

She had to be lying. Had to. So his feelings wouldn't be hurt. He motioned to the chair he'd recently vacated. "So, I guess you heard about my situation. Leto?"

"Among others. Your *situation* is pretty serious. Mortal Status?" She lowered herself into the chair. "I can't believe that old hag still has it out for Mom—I mean Aphrodite." Psyche's gaze darted to the side, and she caught her bottom lip between her teeth. When they'd married, his mother had become hers as well, and the Freudian slip sent a jolt of hope through him. She released her lip. "Anyway. I came down to see if you could use my help."

"What a coincidence, we were just talking about your power of persuasion," said Hermes.

"You were?" She sucked her bottom lip into her mouth again.

Good gods, she needed to stop doing that or else Eros was going to have a coronary. His heart was already having trouble beating at a normal rate. "Um, yes. Yes, we were."

Hermes cleared his throat, wrangling the growing awkwardness under control. "How about discussing next steps over dinner?"

Eros nodded. "Sounds good to me." This was exactly why they were best friends—Wait, what did he just agree to?

"That'll work," said Psyche. "What time?"

"I don't know, six?" Eros shrugged his shoulders. "Does that sound all right to you, Herm?"

"Oh no, not me, I've got a job offer to deliver, remember?

I meant you two." Hermes wagged his finger between them, the grin on his face almost unnoticeable.

Almost.

Eros glared at Hermes before sneaking a glance at Psyche, who was preoccupied with her thoughts. He missed that furrowing of her brow, the gnawing on the inside of her cheek. He even missed the way she rubbed her thumbnail when she over-analyzed something. Right now, she was deciding whether the pros of going to dinner alone with her estranged husband, without the buffer of a mutual friend, outweighed the cons. He pulled at the hair near his temple and shifted his weight from one foot to the other.

Please be a pro. Please be a . . .

"That's fine. I saw a bar and grill a few streets over on my way here. We could go there."

Eros released the breath he'd been holding. "Sure."

Hermes pretended to draw back a bowstring, aiming an imaginary arrow at him. "We all set here, matchmaker?"

"Yep, we sure are." The urge to simultaneously hug his best friend and wring his neck made Eros's lips press thin.

"You're welcome," Hermes sang, tossing a wave over his shoulder before disappearing out the door. An instant later, he popped his head back in. "Oh, wait. Psyche, I almost forgot to tell you the best part of this whole thing. We came up with mortal names." He walked into the room with a proud swagger before ticking his head toward Eros. "You want to do the big reveal?"

Eros sighed, not really wanting to make a bigger fool of himself, before clearing his throat. "I'm going to go by Eron Hartman down here."

"Clever," replied Psyche, promptly nibbling on her bottom lip.

Clever as in I like it? Or clever as in that's the stupidest thing I've ever heard?

"And I'm Robby Winger," said Hermes. "Get it? Robby. Winger."

"I get it," she chuckled. "God of thieves, winged feet. It's very fitting."

"I was thinking about Cary N. Letters, but that's too obvious, right?"

"Right." Her honeyed eyes settled on Eros, and a few seconds of silence passed. He glanced at Hermes, then back at her. Now what did he do? What was he missing?

"Well?" she said. "What should my name be?"

Hermes clapped his hands together and rubbed them back and forth. "I've been thinking about this, you ready? How about Willa Strong? You know, because you've got a strong will . . ."

"Got it." Her breathy laugh made one of Eros's cheeks push up. "Hmm. Willa Strong, huh?" She tucked an arm under an elbow and tapped her lips with a forefinger, pretending she was unsure, but then grinned. "I like that."

The name suited her, all right. Now if only he still did.

Psyche pointed at Eros. "So, you're the matchmaker." Then, nodding at Hermes, she said, "And you're the funny sidekick." The corners of her perfect lips lifted as she laced her arms together. "I guess that makes me the brains."

Eros held the door open for Psyche as they entered the bar and grill. Despite the eating establishment being busy, they didn't have to wait long after putting his mortal name on the waiting list.

"Right this way." The hostess smiled, enamored. She hadn't taken her eyes off of him yet, not since they walked through the door. It was a by-product of his aura. It glowed brighter and stronger than any mortal man in the joint. And it was most likely how they'd gotten a table so fast.

Once their server took their drink order, Eros pulled the Johnson/Simmons file from his briefcase. The table shook when he dropped it onto the varnished wood. Upon impact, the top flapped open and half its contents fanned out.

"Wow. Is that a big file or are you just happy to see me?" A playful smile graced Psyche's lips before the corners of her mouth snapped back down.

He was sad to see it go, considering he used to be able to make that smile appear at will. Now, he wished he'd never taken for granted the way she rubbed the sleep from her eyes in the morning, or how her long lashes fluttered right before they slid closed at night.

The server ignored his attempt to flag her down as she flew past them. In her frantic state of running to the kitchen and returning to several other tables with a large serving tray heaped with plates of food, he decided it might be best not to distract the poor girl. When she came by to set their drinks down in front of them, he caught a glimpse of the panic on her face before she dashed away again. He gathered the folder and stuffed it into his briefcase. "Why don't we get takeout? I'm renting an apartment not far from here. We could eat there."

Psyche eyed him suspiciously. "Why? We're already here —" The sound of shattering plates and metallic twang of silverware bouncing off the tiled floor drowned out the rest of her words.

"Feel like Thai?"

Twenty minutes and two bags of carryout later, Eros scooped a healthy portion of drunken noodles onto a plate while Psyche piled a demure amount of vegetables onto a small mound of rice.

"Glass of wine?" He hoped she'd say yes.

"No thank you. We both know what wine does to me."

His wings quivered when the memory of their heavenly bodies entwined in silk—and each other—flashed through his mind.

Behave.

"How about a Coke, then?" It pained him, but when she nodded he plucked two cans from the fridge before snagging a couple of wine glasses from the cupboard on his way to the table. She tilted her head and gave him a reproachful look as he poured the cola into the glasses.

"What? Fancy is all I have." He shrugged. "How about some music?" He set a glass in front of her before heading over to his laptop.

"No romantic stuff," she called after him. "We have work to do."

He pursed his lips as the cursor hovered over the playlist aptly titled "Romance Mix." She knew him so well. He selected a jazz station and clicked start. The throaty sounds of the alto sax would have to do.

The next moment he was pondering whether he'd remembered to buy matches when, as if by the force of some powerful magnet, his gaze shifted toward her. Why was she looking at him that way? His mouth dropped into an "O" when he realized he'd been staring at the candle sitting on the dining room table.

He wasn't *trying* to be romantic, he just was.

"So, when do the office shenanigans start?" She dabbed at the corner of her mouth with her paper napkin.

"Monday."

She took a sip of her Coke. "Are you nervous?"

"A little." He put down his fork, the desire to finish his half-eaten plate of noodles waning. Oh, but he was good at understatements, wasn't he?

She pulled the open file next to her plate and looked over the paperwork while she finished eating. "I see why."

Eros drew a long breath in through his nose. Pushing it out took considerably less time. "Once I see how the first week goes, I can get a better feel for when to strike."

Her head jerked up. "I wouldn't rush it." The edge to her words was sharp. They always came out snippy when she worried.

He shifted in his seat, struggling to keep his irritation below the surface. Or, at the very least, off his face. It's not like he didn't know his aim would need to be laser-sharp if he was going to shoot so soon. "I'm well aware, but I haven't been given much of a choice, have I?"

Her cheeks pinked. "Sorry, I didn't mean to tell you how to do your job." She lowered her lashes and took another sip of cola. "But isn't that why this account is still open? Because you tried to shoot before they were ready?"

He pushed his plate away, his jaw setting at the mention of his questionable decision-making. "Not necessarily. And it wasn't all my fault, you know, there were other factors involved as well." He couldn't be positive, but now that he thought about it, he wouldn't put it past Hera to have interfered the last three hundred plus years. It wouldn't be unlike her to make sure he failed. And he'd been too dense to know it.

Stupidity: The downside of being a nice guy.

Psyche got up and took her empty plate over to the sink. The weary look on her face made his heart ache. He hadn't meant to be so harsh. Arguing was the bane of his existence. He'd rather make love, not war, even if he did have it in him to fight. He scraped his noodles back into the carryout box as she settled herself onto the couch.

She wasn't saying anything, and it was killing him. "Look,

I didn't mean to get so worked up. I'm under a lot of pressure, which makes me—"

"Grouchier than a hungry Cyclops?"

One corner of his mouth shot up. "Yeah, that."

The open floor plan of the apartment allowed her to watch him set the leftovers in the refrigerator and rinse the dishes. He flicked the water off of his fingers before drying them on a white dishtowel embroidered with tiny arrows. When his hands were dry, he retrieved the file from the table and joined her on the couch in the living room. Her legs were tucked underneath her, bent at the knees, and her arms were folded with her shoulders hunched.

He knew that posture by heart.

Out of habit, he went over to the hall closet, pulled out a fuzzy red chenille blanket and laid it across her lap. Out of love, he went and shut all the open windows. The memory of countless fights they'd had over the thermostat, like any other old married couple, clawed at his heart.

"Thanks." She pulled the blanket up over her shoulders.

"Okay if I light this?" He gestured toward the fireplace. "It's gas, not nearly as romantic as natural, or the candle, so don't worry. Strictly for warmth purposes only."

She rolled her eyes, but then, as if on cue, a shiver rippled through her and she nodded.

He turned the knob and a small flame flickered to life. Soon the fake logs were engulfed in a roaring fire. He smiled as he took a seat next to her, forcing himself to keep a respectable distance between them. Miraculously, his wings behaved as he leaned over and thumbed through the contents of the file.

Where was that strategy flowchart he'd put together? He could have sworn there was a production schedule somewhere. Maybe she left because he'd worked so much. Was that it? "Or was it because I didn't take her out enough?" he murmured.

His shuffling ceased, and he stared at the papers without blinking.

"No, it wasn't because you didn't take me out." She paused to rub her thumbnail. "Let's stick to figuring out how to thaw Liz's heart, shall we? It looks like Leo's not going to make things easy, either."

They were supposed to be strategizing, not picking scabs off old wounds. But the floodgates were open, and he couldn't stop the torrent of questions he'd been desperate to ask all these years even if he wanted to. "Then why?"

"You really want to know?"

He wasn't sure, but he nodded anyway.

"It wasn't because you never took me out, it was because you never let me in. You never let me help you sink one arrow. I didn't feel like I was a part of your life anymore."

He hadn't been expecting that.

Or maybe he had and just didn't want to admit it.

The twinge in his heart made his forehead crumple. It was strange how one could affect the other. Without thinking, he reached out and brushed a thumb over her cheek. "You've always been a part of my life, from the first moment I laid eyes on you. How could you ever think you weren't?"

Had she really thought she wasn't important to him? Even after he'd forgiven her for breaking his trust all those centuries ago? She'd been so easily convinced he was a beast. But she'd been a gullible mortal then, and her sisters jealous. He'd forgiven her, and the whole incident was water under the bridge as far as he was concerned.

And later, after all of that, what about the gifts? The flowers? The love notes? Hadn't it been clear how he felt?

"You were born a god, Eros. The god of love." The blanket

slipped from her shoulders as she placed a hand over his. "I was born a mortal, and although I was granted immortality, I guess I still felt like I was losing you." She guided his hand away from her face and into her lap where she held it. "Yes, even after everything we went through. The tasks, having to go down to the Underworld for that damned box. Earning back your trust. I don't know if this will make sense, but I felt like I was losing you to the very thing that makes you, you . . . Love."

"Why didn't you tell me?" He slid closer.

"I tried. Don't you remember all those times I came to the office? I wasn't checking up on you. I just thought helping you bind hearts would bring us closer together. All it did was make things worse. It distracted you. Besides, I felt ashamed."

His hand found its way to her knee and he squeezed, trying to deliver comfort. He thought his performance had started slipping when she left. *Because* she left. "Ashamed? Why would you feel ashamed?"

"Because I was jealous of something I couldn't see or touch." She wrung her hands, something she did whenever she felt guilty. "It messed with my head, and, well, I am the queen of over-thinking things, now aren't I? I'm nothing if I'm not persistent. We know this. When I want something, I will stop at nothing to have it, even if it means going down into the depths of Hades' Realm to get it. I wanted too much of your attention. You needed to concentrate on your job, not my insecurities."

"I'm sorry." Eros moved closer. The length of his thigh pressing against her shin made him long to take her in his arms and be done with the whole agonizing separation. But it wasn't as simple as that, wasn't his decision, so he resisted. "I still can't believe what my mother put you through."

"Don't apologize. She was protecting you." She patted his hand. "I had to do my part to heal the wound I inflicted. I've made peace with that part of our history a long time ago. I don't blame Aphrodite for making it difficult for me to get you back. For the record, though, I did fall in love with your heart, not your face. Although, I will say it was definitely an added bonus."

She smiled at him, making his own grin come out lopsided. Her hand was on his, soft and warm, and he ached to kiss the tender skin on the back of it. "We made it work before. Why can't we make it work again?"

She shook her head. "I can't ask you to do that. That's like you asking me not to overanalyze things. It's in my nature. Love is in yours." Removing her hand from his, she shucked off the blanket.

He gave her room to maneuver freely when she got off the couch, his wings twitching almost as painfully as his rending heart. She'd drawn the "just friends" line in the sand. "Can you ever forgive me, butterfly?" He swallowed hard as he watched her fold the blanket without saying a word.

"For what?" She placed the blanket on the back of the couch. "Life happens. Trust me, it's better this way. Besides, right now we need to focus on getting your clients to fall in love. Not wasting time figuring out how we fell out of it. I'll see you on Monday."

CHAPTER FIVE

Liz dropped an armload of dirty clothes. The pounding on her apartment door wasn't the light rapping of a friendly social visit. Oh no, this knock had the distinct sound of all business, no play.

She stepped around the bundle and hurried over to the peephole, clamping one eye shut as she peered through the tiny circle of glass. The Borealis Apartments superintendent's wiry frame was even more distorted through the concave lens.

She calmed her breathing and leaned on the door, waiting to see if he would go away. When he released another assault on the dented aluminum, she twisted the lock and opened the door a crack.

"Liz Johnson?" The man squinted as he peered in at her. He reminded her of a buzzard. Beady eyes. Hooked nose. Bald head.

"Yeah?"

"Your rent is late."

Was a simple hello not the standard American greeting anymore?

"Excuse me?" She asked the question even though she'd heard exactly what he'd said.

"You heard me. Your rent is late." He jabbed a finger at the piece of paper he held. "All Borealis Apartments lease agreements state that after three months of nonpayment, we have the right to kick you out. Do I need to start eviction proceedings, Ms. Johnson?"

She was aware she was behind on rent, but threats of eviction for being a few weeks late? She closed the door, so she could let it off the hook, but Buzzard Man stuck his foot in the jamb to prevent her from shutting it.

"Are you listening to me, Ms. Johnson?" He turned the S in Ms. into a drawn out Z.

She kicked his shoe out of the way. Free of its confines, the end of the chain clattered against the door, and the man took a step back when she swung it all the way open.

"Listen here . . . what's your name?" She ground out the words. He'd come here for business? Oh, he was going to get business.

"William Foster," he croaked. His eyes darted between her tattooed arms and nose ring.

She wanted to scream. Some people, like this guy, didn't approve of the choices she'd made regarding her body. News flash. They were her choices, and she was happy with them.

The grimace plastered on his face would have been comical if there hadn't been judgment behind it. But there was, and it was of her. A pity for him she didn't have patience for grown men who'd never learned the subtle art of tact.

"Listen here, Bill, I lost my job and I'm working on finding a new one, okay? I'm late, yes, but you can't kick me out yet. And I don't appreciate your threats. I'll pay what I owe the minute I have the money, so cut me some slack, will you?"

Shock flashed across his face, but he recovered quickly.

"Your sob story isn't going to work on me, Ms. Johnson. If you miss next month's rent as well, I will be forced to start proceedings. Is that understood?" Bill sucked in his cheeks and sniffed. "And I'm also making note of your hostile attitude."

"Be my guest!" She slammed the door and locked it. Frustration and anger burned through her. She didn't want to have to ask her mother for rent money. Number one, it would prove how much of a failure she was and, two, because her mom didn't have it either.

She leaned against the door and let her head fall forward. She needed a job, like yesterday. Seattle was her kind of town, definitely, but even though it had been the perfect place to prove she could take care of her own damn self, it was expensive. Living paycheck to paycheck had been her existence for the last couple of years, and she'd been okay with that. Until now, when she realized just how costly living downtown was, and what little money she'd actually managed to save.

She thumped her forehead before pushing off and flopping down onto the couch. She surveyed her surroundings, which were nothing special and a little worse for wear, but they were hers.

Hers for not much longer if she didn't find another job.

Her gaze landed on the box of stuff she'd taken home from the day she got "let go" sitting on her kitchen counter. There wasn't much in there, just a bunch of pens, a few legal pads, some books on coding HTML and a stapler, but she got up and flipped the lid off anyway.

Memories of that day threatened to give her a migraine, but she continued to rummage through the box, one memory in particular standing out.

It started to rain, the drops making plinking noises as

they hit the window. Liz abandoned the box and grabbed her bag from the kitchen table and began rifling through its contents. Again, not much to look through—wallet, gum wrappers, lens wipes, a ridiculous number of ChapSticks, even more pens, a stray tampon—and she found everything except what she was looking for.

"Dammit." She tossed her bag onto the counter next to the box and shoved her hands into the front pocket of her sweatshirt.

Think, Liz. Where did you put it?

She didn't remember throwing it away, but maybe she had. She pressed her hands deeper into the pocket, her gaze sweeping over her apartment. It stopped on the crumpled heap of dirty laundry.

"Ah!" She sprinted over to the pile and dug through the clothes until she found the pair of jeans she'd been wearing the day she got fired. She pulled them free from the tangled mess and groped the worn denim. "Yes!" She pulled the business card from one of the back pockets.

Follow Your Heart
Belltown, Seattle

She flipped the card over.

Eron Hartman
Mobile: 248-777-LOVE
E-mail: matchmaker@bol.com

She wrinkled her nose at the e-mail address. This guy was cheesy. Extra cheese wrapped in a bean and cheese burrito covered with cheese sauce. She was about to make the mistake of a lifetime, wasn't she?

Too bad she needed to pay rent, like, now. And never mind the fact that she hadn't gotten a response from any of the other places she'd sent her résumé.

She dialed the number.

"Hello, Eron Hartman speaking."

"Hi, Mr. Hartman. My name is Liz—"

"Liz!" The man blew out a breath, almost like he was relieved. "I was beginning to think . . . Anyway, it's nice to hear from you."

He hadn't been waiting for her to call, had he?

She shook away the thought and paced around the tiny living room. She had other things to focus on, like keeping her voice steady. Phone conversations weren't her thing, especially when the person on the other end seemed a bit off. "Your friend Robby gave me your card. He said you might be hiring an IT tech for your company."

"When can you start?"

She stopped pacing. Perhaps "off" was putting it mildly. "Don't you want to interview me first?"

"Yes, of course, I need to interview you. How about tomorrow morning?"

The man didn't sound old enough to be senile, but she was starting to wonder. "It's Sunday, but I guess that works okay." If it helped her chances of getting the job—and Bill off her back—she'd interview whatever day this guy wanted. She must really love Seattle if she was willing to take a shit job at a flower shop to stay.

"Great! I'll see you then."

"Mr. Hartman! Wait!" she shouted in order to get his attention before he hung up.

"Yes?"

"Where should we meet? For the interview?" Silence gave way to an uncomfortable absence of words. "Mr. Hartman?"

"Please, call me Eron. The shop is still a mess. Any other suggestions?"

Ball's in your court, Liz.

"Starbucks on 1st Ave and Battery in Belltown? 9:00 a.m.?"

"Perfect. See you then. Goodbye, Liz Johnson."

She stared at her phone, bewildered by the strange conversation she'd just experienced. What was she getting herself into? More concerning than Eron Hartman seeming a few cards short of a full deck was the fact that she didn't remember mentioning her last name.

Liz slipped inside Starbucks to wait for who she hoped would be her new boss to arrive. She'd walked down to the coffee shop an hour before her interview to mentally prepare. She disliked interviews, but she despised being late even more.

The aroma of freshly ground coffee beans was divine, and the din of other people's conversations comforting. It meant they were talking to each other and not her. She shed her wet coat and hung it on a nearby hook to dry. Next, she chucked her bag on the chair beside her and pulled out her old copy of *Tales of Edgar Allen Poe*. She liked her reading material grim.

Absorbed in swinging pendulums and tell-tale hearts, she lost track of time. Her internal timer buzzed, causing her to glance up at the real clock. 9:12 a.m.

Figures, he's late.

She was about to resume reading when a man with wavy blond hair rushed into the coffee shop. After a cursory look around, he spotted her. A smile rounded his cheeks, one more than the other, and he headed over to where she sat.

"Liz." It was a statement, not a question.

"That's me." She closed Poe and tucked him into her bag.

"Eron Hartman." The man held out his hand. "Sorry I'm late." He had killer dimples, and his eyes were the bluest she'd ever seen. Like, ever.

"Nice to meet you." She shook his hand, doing her best not to sound like she felt, which was far less enthused than she should be for the prospect of being able to pay rent. She didn't like talking about herself. Unfortunately, that's what people on interviews did, and she was about to do a lot of it in the next few minutes.

"Thanks for meeting me on a Sunday. Can I get you another?" Eron nodded at her empty cup.

"Sure. Grande iced mocha no whip. Thanks." Good. She had a few more minutes to think of something spectacular to say that would land her a job. What, exactly, that spectacular something would be, she didn't know.

She tried not to gawk at her potential new boss as he approached the barista at the front counter, but couldn't seem to help herself. There was something about him. Something she couldn't quite put her finger on.

Threatening? No. Intimidating? No. Was he glowing? Maybe. Or was it an illusion caused by the early morning light coming in through the window? She squinted at him one more time before looking around at the other patrons. Everyone sipped their coffee without a second glance, their faces buried in their smart phones. Nope. No one noticed anything strange about Eron Hartman but her.

She dismissed the thought as he made his way over to her table. She'd only just met him, and he hadn't exactly made a bad first impression. Plus, people didn't literally shine. She ought to give him a chance. Correction. She *had* to give him a chance. She offered him as much of a smile as she could muster, which was weak at best, as he set her coffee down in front of her.

"So, why don't you tell me a little bit about yourself." He pulled out the chair across from her and sat.

There's really nothing worth telling.

"I have a degree in Information Technology from Lawrence Tech. Like I was telling Robby, I have extensive experience in end user support."

"Great, but what about you, Liz Johnson? Tell me a little bit about *you*."

Please, God, not another come on. She blinked, trying hard not to purse her lips. Why hadn't he stuck to the standard interview questions, like *"What weakness of yours would you consider a strength?"* or *"Tell me why I should hire you, Liz?"*

"I grew up in Chicago," That was as much personal information as he was going to get. "I've always liked computers, so getting a degree in Information Technology seemed like a natural fit."

"Why are you so opposed to love?"

"Excuse me?" Okay, now he was crossing the line. That was definitely not a standard interview question.

"So, are you opposed to love?" He rephrased his question before taking a sip of his Frappuccino. "I do own a flower shop, after all."

"I guess you could say I'm indifferent to it. This is an IT position, right? I won't be doing sales, will I?"

"No, no, of course not. You'll, I mean, whoever we hire, will be running our Internet from behind the scenes."

"You know IT doesn't actually *run* the Internet, right?" She dipped her chin. Seriously. Under what rock did this guy live?

"Of course. That's what I meant." Eron combed his fingers through his hair.

"Okay. I know HTML, too," she continued, "so, if you need any kind of coding done for your website . . ."

"Great, I'll keep that in mind. Would you be able to start tomorrow?"

She stopped her lips from tipping into a smile. Rule *numero uno*: Never show emotion. "Uh, sure."

Eron grabbed her hand and shook it so hard her elbow thumped the table. "Great. Then you're hired."

CHAPTER SIX

Leo ducked, the saltshaker skimming the top of his head before exploding in a cascade of white crystals against the wall behind him. Cat-like reflexes. One of the two absolute necessities every man needed when it came to women.

"You're a cad, Leo Simmons, do you know that? A selfish cad!"

He glanced around for the manager of one of London's trendiest Indian restaurants. Ah, there in the far corner, arms folded, lips pursed, face a darker shade than normal. He was going to give Anish an aneurism one of these days.

He scanned the crowded dining area. As expected, the other couples whispered between themselves, their samosas forgotten. Even in the dim lighting he could see the women glaring at him, in solidarity with their about-to-be fallen sister, no doubt. The men shook their heads, the look of pity on their faces unmistakable.

He didn't need their sympathy. He'd been here before, in this same position, many times. It wasn't anything he couldn't handle.

He reached across the small table, taking care to avoid the lit votive between them. No need to catch a brand new Armani shirt on fire over this. "I'm sorry, Madeline, but it's an opportunity I can't refuse. I hope you understand." He brushed his thumbs over the backs of her hands and squeezed, hoping it would prevent any more violent outbursts.

Anish shot him a prolonged sideways glance, the message clear. Complete this break up without making a bigger scene.

Madeline pulled her hands from Leo's and set them in her lap under the table. Troublesome. Not many women voluntarily let go when he took their hands in his. He took inventory of the cutlery. Two forks. Two knives. All still on the table. At least that much was going for him.

Her voice was soft and low, but the desperation in it was loud and clear. "Oh, so that's all you care about? More money? Being some big marketing director in Seattle? What about us, Leo?"

The second absolute necessity a man needed when it came to women was charm. Also known as the ability to talk one's way out of—or into—anything. Right now, his goal was to talk his way out of this relationship, if one could call three months of shagging with a strict no overnight stay policy a relationship, without acquiring great bodily harm.

Some women were criers. Some women were yellers. Madeline was proving to be a thrower.

"Look, you're an amazing woman, but I'm not ready. Perhaps I will be someday, but not right now. It wouldn't be fair. You deserve better." He performed his trademark slow-blink—it accentuated his long lashes, which he'd discovered several years ago was to his advantage—before casting his eyes downward. "This move is really important to me. I need to prove to myself . . . To my father . . ."

The sadness in his voice was a sham, but the words that

came out of his mouth were true. Sort of. He wasn't ready to settle down, that much wasn't a lie. Not that he didn't think it *could* ever happen, more like he'd never met anyone he thought *would* make it happen. The white picket fence, kids, a dog that was a cross between a golden retriever and a poodle, he didn't see any of it in his future. Why didn't the women he dated get that? It's not like he didn't warn them.

Besides that, he wasn't sure he was going to accept the job in Seattle. The money was impressive enough to make him consider it, but leaving London to be the marketing director for a foreign start up seemed a little risky.

It was the part about his father that was a lie. He had no desire to prove anything to Donovan Blackwell. Why should he? The man could hardly be classified as a father. Rich and powerful advertising executive, yes, but father? No. Sperm donor was more like it.

Of course, Donny boy threw enough money Leo's way to keep his old-money, cash-cow wife in the dark about his extramarital affairs, one of which had been Leo's mother, but he certainly hadn't had a hand in raising him. The only thing the man had a hand in was reminding Leo he wasn't good enough to be considered a Blackwell.

Actually, there was one good thing he had gotten out of the deal: The ability to attract beautiful women. Lots of them, which meant being lonely was never a problem. He'd inherited that bit of DNA, all right. If Madeline wanted someone to point the finger at for the way he'd turned out, she could blame the bastard who gave him life.

Madeline's tears glistened in the candlelight. "I understand completely." She sniffed down her unshed emotion. "That's why I think I should go with you."

Bugger, a little too much charm.

He shook his head, but his voice came out smooth and steady. Practiced. "I don't think that would be a good idea. I'll be working all the time, and you'll be alone in a strange city, in another country."

"But, Leo, I'd sacrifice anything for you. I lo—"

"I'm sorry, Madeline. I think it's best if we just end things now." He couldn't let her say the "L" word out loud, for her sake. He didn't deny he could be a selfish arsehole, but he wasn't a total prick.

Leo eyed the wine glass closest to Madeline. She'd drained its contents a while ago, but her hand had migrated back onto the table and her fingers where now curled around the stem. The knuckles of her other hand, the one gripping the cloth napkin like an eagle talon, were white.

He went over his options regarding which way to move when she launched the glass at him. Experience told him to go right. Sure enough, it whizzed by his left ear, shattering against the reclaimed brick behind him.

A collective gasp, followed by a round of snickers, came from the patrons watching his nightmare happen in real time. His hand found its way to the back of his neck and rubbed. Why wasn't his usual bag of tricks working?

He made eye contact with Anish, who was all but sprinting over to their table. Shite. He loved the tikka masala here and had planned to come back at least once more before he left—if he left. The restaurant manager's mustache twitched from the colorful curses in Hindi he was muttering under his breath.

Maybe not. Coming back might put Anish straight over the edge.

He sputtered to a stop in front of Leo and stretched one arm toward the door. His voiced was strained, but he managed to keep most of his cool. "Please, go. Find someplace else to break up with your girls, Leo. I can't afford to keep replacing wine glasses."

Madeline leaned back in her chair and blinked up at

Anish. "Glasses, as in plural? How many times has he done this?"

Anish cleared his throat, deferring to Leo.

She trained her viper's stare on him. Head cocked back and swaying like a cobra, she waited for an answer. His mind raced. What tactic would be most effective at this juncture? He opened his mouth, praying this wouldn't be the moment his charm failed him.

"Save your breath." She slid out of her chair. "I feel sorry for the next girl, I really do. She's going to have to be one tough bitch to put up with a heartless bastard like you." She hooked the strap of her Fendi bag over her shoulder and held it behind her back with an elbow. "You know what? I believe I just dodged a huge bullet." Her hand snaked out and snatched his wine glass off the table. "Goodbye, Leo."

The remains of his expensive red splashed down the front of his even more expensive shirt, and the click of her high heels punctured through the raga music playing softly in the background.

A man strolled by, his sinister laugh filled to the brim with judgment. "That went splendidly, yeah?"

Leo bristled, but continued to sop the wine off the table without looking up. He didn't need to—he'd know that spiteful sound anywhere. He hadn't noticed Donny boy sitting in the restaurant's darkest corner, although it wasn't a surprise. The man had a knack for emerging from the deepest recesses just to grind in Leo's failures.

He caught a whiff of cheap perfume, confirming the woman on Blackwell's arm wasn't his wife, but probably the advertising agency's newest hire.

When his efforts to clean up the mess proved futile, Leo threw the stiff, cloth napkin, wholly unsuitable at absorbing anything, down and reached for his billfold.

Anish shook his head. "No, no, just go. And, I'm sorry, but please do not come back unless you are alone."

Leo took out three one hundred pound notes anyway and pressed them into Anish's hand. "Well, that won't be too difficult, mate. You'll be happy to know, as of this very moment, I'm leaving London."

The evening's events gnawed at him all the way back to his flat. Even if the night ended in a decimated wine glass or two, he was never proud afterward. He was still a good guy, deep down *somewhere,* despite what kind of monster the resentment for his father had created. He just hadn't checked in with that guy for a while. Maybe he'd find him in Seattle.

To make up for his lack of company, he poured himself two fingers of scotch. One for each of the only words he'd heard Madeline hiss at him before walking out of the restaurant.

Heartless. Bastard.

Leo snorted and undid the buttons of his shirt. Like she hadn't known. He swiped his drink off the wet bar and headed for the bedroom. His conscience scolded Monster Leo, and his sip turned into a gulp. It was annoying the way the two were constantly at each other's throats.

Start packing, that's what he should do now that his mind was made up. It wouldn't take long, because he wouldn't be taking much. He'd leave most of his belongings, his latest ex's emotional baggage in particular, behind. He had enough of his own.

He took another sip of scotch, the liquid burning his throat with a sharp sting. Did he like that he'd turned out to be a younger version of his father? No, but at this point he couldn't stop. Old habits die hard, as they say. Commitment wasn't worth the risk. He'd already lost too much as it was.

He pulled open the nightstand drawer and fished out a worn photo strip. His eight-year-old self and his mother made silly faces up at him. They both looked so happy, neither one knowing they only had seven more years left together.

Twelve years gone. Had it really been that long? Must have been, because age fifteen was the last time he remembered caring about anyone other than himself.

She'd been his whole world, teaching him right from wrong, which direction his moral compass should point. And the powers that be took her away when he had needed her most. Without her, he became more like his father every day.

The doorbell rang, chasing the memories from his mind. He realized who must have come calling when it rang a second time. By the third ring, Monster Leo was already prowling up from his lair.

Leo tucked his emotions away for safekeeping as he shrugged out of his shirt. His bare feet slapped the expensive travertine tile as he hurried through the kitchen, and the ruined garment went into the trash on his way to the door. His conscience begged him to dig it back out. But why bother? That stain was never coming out. And he would never have the inclination to put in the effort. Effort got him nowhere. Now, charm on the other hand . . .

A grin stretched his lips when he checked the peephole. He pulled his muscles taut so his abs hardened and bunched in all the right places. They were going to earn their keep tonight.

He opened the door and gasped, just light enough to sound surprised. "Madeline? I thought you never wanted to see me again."

"I was angry." She peered up at him sheepishly.

He raked a hand through his hair, torn between right and wrong. "You threw wine in my face."

Her forehead creased, her despair bordering on panic that he'd send her away without forgiveness. "I'm not proud of the way I handled things."

Before his conscience could pipe up again, he performed his *coup de grâce*: a slight downturn at the corners of his mouth. No woman could resist it. "You called me a heartless bastard."

"I know." The regret in her voice thickened. "I don't know what came over me. I know I have to let you go . . . so you can prove to your father . . ." Her eyes welled with tears.

"Shhh, it's all right." He held her to him, knowing what warm male skin, still bearing the faintest scent of cologne, did to women during an emotional crisis. "I know it's hard." Monster Leo caressed the back of her head. "Have you come to say goodbye, one last time?"

She nodded, her hair brushing against his bare chest. Her breath, as hot as it was desperate, danced across his skin when she spoke. "Will you at least call and let me know how you've settled in?"

"Of course I will." He released her just long enough to push the door open wider, an invitation to ignore the truth. She hurried past him, intent on accepting it.

Fine. He *was* a total prick. Like father, like son.

CHAPTER SEVEN

The tap on Liz's shoulder was light, and when she pulled out her ear buds and dragged her eyes to the man standing next to Eron, everything stopped, including her breathing.

"Liz Johnson, this is Leo Simmons, our new Marketing Director."

The second she locked eyes—gray ringed with blue—with the new guy, her heart attempted a maximum-security prison break, forcing her to wrestle in a small breath before clearing her throat.

Butterflies played leapfrog in her belly, and she sucked in tight, intent on squishing the annoying bastards. But the way the new guy's gaze held hers only encouraged their games. Their swarming was ridiculous, and she had half a mind to flip him the bird. Eron too, actually. Maybe then they'd stop staring.

She might find herself out of a job again, though, so she refrained.

Leo, all tall and dark-haired, returned her tight smile with a dashing one. "Nice to meet you."

Oh God, this guy *would* have an accent that simultaneously sounded like heaven and felt like hell.

A lopsided grin climbed halfway up Eron's face, reminiscent of an evil scientist waiting to see which minion volunteered to be the test subject for the Death Ray of Destruction.

Not it.

The urge to scratch the hives breaking out on her chest made her fingers curl, and a thin layer of sweat formed between the bridge of her nose and her glasses. Having no way to discreetly wipe it away, she settled for letting her frames slide down her nose and pretending to be unimpressed. "Yep. Nice to meet you."

Despite the fact that she'd just met this guy, she couldn't stop glancing at the way his dark hair curled over the top of his ears. The sense that she knew him, had seen his face somewhere before, gnawed at her. And his eyes, framed by the thickest lashes she'd ever seen on a man, did they widen in recognition as they swept over her face, stopping on her nose ring for the briefest of moments before making their way down to her tattoos? She watched the tip of his tongue dart out over his bottom lip before disappearing again.

Nope, that wasn't recognition. It was an assessment.

She pushed up her glasses, discretion be damned, and when she refused to say anything more, Eron's smile dropped into a frown.

"Well, then, I guess that'll do. We have quite a road ahead of us, so we best get started." He gestured to the workstation opposite hers. "Leo, this is where you'll be making the marketing magic happen."

Jesus H. Christ, it figures.

She hadn't minded that there were no cubes, or that the workstations were set up in that irritating community style that was supposed to foster more productivity but really only produced more distraction—until now. The only thing separating them was a glass partition. It was frosted for some semblance of privacy, but she'd still be able to see him. And he'd still be able to see her.

She'd liked her personal space while it'd lasted, but now the office, with its cool exposed beam ceiling and brick walls, seemed cramped. It was bad enough that everyone would know just how small her bladder was when she used the tiny unisex bathroom several times an hour. But now the new guy would know the insane number of times a day she got up to get a snack from the kitchenette, which she had already stocked. All her quirky workday habits would be fair game for ridicule.

After a few more seconds of awkward silence, Eron swiped a hand through his curls and turned to go. "Okay, I'll be in my office. You know, if you need anything," he called over his shoulder. His meandering was torture, and he kept looking back at them as if to check that they were still there.

Liz slid her chair over so her computer monitor blocked her frosted view of the new guy. The employee handbook—a one-page printout—occupied her mind for exactly one minute until lunch filled her thoughts. She looked around for the clock.

Ah yes, the clock, the one which happened to be hanging on the wall behind him, Leo What's-His-Face. And, *of course*, it had to be hanging low enough so that his big, fat, incredibly handsome head obscured it.

The new guy wheeled his chair away from his desk and angled it toward her. "So, this is your first day as well?"

A burst of heat surged through her, threatening to incinerate any trace of a cool, calm or collected exterior. He looked like a male model in his expensive suit. What the hell was he doing here and not on the pages of a magazine?

She kept her expression blank, and hoped like hell he

couldn't hear how hard her heart was pounding. It wasn't so much that she didn't have an answer, but more that her vocal chords had decided to hold her voice hostage.

Undeterred by her lack of answer, Leo got up from his chair and stood over her with his hands in the pockets of his tailored dress pants and asked, "Are you from Seattle?"

She forced the words out before the edges of her teeth nipped at the tender flesh on the inside of her cheek. "No, Chicago." She hoped she looked bored. Or busy. Both would be ideal.

"Have you been in Seattle long?"

"Not really."

More silence passed between them, and he tilted his head. Maybe it was the intensity of his stare, or the way his thick lashes feathered his cheeks when he slow-blinked, but out of nowhere, a wave of bashfulness washed over her, bringing with it the urge to lower her own gaze.

Eff that.

She kept her eyes trained on his, narrowed and piercing. Rule *numero dos*: Never let them see you sweat.

His look turned confused, and she bit the inside of her cheek harder. Good. No, wait. Not good. She didn't want him to be anything by her, flummoxed or otherwise.

Leo stood straighter, and . . . pushed out his chest? Oh, for Christ's sake, she thought guys only did that in the movies.

He trapped his tie between his thumb and forefinger just below the knot and slid them down the length of the silky fabric. "Well, in case you couldn't tell by the accent, I've come all the way from London."

She pursed her lips and threaded her arms across her chest.

Yeah, so you're wearing a nice tie, buddy, get over it.

And was she supposed to be *impressed* that he was from London? Or that he looked killer in that suit?

"Oh, really? Well, I hope that works out for you."

Hello, Cautious Liz. It's about damn time. Because this new Liz? She was acting weird. She was sweaty, and obviously in need of a stern talking to. This guy looked like the type who wasn't used to women only offering one- or two-word answers to his questions. He looked like the type who was used to women flirting and gushing like total idiots around him.

"Me, too." He raised an eyebrow before sauntering back to his side of their desk.

Her hands curled into fists, but she forced herself to ignore his comment instead of playing into his trap. If she wanted to catch up on her rent, she would have to see him all day, every day. There was no getting around that. Ignoring him would be easy. Not responding would take every last ounce of self-control she possessed.

Because that comment, it clawed its way under her skin with astonishing speed. And that look was all the proof Cautious Liz needed. In less than an hour—no, in two words—this guy, this Leo Simmons character, had revealed his true nature. He was a player. And she was having none of it. She'd dated enough guys like Leo to know he was bad news. So, take that, Weird Liz. This guy was used to women simpering after him, falling under the spell of his dreamy eyes and swooning over his irresistible British accent. Guaranteed.

Good luck, lover boy. No way I'll end up a crying mess on the floor.

Liz focused on her work for the rest of the morning, slamming her mental door shut on Weird Liz's curiosity about Mr. I've Come All the Way From London. Noon came and went and, after staving off hunger for as long as she could, her stomach began to growl in protest. She'd wanted to venture out over an hour ago, but, fearing she'd make eye contact with him again, she'd pretended she wasn't interested in getting lunch. Apparently, he was doing the same, because he hadn't moved either. He'd continued to tap away at his keyboard.

She couldn't take the incessant clacking much longer. She had to eat. Things did not work out well for other people when Liz Johnson's blood sugar was low. She pulled open a desk drawer and grabbed her bag, deciding that, no, she didn't even know this guy, so it was *not* rude to leave without saying anything. When Eron's office door swung open, her chance to slip out unnoticed hung in the balance. She made a break for it and bolted out of her chair, but he flagged her down.

"Going somewhere?"

"Oh, hey, Eron. Yeah, I'm leaving to grab lunch. I'll be back in a few minutes, okay?" She headed for the door that exited into the alley.

"What? Neither of you have had lunch yet?" He sounded a little too excited about that fact, and it grated on her nerves a la commercial-grade meat slicer.

Leo stopped typing and wheeled himself out into the aisle. She glanced at him, hoping the look on her face would deter him from asking to tag along.

"Mind if I join you?"

Goddammit.

She loathed being put on the spot. "I'm just . . . running out . . . real quick." A floundering Doug popped into her head, and she couldn't say with certainty whether she appeared as though she were that same fish gasping for air.

Karma was such a bitch.

"Perfect. I've got to get back to this marketing plan, but I could use a break."

"Yes, of course!" said Eron. "Take a break. Go have lunch. In fact, you know what? It's your first day, why don't you two take a long lunch? That marketing plan can wait. There's got to be a nice Italian place around here somewhere. Sit, talk, have a glass of wine, get to know each other."

Liz shot Eron a look, trying her best to put the brakes on whatever train wreck was about to happen. "I don't plan on being long. There are a couple of e-commerce software programs I want to take a look at. And I'm sure you're super busy, right, Leo?"

"Well, he is our boss, love. If the man says take a long lunch, I say we take a long lunch." He'd grabbed his pea coat from off the standing coatrack and was already fastening the buttons.

She clamped her lips into a tight line. God, he was so annoying. Of course he would wear a pea coat, one that accentuated his stupid broad shoulders. And did he call her *love*?

"Fine," she said through clenched teeth.

He flashed a devilish grin and held out her jacket. She wrenched it out of his hand.

Eron herded them toward the door as she shoved one of her arms into a coat sleeve. "Good, because it's mandatory. Think of it as a team-building exercise. Now go and have a nice lunch."

She liked her new boss, but what was this mandatory team-building bullshit? The minute her Converse hit the street, she was off like a bat out of hell.

CHAPTER EIGHT

For being so small, she sure walked fast. She should try out for the Olympic race-walking team. She'd gold medal. Wait, she wasn't trying to lose him, was she? Curious. It was usually the other way around. He'd have to fix that straight away.

Light-brown locks with the ends dyed blonde trailed down her back. The faster she walked, the higher they bounced. The purple knit hat atop her head kept her in his sights, and Leo stepped up his pace to close the distance she was determined to create.

He reached for her shoulder. "Excuse me, Liz?"

Tap, tap.

"Liz?"

Tap, tap, tap.

"Liz!"

She whirled around, her head tilted upward, delicate brows angling over pretty brown eyes. "What do you want?"

For starters, he wanted to know how it was possible he'd made it this far past noon without a single smile from her. Next, how long it would take to change that.

True, she wasn't his usual type—Monster Leo liked his girls at least five-foot-eight—but there was something about those dark, brooding eyes that intrigued him. It wasn't her personality, that was for sure. "Lunch. I'm famished. Why don't we find an Italian place like Mr. Hartman suggested?"

"Look, I've got shit to do, okay? I told you that." She resumed walking, but called over her shoulder, "You didn't really think we were having lunch, did you?"

He did, actually, and in three strides he was at her side to make sure she knew. "I thought perhaps, since I'm new here and it's my first day at a new job in a new country, and I know absolutely no one except for my boss and a co-worker who enjoys running sprints on her lunch break."

"Okay, okay. Fine," she said, glancing at him before refocusing her gaze on the sidewalk up ahead. "But I'm not going to an Italian place."

There, that was better. "Splendid. Where would you like to go?"

She twirled one end of her thin scarf tighter around her neck before plunging her fists into the pockets of her green, army-style jacket. "We can grab something at Pike Place Market."

"Very well, Pike's Place it is."

"Pike Place."

He stopped. "Pardon?"

She kept walking. "Just Pike," she shouted back at him. "Not Pike's."

He caught up to her for the third time. Her pace had gone manic again, but he matched it with ease. She cocked her head up at him. "I know, let's go to Saffron Spice. You like Indian food, right?" The fake enthusiasm followed by a smirk told him she assumed he hated it.

"I love spicy dishes."

It was her turn to stop. She rolled her eyes at him. "Very funny."

He kept walking but glanced back at her. "You seem surprised I like Indian food."

She groaned before catching up to him. He couldn't keep the grin off his face as he pulled his phone from his coat pocket and entered Saffron Spice into his GPS app.

"Don't bother. It's right over there" She pointed at a two-story brick building on the corner of 1st Street and Pike, "Economy Market Entrance" in white letters on its green awning. "Around the corner from the gum wall." She waited for a vehicle to pass before darting across the intersection.

"The what?" He matched her step for step, staying close behind.

"The gum wall, in lower Post Alley. You've never heard of it?"

He shook his head as he held open one of the doors that led into the market. Did the accent not indicate he wasn't from around here?

Aromatic spices mingled with the scent of brewing coffee and baked goods. All sorts of food stalls lined the wall, and numerous conversations echoed off the high ceiling, bouncing against each other and adding to the whirl of machinery humming in the background. When he approached the counter for Saffron Spice, a young woman abandoned her pile of carrots and mangos to turn off a large juicer. He scanned the menu until he found his favorite.

"I'll have a chicken tikka masala, please. An order of vegetable samosa and whatever this ill-natured young lady is having."

Liz huffed loudly, arms wrapped around her waist. "You don't need to buy me lunch."

Of course he didn't *need* to, but he knew better. Women

said one thing, but always meant another. "I want to. Please, I insist."

Her face flamed red, and crimson splotches were just beginning to peek above her scarf. She pursed her lips at him before giving the woman her order. "Chicken tikka masala, please."

"Excellent choice. It's my favorite. Yours, too?"

Her jaw tightened, the muscles working as she ground out an answer. "Yes."

God save the Queen, he'd asked a simple question. Capitalized on an opportunity to learn more about her. Her cheeks should have blushed a pleasant shade of pink, not flamed an angry red. She should have giggled or bit her bottom lip or both.

Bloody hell, she was maddening.

They waited for their food in silence. No idle chit or chat from this one. The lack of conversation made him fidget with his tie while scanning the dining area for a place to sit. He didn't see much. One seat open here, another open there, but nothing with two seats across from each other. The proper way to dine.

Liz shrugged. "It gets crowded in here. We can go to the waterfront. They have tables out there." She bit the inside of her cheek before continuing. "I can take you through Post Alley if you want to see the gum wall."

The memory of visiting random places—backyard art installations, museums and curiosity shops—with his mother, for no other reason than to say they'd seen them, made his throat tighten. "Sure."

Great. A stroll through memory lane in front of someone he'd just met. Now was not the time to be sentimental. He walked over to the counter and leaned in to get the woman's attention. She looked up from scooping fragrant basmati rice into a container. "We'll take that to go, please."

Even though they were standing close by, the woman bellowed, "Simmons!" when their order was ready. Perfect timing. The silence had started to get awkward.

Liz led the way out, even holding the door since he was carrying lunch, and he was please she refrained from taking off and leaving him behind again. He had what she'd come for, so if she wanted to eat, she'd have to stick around.

One point for Monster Leo.

"So what do you think of Eron?" He tried making conversation as they walked down the sidewalk and further into the market.

"He's weird, but nice." She stopped in the middle of a short alleyway, hands stuffed in her pockets and looking bored. "Here it is. The gum wall."

A brick wall plastered with chewed gum, from street level to an arm's length above his head. "Well, this is unique. Quite distasteful, yet I do suppose it has a certain charm to it. Colorful as well, so it has that going for it. Don't you agree?"

"Yep. My thoughts exactly."

Why did he get the feeling she wasn't referring to the wall?

He followed her out of the alley and along the back of the market, past Pier 57 and a giant Ferris wheel to a small park.

Liz marched over a grassy area and hopped down onto the park's cement patio, making her way over to one of the few open tables left. Leo pursed his lips at the graffiti-laden concrete wall that kept park goers from falling onto the rumbling freeway below. A sigh escaped. At least he could rest his takeout on a flat, if not sanitary, surface.

Surprisingly, the tikka masala was as good in Seattle as it was in London. However, the wind, along with the pigeons eagerly cooing amidst the sea gulls feigning interest, made his current surroundings a less than desirable place to enjoy lunch. He would have been content to stay inside the market.

"I'm intrigued by the giant Ferris wheel," he said, finishing the last of his bottled water. "Shall we go for a ride?"

"Hell no." She snorted, her flippant response batting his attempt at conversation on the nose. He paused, his eyebrows involuntarily tipping down for an instant before he pulled them back into place. He wasn't kidding. He really did want to ride it.

Had he ever worked this hard to get a woman to talk to him? They should be halfway through her childhood by now. Perhaps lunch had been a mistake. Maybe he was barking up the wrong tree. He found it unattractive when women made unrefined noises like huffs and puffs and snorts, anyway.

Except, her huffs and puffs and snorts didn't set his teeth on edge like it did with others. Her huffs and puffs and snorts were somehow less obnoxious and more kitten-like. An evil kitten, but still.

She didn't want to ride the Ferris wheel. Interesting. With the tattoos and nose ring, he'd pegged her for the adventurous type. The fact that he kept missing the mark made him want to figure her out all the more. But she refused to engage with him at every turn. And he was growing impatient. "So what's your story?"

"I don't have a story." Her lids fluttered in a restrained eye roll before she looked out over the water. "And if I did, it would be none of your beeswax."

He'd hit a nerve. Time to smooth things over with a bit of flirtatious teasing. "Oh, beeswax? That's more serious than plain old business, yeah?"

"Yes."

Look at that little lip curl, so sneer-like. She was cute

when she was annoyed. "Do you say anything else besides one word answers when you're irritated?"

"No."

He gathered both their empty containers and crumpled napkins. "So I should refrain from asking any more personal questions, then?" He dropped the garbage into the trash can.

She gave him an unrestrained eye roll this time. "I don't think that's possible for you."

"This may be true."

Was that a chuckle she almost let escape?

She glanced at him before getting up from the table. "Mind if we stop at Starbucks on our way back? I'm pretty sure I'm addicted." She stuffed her hands into her coat, and then she . . . smiled. His belly did a strange little dip. It hadn't been anything he'd said—she'd been proud of her own cleverness—but bloody hell it looked good on her.

It also confirmed she wasn't a cyborg.

"Are you giving me a choice in the matter, love?"

Her smile vanished. "No."

He winced at the abruptness of her departure. He'd said something wrong, that much was clear, but never having experienced this particular reaction from a woman, he found it impossible to imagine what that something had been.

Minus a thousand points for Monster Leo.

How on Earth could she be so unaffected by him? He didn't understand, at all. He'd exhausted a considerable amount of charm in just this one lunch alone. And it had yielded him nothing. His accent, at the very least, should have garnered *something*. It was the one thing he thought would have been a sure-fire panty dropper here in the States.

Speaking of panties, it was official. He was attracted to her, very much so. But it was more than that. He'd eaten lunch outside, in the chilly Seattle weather, out of a take-out container with a plastic fork. The thought alone was a personal affront to his refined sensibilities for civilized dining. And he'd agreed without protest.

Even more perplexing was that, somewhere between 9:00 a.m. and now, the challenge of getting his first American conquest to smile became more arousing than getting into her pants.

CHAPTER NINE

Liz grabbed the back of her chair and twisted, her vertebrae snapping and popping like firecrackers. She elongated her spine and stretched her neck from side to side until that cracked, too. Of course it wasn't an excuse to sneak a peek at Leo. Why would she even *care* what he was doing?

From her low vantage point, she could only see the tips of his dark hair spiking up over his monitor. Rich, dark brown, thick and glossy. He had the effortlessly mussed look down pat.

Now if he could just work on not being so full of himself.

She didn't notice the clacking from his keyboard stop until the smooth baritone of his voice penetrated her thoughts. "That can't be good for your back, love. Speaking of things that are questionable for your health, shall we go to the market again this afternoon?"

Her heart flew into her throat when she ducked behind her monitor and grinned. Not that she was going to say yes or anything because, God, he loved to hear himself talk, but his eagerness to go to lunch a second time was more satisfying than it should be.

Stop it, Weird Liz. Get back in your cage.

Before she could properly refuse him, a woman poked her head through the curtains that separated the retail shop up front from the studio workspace in the back.

"Hey there, sorry to bother you guys, but is Eron around?" She pushed the heavy fabric aside so the rest of her body could pass through. She was tall, notably so, and slender, blessed with enviable muscle tone from what Liz could see. Bangles adorning her wrists, long hair parted down the middle and hoop earrings gave her a bohemian vibe Liz liked. Basically, she pulled off the flowing batik skirt and distressed tee look like an Amazonian badass with an excellent sense of style.

Liz clenched her teeth when Leo bolted out of his chair. He hadn't tripped over himself when he'd first met her, had he? She sifted through the stack of mental notes she'd filed away. No, he'd simply stared at her. So that meant he was acting like a fool, and his current display of male prowess was, quite frankly, pathetic.

"He's not in yet. Must be running late." Leo was by the woman's side in a few strides of his long legs.

Those thighs. They could probably hold about 125 pounds, give or take, against a wall in a fit of passion, right?

Cage. Now.

The woman smiled, a dazzling sight. "Ah, yes, that sounds about right."

Leo pushed his shoulders back, encouraging their visitor to take in the full expanse of his chest. "Are you here for an interview?"

Liz groaned loud enough for him to hear as she turned toward her computer. Someone had to let him know how ridiculous he was. The peacock was showing off his feathers again. At least he knew which plumage to draw attention to, she couldn't begrudge him that. As far as male pectorals went, they looked grope-worthy even from under his Armani dress shirt.

"Oh, I've already got the job. Eron and I are old friends. I'm helping him manage the front for a while. I'm Willa."

Leo clasped onto her outstretched hand with both of his, as if she might get away, and shook. "Delighted to meet you, Willa. Leo Simmons."

Two hands? My, my, aren't we excessive?

Liz lifted her ear buds from off her neck and looped them over her head. Fine, she'd go meet the new employee. Someone had to save the woman from Leo's shameless mating ritual.

"I'm Liz Johnson, your IT department." Liz was content to keep her fingers tucked into the pockets of her jeans, but Willa extended a hand. It was warm and dry compared to Liz's cold and clammy one. Warm hands, warm heart, wasn't that the saying?

Sounded about right. Liz's hands were ice.

"Nice to meet you," said Willa. "I love your nose ring. I've always wanted to do that. I was too scared to get one when I was younger. I mulled it over in this crazy brain of mine for centuries, and now, well, I'm too old for that kind of thing."

Liz glanced down at the beat-up Converse on her feet. "Uh, thanks?" So she had a nose ring, which accounted for *some* cool points, but she felt nowhere near as captivating, or stylish, as Willa. And centuries? Liz hoped this woman didn't turn out to be a drama queen with a penchant for exaggeration.

Leo already had that position on lockdown.

"Well, it's nice to meet you both. I've heard so much about you." Willa sighed. "I guess I'll get acquainted with the ordering system while I wait for Eron to get in."

There it was again, that odd feeling spinning in the back of Liz's mind, just out of reach. What could Eron possibly have told Willa about Leo and her? He'd been their boss for all of two whole days.

"I can show you how to log on if you want," volunteered Leo.

"Sure, but no offense, wouldn't you do that?" Willa turned her liquid gold eyes on Liz. "I'm assuming, being the IT person, you need to set me up with a password and stuff, right?"

Liz shifted her gaze toward Leo and lifted an eyebrow. "Yeah, Leo. I should probably be the one to run through the system with her."

She liked this Willa. She wasn't the eyelash-batting kind of woman. Maybe, other than her having flawless olive skin and Liz being close to translucent, Willa was a woman after her own heart. Comfortable in her own skin enough not to use feminine wiles to get what she wanted.

Plus, what Liz liked most, she seemed unaffected by Leo's charm.

Take that, lover boy. Oh for two.

Willa turned to go up front. "Go ahead and finish up whatever you guys were working on. I'll be all right for a few minutes." She looked back at them, smiling as if she knew something they didn't, before disappearing behind the curtain once more.

"Nice try," Liz mouthed to Leo as soon as Willa was gone.

"She seems nice." He strutted back to his desk, ignoring the fact that Willa had just shot him down and Liz had rubbed it in his face immediately after.

"Yeah, and thank God she's not one of *those* kind of girls." Liz followed him toward their conjoined workstations, glancing at his backside. She tried to pry her gaze off of him, but it refused to leave the well-defined contours of his glutes.

He flipped around, planting himself directly in her path. She squeezed her own glutes in order to keep from crashing into him, which wouldn't have been all that bad, really, because then she could have tested the theory that his torso was also rock hard.

"What do you mean *those* kind of girls?" His head was cocked and his arms were folded, but he had an amused smile on his face.

"You know, *those* kind of girls—the kind of girls guys like you can't seem to get enough of." She hustled around him, her heart skipping a few beats.

"What do you mean *guys like me*?" Now he was behind her, so close it made the back of her neck prickle and goose bumps skitter down her arms. Thank God she'd decided to wear long sleeves that morning.

He scooted in front of her again and parked his hands on his hips. She struggled to banish the thought of those long fingers parked on *her* hips. "Good looking guys who think they're God's gift to women." She turned up her chin at him. If he wanted the truth according to Liz Johnson she'd give it to him, fine-ass body or not.

"You think *I think* I'm God's gift to women?" He laughed, placing a hand on his chest as he sat down.

"You said it, I didn't. But hey, at least I don't have to worry, right? Because I'm not one of *those* girls." She sniffed. Leave it to him to pretend he didn't know he was exceedingly attractive.

She'd never been one to carry three shades of lipstick or emergency fake eyelash glue in her purse. In fact, other than a tube of lip balm in her pocket, she didn't wear makeup at all. She kept things plain and simple for a reason. She had no desire to pretend she was someone other than who she was, just so she could impress guys like him.

At least, she never had before.

She suddenly found herself at his side of their workspace, standing over him with pursed lips. He leaned back in his chair, fingers laced behind his head and a grin so wide she could practically see every one of his perfect pearly whites. He reminded her of the Cheshire Cat in *Alice in Wonderland.*

Or was it more like the cat that had just eaten the canary?

"You're right, love, I am rather good looking. As for God's gift to women, well, I wouldn't disagree, but I don't kiss and tell, so you'll have to find out for yourself."

The suggestive look on his face blew on the coals smoldering inside her, the ones she was trying to ignore, and the way he lifted that one eyebrow, implying how good of a lover he was, stole the strength from her knees. "Fat chance, buddy."

She scurried back to her desk before her legs could give out.

His amused snicker filled her ears, prompting her to mock him silently from behind the safety of the partition that separated them. She rested her forehead on her palms to clear her head. There was no way she was going to find out whether he was God's gift to women, because there was no way she *wanted* to find out.

If that was true, then why did her breathing go shallow every time she thought about the gift that God had given him? And why did her heart keep insisting on freaking out afterward?

CHAPTER TEN

When Willa asked her to go to lunch, Liz could have kissed her. She may have even agreed to make out, since she was purposely avoiding Leo. One, he talked too much, which was annoying—he thought he was so smooth—and two, her body responded to all that talking. That voice. It did something to her heart, her stomach, her . . . well, that and her frigging tongue and brain couldn't get it together enough to formulate complete sentences.

It was safer not to be alone with him, for both their sakes, because when her mouth finally did start working, there was no telling what might come out of it. She might say something that made him think she was being *friendly*.

Third, she was running out of excuses why she couldn't go to lunch with him, and fourth, she'd been in Seattle almost two and a half years. It was about time she made a friend.

"So Eron and Leo have become pretty chummy, huh?" Liz managed to say before stuffing one end of her food truck veggie dog into her mouth. Part of her was thankful Eron had asked Leo to lunch every day for the past couple of weeks. The other part of her was . . . she didn't know, exactly.

"Eron makes friends easy. It's one of the best things about him."

"Well, that's high praise. How long have you known each other?" Maybe she could get some pointers on how to work with a guy without wanting to strangle him.

"Oh, we met ages ago. H—Robby and Eron have known each other even longer."

The sad look on her face told Liz there was something more to that story. It also indicated that Willa didn't want to talk about it. Time to change the subject. "You mentioned you're from Greece?"

"Yes, do you know where Mount Olympus is?"

Liz had never been that great at geography, but she ventured a guess anyway. "In the Balkans?"

"That's right. I grew up there. I had a lovely childhood. Privileged, even."

"Wow, and you left it to come here," said Liz between chews, trying her best not to smack her lips.

A wistful expression lit Willa's face. "I did." The delicate tinkle of her metal bangles sounded as she lifted her arm to brush a stray strand of hair the late May breeze had blown into her face.

Liz glanced at Willa's untouched veggie dog.

"Are Robby and Eron from Greece, too, then? They both kind of have that Greek god thing going on. Robby more so than Eron, but I guess I wouldn't consider either one of them an eyesore."

They had nothing compared to Leo, though.

Shut up, Weird Liz.

Willa's smile reached her eyes. "Mmm hmm." She bent her head back so the warmth of the sun could caress her face.

Liz followed suit and, stretching her legs out, the palest

ankles known to man slid out from underneath the pant legs of her jeans. No, it probably wasn't a bad idea to get some Vitamin D while the sun was out.

"But enough about me," said Willa. "What about you? How long have you and Leo been dating?"

"What? No." Liz shook her head and got up to throw her trash into the nearest garbage bin. Whatever gave Willa a ridiculous idea like that she hadn't a clue. "Leo and I are *not* together."

"Is that so?" Willa abandoned her basking. Beautiful almond-shaped eyes, a truly unbelievable shade of gold, held hers. "You could have fooled me. I see the way you two look at each other."

That was interesting. Because Leo was a pain in her ass. He had annoyed her somehow, some way almost every single day since they started working together. How was it possible anyone could think they were dating? Except, he did flash his perfect smile at her a lot, and he always said good morning, even though she growled at him most of the time. Maybe there was something . . .

No, Weird Liz. No.

She snorted, breaking eye contact. "I don't know what you're seeing, but it's not anything special."

"I don't know, you may not like him, but he sure likes you." Willa shot her a sideways glance before handing over the veggie dog Liz had been eyeballing.

She accepted it even though it had sweet relish on it, the worst condiment ever, and took a bite. "No he doesn't," she said through a mouthful. "I'm not his type—ugh, how can you eat this stuff?"

Willa clicked her tongue. "And just how do you know you're not *his* type?"

"Trust me, I know." She took a swig of Willa's lemonade

to rid her taste buds of the offending relish that clung to the inside of her mouth.

"What do *types* mean anyway? Your one true love could have the face of a beast for all you know. It's what's inside that matters," said Willa, placing her fingertips to her chest, right where her heart was, and curling them inward, as if she could actually hold it. "In fact, I fell in love with someone without knowing what he looked like."

"How could you have possibly not known what he looked like?" Liz couldn't help asking. Because, who does that? Facebook, Twitter, Instagram, Google Images . . . there were plenty of ways to gather visual intelligence on a person. "So, you guys just emailed and chatted online?"

A butterfly landed on Willa's knee. "Something like that." She held out her hand and it fluttered onto her knuckle. Then, taking flight as suddenly as it had landed, it was gone. "The point is it wasn't his looks I fell in love with."

"Okay, that's code for fugly. I take it he had a slamming bod, then?" Her mind wandered into dangerous bare-chested Leo territory. Was it smooth, or did he sport a man sweater? She preferred smooth, but she could get onboard with *some* chest hair.

"I fell in love with his heart," said Willa.

Liz mashed her lips together, embarrassed she'd assumed Willa would be so shallow. That she, come to find out, was shallow. Liz averted her gaze, following the bouncing path of a bright blue butterfly passing in front of them. Her eyes flicked toward another, this one a buttery yellow, fluttering overhead.

What the hell's with all these butterflies?

Liz turned her attention back to Willa. "Are you still together?"

She shook her head, sadness weighing down her eyes. "No."

"What happened?"

Liz hadn't meant to be nosey—she disliked nosey people —but the question slipped out before she could stop it. She clamped her mouth shut. What was *up* with her today?

"It's a long story." Willa sighed. "One for another day. Let's just say, in the end, we grew apart."

When she didn't elaborate, Liz took the hint and backed off. Even though she really wanted to know, the last thing she wanted to do was upset her new friend. Willa was sweet and genuine. And still hurting. Besides, Liz could fill in the blanks. Relationships were messy, heart-breaking ordeals, and if a beautiful soul like Willa couldn't find—and keep— love, what the hell kind of chance did she have? In her opinion, it was better not to know what it felt like to have a broken heart, which was why she needed to stop thinking about Leo. They'd never be friends, let alone lovers. "Well, who needs love anyway, right?"

Willa's head snapped in her direction. "Everyone needs love."

Liz flinched, not expecting the reaction she got. In fact, she'd expected Willa to agree. To back her up that Cupid and Valentine's Day were utter nonsense, made up and marketed to sell millions of dollars worth of flowers and chocolate to a bunch of idiots.

But it was obvious Liz had hit a nerve, so she searched Willa's face for any clue as to why her dismissal of the dreaded "L" word had upset her friend so much.

A strange, soft humming filled her ears when their eyes connected. The sound was just loud enough to block out the ambient noise around her. She could see the branches with newly unfurled leaves swaying gently in the breeze, but their rustling had gone quiet. Same with the footfall of pedestrians walking by and the taxis weaving in and out of traffic and honking—she hardly noticed. It was as if someone had turned the volume on life down to barely above a whisper.

With Willa's eyes locked on hers, Liz felt the skin along her forehead and around her temples begin to tingle, as though her scalp had fallen asleep. Pressure, like small, delicate fingers searching for entry, added to the sensation. When the phantom fingers made their way past skin and bone and into her head, a host of strange thoughts and ideas tumbled around in her mind before assembling themselves into order.

He's the love of your life.

He's always been the love of your life.

Lives, actually, and he's loved you in every one.

Deep down you love him, too.

The onslaught was quick, and it felt as if her will was engaged in a battle against someone else's. She was left at the mercy of an outside force telling her what to think, how to feel.

You're destined to be—

This is insane, Liz, get it together.

She knew how she felt, and this little mental breakdown, this massively loony discussion she was having with herself wasn't going to change a thing. She hardened her resolve and evicted the preposterous thoughts from her brain.

She didn't break eye contact—she couldn't—but her eyes narrowed out of habit, and she fought to keep her take on love straight. "Yeah, sure, some love is all right, like a mother's love. I'm talking about *love* love. That kind of love always gets too complicated, so who needs it? It's easier to be alone. Then you don't have to worry about anyone letting you down. Or leaving." Liz shrugged, and with the last of her mental strength shoved out the absurd notions running amok inside her head.

Willa flinched, as though she'd actually *felt* the push. A

determined look flashed across her face, and as quickly as Liz had thrown them out, the thoughts came rushing back. Her throat tightened, and her lips parted. Had these thoughts always been there, fighting so adamantly to be heard? Because now she wasn't sure her argument still made sense. Now her argument against love seemed sort of flimsy.

Although it seemed impossible, Willa's gaze intensified. If Liz thought she couldn't look away before, the strange feeling was ten times stronger now. At this point, she couldn't even blink, no matter how hard she tried, and her face twitched with the effort.

Liz swallowed hard, the struggle continuing inside her head until there was only one thought that prevailed. One idea that grabbed a hold of her and refused to let go, swinging its iron hook up and over the ramparts of the fortress of self-imposed solitude she'd so painstakingly built. Try as she might, she had no other choice but to stare back into Willa's lovely golden eyes and listen to what the voice inside her head was telling her.

Give him a chance.

CHAPTER ELEVEN

Liz got the feeling someone was watching her. Sure enough, Leo was staring at her from over the top of his monitor, waiting for a response. When he motioned for her to take out her ear buds, she contemplated pretending she hadn't noticed. She'd already made eye contact, though, and once those steely blues were locked on hers, she had the worst time looking away.

But she totally could if she wanted to, so whatever.

She pulled out her ear buds and set them on her desk. "I'm sorry, did you say something?"

He nodded, his face heavy with something she hadn't ever seen in the three months they'd been working together. Worry? Concern? It made her response to his nonverbal answer come out louder—and snappier—than she meant it to. "Well, what is it?"

"*Shhhh*!" He craned his neck and looked around to make sure they were alone. "I'm trying to be discreet."

"Well, *pardon me,* Lord Shropshire." She immediately winced at how harsh the words sounded. A tiny sigh of relief blew past her lips when he frowned at her in that foppishly dandy way of his.

"Your British accent is deplorable."

"*You're* deplorable. What do you want? I'm busy." She paused the Youtube video she'd been watching while waiting for a software update to finish loading and minimized her browser. "And why are we whispering?"

"Because the walls of our boss's office are paper-thin. Have you seen him today?"

She lowered her voice, complying with his request. For the time being, anyway. "Eron? Yeah, but only for a second when he got in this morning."

"Did you notice anything odd about him?"

There was that look again. Or was she imagining it?

"I've noticed a lot of odd things about him." She held up a finger. "One, the dude glows. It's barely noticeable, but if you look really—"

"I'm serious, love. You've noticed nothing strange at all?" He walked the three steps over to her side of their desk and propped himself on the edge, his handsome features thoroughly crumpled.

Concern. It was definitely concern.

She tried to stay focused, but he was close enough to invade her personal space. It wasn't unpleasant, but it was too close for comfort and making it hard to concentrate. Besides, the longer he sat there, the more chance she'd side with Weird Liz and fantasize about jumping into his lap. So far, she was in agreement with Cautious Liz, whose vote was to push him as far away as possible, starting with off her side of the desk.

She leaned back in her chair and calmly adjusted her glasses before folding her arms. It wasn't to appear unbothered—she had that down—so much as it was to muffle the sound of her galloping heart, which, by the way, insisted on breaking into a run any time he was within an arm's reach. Sometimes, all he had to do was rub the underside of his jaw for it to start acting up. He did that when he was thinking, rubbed his jaw.

And he was doing it now.

Her toes curled inside her Converse, and she pressed her knees together to keep them from bouncing. She would ignore it, whatever *it* was. "Okay, Sherlock Holmes, you obviously have a specific oddity in mind, so spill it because I haven't got all day."

Yes she did.

Stop it, Weird Liz.

Leo leaned toward her. "I saw Eron coming back from lunch . . ."

He leaned closer still. The way he smelled—woodsy, but not sweaty lumberjack woodsy, a touch of warm spice and a hint of something else Liz couldn't place, but it was intoxicating whatever it was—made her brain semi-nonfunctional. Shit, there *it* was again. "And?" she said, trying not to salivate like one of Pavlov's dogs while inspecting his broad shoulders without being noticed. Her gaze flicked over his chest, then back up to his face, his five o'clock shadow beginning to make an appearance.

Oh, Christ. Deliver me from sin.

"He was wearing two suit coats."

She burst out laughing, mostly to eject the devilish thoughts possessing her mind. Though, some part of her did think his concern over their boss's attire was actually funny.

Leo straightened, indignant. "I'm delighted you find me so humorous."

She tried to stop, truly, but her efforts proved futile. She did find wearing two coats strange, but she wasn't sure Eron could be classified as normal. He was an odd duck. Maybe he was an odd duck with poor circulation. She wiped at her eyes and tried keeping her mouth shut, but a few chuckles managed to escape. "Did you ever think that maybe he's cold?"

"Bloody hell, Liz, what are you talking about? It's the middle of June!" His hands flew up before dropping back down to slap his thighs.

Good God, the theatrics. Clearly, another desperate attempt at getting her attention. She slid open a desk drawer to retrieve her bag. Manufactured drama never went over well with her, but for some reason, she found herself only mildly exasperated.

What are you up to, Weird Liz?

"Right. I see what you're saying, who'd be wearing two coats in June." She rummaged through her bag for some mints. His close proximity had made her mouth go bone dry. "You Londoners know nothing about humidity, obviously. Have you ever been to Florida in June? Seattle is a piece of cake compared to that." She thought about offering him a curiously strong mint, but that might give him the impression they were on friendly terms. She threw the tin in her purse and slammed the drawer. "Maybe our man just wants to make a fashion statement."

He ignored her sarcasm, and she blinked, a little stunned. He usually rose to the challenge.

"What if he's sick?" he continued, leaning forward and gripping the edge of the desk. His gaze shifted to the floor. "I've noticed he's looking a bit under the weather lately. And he's always tugging at his back. I don't think he's well, Liz."

He was serious. So serious, her annoyance drained away. She did think Eron looked rather frazzled as of late. She'd thought he was just stressed out, from starting a new business, but maybe Leo was on to something. "You think he's sick? Like, *sick* sick?"

Leo looked at her with those mesmerizing steel-blue eyes.

"He was acting weird at lunch yesterday. Fidgety." Leo clasped his hands in his lap until his knuckles turned white. "He kept talking about destiny and making the best of one's circumstances."

When Eron's office door swung open with a loud *whoosh,* they were both caught off guard. They leaned in unison—Leo to the side, her backward—to determine their boss's exact location.

Liz plastered a smile on her face as she watched Eron pour a cup of coffee before showing a powdered donut no mercy. His enthusiasm for donuts was comical, and if anything could make her crack a genuine smile, it would be the gusto with which he enjoyed eating them. A close second would be the awkward way the two coats made his arms move, like he had mechanical elbows.

Leo hopped of the desk and stood, the top of his thigh at eye level. "Good afternoon, mate."

Hips, eleven o'clock. Don't look.

She looked.

Dear God, what's wrong with me?

"Hi guys. How's it going?" Eron grinned while adding an obscene amount of cream and sugar to his coffee. Her teeth ached just watching.

"I should have round three of the marketing plan finally worked out by end of day. Fancy having a look at it first thing tomorrow morning?"

"Ha! You know I don't get in first thing." Eron rolled his eyes. "Good one, Leo. What a funny guy, isn't he a funny guy, Liz? A good sense of humor is such an important quality in a man, wouldn't you agree?"

"Are you feeling okay?" asked Leo, eyeing their boss's choice of clothing for a hot summer day. "Have you caught a chill?"

Liz waited, looking from Eron to Leo and back again.

When Eron's forehead creased in confusion, her annoyance reconstituted itself. "The reason for the two coats."

Eron squinted before his mouth dropped open. "Oh! Yes, I'm *freezing.*" He shivered, the display obviously fake, and set down his mug to rub his arms. He forced out a weak cough before abandoning his coffee, the conversation and, most out of character, the donuts. With his back facing the wall, he inched his way toward his office. After groping around for the handle, he opened the door and darted inside.

Liz might have believed he was merely cold, or perhaps that he was simply strange, if it hadn't been for the two small lumps she'd seen in the instant he'd turned to slip inside his office.

Leo pursed his lips and shot her a look that said, *"I told you so."* One hand found its way to the back of his neck and squeezed. "Maybe we should tell him, you know, that we know, just so things aren't so awkward."

Oh, hell no. She wasn't letting Leo drag her into this. They had no business getting involved in Eron's personal life. He was nice, but he was their boss, and that was it. They were not required—*she* was not required—to care beyond receiving a paycheck every two weeks. "Tell him we know what? We don't know anything."

"Did you not see him, love? It's clear there is something wrong, and it's obvious he's trying to hide it from us. Have you no soul? Don't you think it would be easier on him if he knew we knew, and that we're here to support him, no matter how bad it is."

She tried not to hear what he was saying, but plugging her ears like a child stopped being an option in the second grade. The words found their mark despite her reluctance to hold still and listen, and something foreign began to tug at her. As quirky as he was, Eron had grown on her, and she didn't want Leo's suspicion to be true.

But that wasn't the only thing bothering her.

Liz nipped at the inside of her lip to stop a grumble from coming out. This couldn't be happening. Could not. This was Leo, egotistical jerk, self-proclaimed God's gift to women, and he was actually thinking about someone other than himself?

Another chink in the armor.

I swear to God, Weird Liz, you're a dead woman.

"But what if he doesn't want us to know? I'm not sure I'd want my employees to know if I was sick." She tossed another argument at him, making one last effort to avoid getting involved.

"I've never heard him talk about family. It's seems wrong for him to go through something like this alone, yeah?"

She sighed. Leo was right and she was an emotionless monster, apparently. "Yeah," she said, nodding in agreement but feeling like she was trying to stand on shaky ground. Or, it could have been that various appendages were actually trembling. Either way, it felt odd to be on the same page as Leo. If she was forced to tell the truth, it might have even been a good kind of odd.

A right kind of odd.

She chewed on a fingernail while waiting for lightning to strike either her, or more preferably, Leo. There had to be a way to let herself off the hook, prove his assumptions were wrong. A way to slip out of his charming clutches and go back to the place she liked best. Minding her own damned beeswax.

She got up, grabbed Leo by the arm and pulled. "I might know a way to find out if anything's up for sure. Come on."

The firmness of his bicep, his skin separated from hers only by the thin layer of an expensive cotton blend, practically begged her to squeeze it. So, she did. Just a little.

Leo's gaze darted to her hand, which coincidentally, now

had a mind of its own and was groping his forearm. He bit his bottom lip and smiled. Just a little.

A burst of adrenaline exploded like a grenade, sucking all the air from the room.

What the hell are you doing, Weird Liz?

She dropped his arm like a scalding hot potato and took off for the front. He was mere steps behind her, so she turned on the afterburners. She refused to give him one stinking ounce of satisfaction by pointing out her keen interest in his male musculature a few moments ago. He wasn't going to get the chance to utter a single word about it.

Liz hurried up to the front counter, still trying to wrangle her breath, and what was left of her dignity, under control. "Hey, Willa."

Leo sidled up next to her and smirked. She couldn't see it because she refused to look at him, but she could *feel* it, and it made another round of hives start buzzing up her neck.

Bastard.

Willa looked up from her book on Greek mythology. "Oh hi, guys, what's up?"

Liz wasted no time cutting to the chase. "Question for you. How tight are you and Eron?"

"I don't know, pretty tight, I guess," said Willa, using a receipt to mark her place.

The coolers, packed with buckets of fresh cut flowers, hummed, and the late afternoon light shining through the front window stretched across the tiled floor. Business was good, better than Liz thought possible for a flower shop. Robby had been right. People did like getting flowers, which meant Eron couldn't be stressed out about business.

Shit.

"Because you've known each other for a long time, right?" asked Liz.

Willa slid her book to the side, giving them her full attention. "Yeah, why?"

Leo jumped in before Liz could continue. "Would you say you're tight like tell-each-other-*everything* tight?"

Liz pursed her lips at him. Really? Right now, she needed him to be quiet, not gumming up the intelligence-gathering works with his sticky sweet charm. She didn't need a Laurel to her Hardy, nor did she ask for a partner in crime. She was perfectly capable of committing them on her own.

"I suppose so." Willa shrugged then scrunched her forehead. "What are you two getting at?

"We know about Eron," blurted Liz. Honestly, did she even have *any* cool points left right now?

Willa blinked, drawing herself upright. "Oh my gods, you do? He told you the truth?"

Liz glanced at Leo, whose unnaturally handsome, freakishly unblemished face had suddenly gone pale.

"It's true, then, isn't it?" His voice was barely above a whisper. "Eron could die?"

Now the color drained from Willa's face.

Liz shifted her weight from one foot to the other. Son of a bitch. He was right, and the look on both their faces squeezed her deadened heart into action, forcing it to pump sympathy into every nook and goddamned cranny against her will.

Christ, did the universe not understand she was no good at this shit? This is why she never allowed herself to care, about anything. Why she always used sarcasm as a shield and the bitter truth as a sword.

"Look, the tumors on his back are hard to miss, and they look like they're getting bad. He doesn't have to hide it around us, both Leo and I understand."

Leo nodded. "It's not his fault. No one can control . . ." He swallowed hard. "It's just . . ."

The grief emanating from him was so palpable Liz almost reached out and took his hand, but uncertainty stopped her and she tucked both of hers into the back pockets of her jeans instead.

"He's such a great guy, with a real big heart and everything." She finished Leo's sentence for him, at least. It seemed the right thing to do. It also made the lump in her throat grow.

There was only one option left. Dump as much indifference on these burgeoning feelings as possible, before they could turn into bona fide emotions. "Lots of people get sick. At least he's keeping a positive attitude about it. I mean, even cancer can't get him down, am I right?"

Leo dropped his shoulders and tilted his head. Okay, so she could use a lesson in charm *and* grace, but at least the color was coming back to Willa's face.

"Oh, *whew,* for a minute there I thought you guys . . ." Willa shook her head. "Never mind. It's probably best that you don't know the specifics. Anyway, to answer your question, yes, there are some things that get him down. And mad, too, but it takes a lot for him to lose it. When he does, though, let's just say he's got his father's temper." Her pretty features suddenly darkened. "But his temper isn't what's so infuriating. No, that would be his pride. All he has to do is say, 'I need help,' but no, he can't say those three little words, not even to save his own relationship. It's enough to make you want to say *forget it,* you know?"

Liz widened her eyes at Leo. Recovered enough to understand her silent plea for help—closing the lid on the can of worms she had just opened—he took the reins. "Yeah, so if you could tell him both Liz and I are here for him."

"If he needs anything at all, let us know," said Liz, trying not to react to Leo's hand resting on her back.

Resting comfortably—*like no big deal*—as if it belonged there.

Calmer, Willa pulled in a deep breath. "That's very sweet, I'm sure he'll appreciate that. He's up against a real tough situation right now, but everything's going to work out fine. He'll make it through this. I know he will. He has to." Willa's watery eyes took Liz by surprise. "Because I can't imagine the world without him."

It appeared Willa and Weird Liz had been swapping notes on how to be an emotional mess. Willa had run the gamut of emotions in mere seconds, dragging Liz along for the ride, and she couldn't help but feel a bit turned inside out. "I didn't mean to upset you," apologized Liz. "I shouldn't have brought it up."

"No, it's okay." Willa dabbed at the corners of her eyes with a knuckle. "It's just that I love him so much. You know, as a *friend*, of course, and I don't want to lose him again."

Again?

The way Willa talked about Eron, the way she looked at him. The conversation at lunch a while back. It all clicked into place. Willa was in love with Eron. How had Liz missed it?

"Eron is the guy you fell in love with. He's the heart-not-the-face guy, isn't he?" Liz glanced at Leo, and he gave her a look, one that said he was in the dark, so she shot him one that told him she'd explain later.

And they were on a communicating-via-facial-expressions basis now?

Willa sniffled loudly, her breath doing a triple hitch. "I'm afraid I messed things up again and now it might be too late. I might lose him forever."

"Don't say that." Liz did her best at finding the right words to comfort Willa. "Life isn't always rainbows and gumdrops, but if you really love him, it's worth trying to make it work, isn't it? Forgive him, for whatever he's done. He's only human."

Oh my God, did I really just say rainbows and gumdrops?

"He's my whole world. I don't want to hurt him any more than I already have, but he's so stubborn sometimes," said Willa, a tear clinging to the corner of her eye, ready to roll down her cheek.

Liz rushed around the counter and pulled her into a hug. "Don't cry. You still have time. Say you're sorry. Let him know what he means to you. Tell him how much you love him."

Leo stared at her with another look she'd never seen before. Given their newfound ability to read each other's minds, it was clear he was conflicted, trying to reconcile her two sides, the irascible one and this terrifying new one, the one with half a heart in working order.

To be perfectly honest, she struggled to reconcile them, too. Who was this staunch advocate for love speaking right now? Liz Johnson didn't care about true love or love at first sight, holding hands, kissing in the rain or any of that crap.

Did she?

CHAPTER TWELVE

Leo led Liz through the curtain and into the back. Her hand was small, but it fit, and without thinking, he brushed a thumb over her knuckles. He realized what he'd done when she stopped dead in her tracks. Eyes wide, she withdrew her hand from his, like she'd been zapped with a spark of electricity. He couldn't blame her. He was just as shocked.

He tucked his hands into his pockets, the feel of her skin still on them. "What did you mean 'Is Eron the heart-not-the-face guy'?"

She held a finger to her mouth. His gaze dropped to her lips. Were they as kissable as they looked? No. He needed to stop these ridiculous thoughts. The teeth behind them would surely bite him if he tried.

The prospect made Monster Leo growl with excitement.

She slid past him while he struggled to gain control over his warring thoughts. Bloody hell, what was wrong with him? He'd just learned Eron was sick, which had shaken him considerably. Perhaps more than it should have for only knowing the man a few months, but the news had hit way too close to home nonetheless.

He followed when she ticked her head toward the side door, not surprised when she stopped at her desk first to grab her iced mocha. The tattoos moved with the muscles of her arm when she reached for the cup, and he couldn't keep his eyes from her curves.

Once they were outside and out of earshot, she leaned against the dirty brick, sipping her coffee and waiting as if it had been *him* who'd suggested they go somewhere more private. It appeared the Liz he'd witnessed wrap her arms around someone in need of comfort had been banished back to her dungeon.

He cleared his throat, forcing his disappointment into submission so the mask that hid his own emotions could fall into place. "As a certain ill-tempered someone once barked at me, and I'm paraphrasing here, I haven't got all day, so spill it."

"Calm down, Winston Churchill. Don't get your—what do you guys call them? Knickers?" She latched the hand that wasn't holding her coffee onto the opposite bicep.

Leo swallowed, trying to keep his gaze from her chest. She was wearing a concert tee for heaven's sake, nothing remotely sexy, but suddenly, the fact that it'd been months since he'd had a bedmate was all too apparent. "Yes. Knickers." He inhaled, closing his eyes and pinching the bridge of his nose. His conscience wanted to punch the wall. Monster Leo wanted to shag her up against it.

"Yeah, those. Don't get them in a twist."

His hands found their way into his pockets again, and he rested one shoulder on the wall next to her. She stiffened, looking as though she was ready to flee—or vomit—and his ears warmed. It was beyond frustrating the way she went from playfully calling him English monikers to scowling at him in silence. He never knew from one moment to the next what he was going to get.

Frustrated, he snatched her half-full drink out of her hand. That'll teach her split personalities to mess with him. Besides, he was feeling in need of some attention.

"Hey!" She reached out to retrieve her drink, but he lifted his arm, holding it high above her head. Her jumping was useless. There was no way she could reach it, not unless she climbed up his waist and onto his shoulders, which wasn't an unpleasant thought.

"Start talking, love." He pressed his lips together so he wouldn't laugh as she swiped at the cup again. When her arm crashed into his elbow, she lost her footing and stumbled into him—also not unpleasant—bracing a hand against his chest. Without thinking, he caught her.

Positive that rapid-fire insults were about to commence once she'd realized what he'd done, he prepared for battle. When nary an insult rang, he released his breath.

But not her.

Her gaze inched its way up his neck, to his mouth, then finally, his eyes. That feeling he sometimes got, like he'd known her forever, caused his heart to jab mercilessly at his ribs. The grip on her iced mocha loosened, dangerously close to slipping from his fingers and dropping onto the pavement. She'd be upset, but she'd forgive him because, for Monster Leo's patented brand of kissing, he'd need both hands free.

Wait. He was going to kiss her, then?

He knew the way women's eyes darkened with desire for him. Old hat at this point, really, but the way *this* woman's pupils dilated so completely, as if they were on the verge of drinking in his entire soul in one gulp, that was new.

Yes. He was going to kiss her.

He leaned in, just a touch, dropping his gaze to her parted lips before dragging them back to her eyes. In his twenty-seven years, had he ever encountered such an alluring shade of brown? His own lips fell open at the realization that, no, he had not. When she drew in a sharp breath, every muscle in his body tensed.

Those eyes, the way they darkened when her mood did, or brightened on the rare occasion he managed to make her smile, that was new, too. Other women, with their unremarkable hazel and vacant blue eyes, followed wherever he led. Not the woman standing in front of him. This woman was doing the leading. The burning question was, would he follow?

He'd decide later because right now the defiant tilt of her chin, so at odds with the way her hair framed the soft curves of her face, commanded him to the brink of his own destruction. He drew closer still, searching her face for . . . what? A sign? Permission? He wanted to kiss her, but did *she* want him to? He wasn't sure. It had never been an issue.

All he knew was somehow, even standing in a cramped side alley, where car exhaust mingled with the salty breeze coming off the waterfront of Elliot Bay, the thought of caring for someone other than himself seemed possible.

Remote, but possible.

As if she heard his thoughts, she went rigid in his arms, and like a jet engine in reverse screeching to a halt, that was all the sign he needed. She should have moved into him, not stood there like a marble statue.

The moment lost, he released her and took a step back, feeling like an awkward teen all over again. Except, he'd never been this clumsy with girls.

Liz wrapped her arms around her waist and scowled at the concrete as she pressed her back into the dingy brick behind her. She kicked at a weed that had persevered despite not having the good sense to grow in a more hospitable environment. Perhaps *that* was his sign.

Liz was inhospitable, so don't even try.

His mind raced for something to say, for a way to play the last ten minutes off like he'd only meant to keep her from an embarrassing tumble. Anything that would save him from admitting he'd slipped up. "I'm holding your coffee hostage until you tell me what that was all about in there."

So, something daft, apparently.

"Your threats don't scare me, you know. I can go get another one." Her tone was flat. Disappointed.

Had she *wanted* him to kiss her? Because, bloody hell, he would have kissed her if he thought that's what she had wanted.

Too late now. Best to carry on like he hadn't even wanted to in the first place. "Yes, but it would be such a shame if this one were to accidentally . . ." He popped the lid off and tipped the cup so the liquid came dangerously close to pouring out.

"I dare you."

He snapped the top back on and handed it to her. "Fine. Have it your way, Queen Victoria." She smiled at that, and his own grin widened.

Reacquainted with her iced mocha, the green straw slid between her lips and she took a long sip, as if the liquid inside was the source of life. Sufficiently revived, she finally got to the reason why they were standing in a filthy alley in the first place.

"Okay, so one time at lunch Willa mentioned how she fell in love with some guy she'd never seen before, and how it was his heart and not his face—"

"How, may I ask, did the subject of falling in love come up?"

She pawed at her glasses. "No, you may not. And I don't know, it just came up, but that's not the point."

"I'm not buying your lies, Liz Johnson, but go ahead. What's this point you speak of?"

She unleashed one of her kitten huffs. "Okay, so it's obvious Eron and Willa used to date. And according to her, she fell in love with his heart, not his face, because they talked over the phone for a while or some crap like that, she didn't really explain." She took another sip of her iced mocha. "But then they broke up. I don't know why, she wouldn't go into detail, but she still loves him. I mean, why else would she react that way, all crazy emotions and shit?" She glanced at him before fixing a blank stare on the opposite side of the alley. "You know, pretending not to care as much as she does."

The feeling he'd missed something important nagged at him, but he couldn't, for the life of him, do anything other than stare down at the cracks in the concrete. Finding out Eron was sick, seeing a different side of Liz, a softer side, then ruining it, chasing her away by trying to kiss her. It was all too much, and her voice floated away with the breeze.

"She should, though, because who knows how long . . ."

Each word faded, until he could barely hear anything at all.

"Because life's a bitch, right? And then you die."

That he did hear. The memories of his mother wasting away in a hospital took over, and the weight of the last hour crushed him, shoving his head and shoulders down. Why did it have to be *his* mum? And Hadn't he always known it would come to this? He'd never allowed himself to grieve. The anger, the resentment; he'd let them go unchecked. No wonder Monster Leo ran the show. It had been easy for him to become the ringleader.

And now here he stood, on the verge of losing the control he swore by. At work, in front of a woman who he wished more than ever he could hide it from, but who saw him for exactly what he was: A selfish arsehole.

He hadn't always been that way, and he wished Liz knew that. He blinked at the top edge of the building where it met the sky, groping the bricks behind him to keep steady. For her to know, he'd have to tell her. No, he'd have to *show* her, and that required effort. It demanded of him something he hadn't been able to do in a long time, to be the person he was *before,* the optimistic boy who had the potential to be a good man.

But it was too late for that, wasn't it? The only thing he could do now was will his emotions to fall in line and soldier on.

Monster on.

"Leo? Are you okay?"

The feel of her hands on his shoulders, accompanied by a gentle squeeze, was enough to calm him. Bring him back to the present. To the woman he never would have guessed could ground him so easily.

He gathered himself and scrubbed a hand over his face, hoping it would wipe away any evidence of how badly the news about Eron had affected him. When he refocused, her brown eyes, wide with alarm, were staring up at him.

"What did I say?" Her brows angled in toward each other. "Whatever it was I'm . . . Oh no, please don't tell me you've lost someone to . . . ?"

He wished he could take Liz in his arms. Hold onto her and bury his face in her hair. To be comforted by her. But he couldn't be sure it wouldn't be purely for his own selfish reasons, so he refrained. He swallowed hard before choking out the next two words. "My mum."

"I'm so sorry."

And like that, the world turned on its axis. The warm and caring Liz was back, and her arms were around him, of their own volition, not because he'd charmed them into it. Grateful, he leaned into her, taking this unexpected gift from the universe and savoring it. The feeling of her body pressed against his was more perfect than he'd imagined. No silly names. No distance between them. Just him and her, fitting together like puzzle pieces.

CHAPTER THIRTEEN

Eros opened his office door a crack and listened. Per usual, Leo was punishing his keyboard. For the love of Zeus, the man was prolific. He closed the door, softly so the latch didn't give away his spying.

"He needs to ask her out on a date."

Hermes, sprawled out on the love seat, scrunched his face into an expression that suggested he thought otherwise. "Are you sure?"

The seed had been planted, but it needed watering. Matchmaking 101.

"I'm on an accelerated timeline, remember? It's obvious they're into each other but holding back. They need more alone time *outside* of work. Trust me, I know these things," said Eros, pulling the top drawer of his credenza open. His chest filled with a mix of longing and regret as he looked down at his bow, which had sized itself to fit the cramped space. "If I let it go too long, she'll freeze over again. They need to go on a date. And I need to know the time and the place so I can be there.

He reached down and caressed the bow's gilded curves.

The thrum of power that usually pulsed through his fingers, his chest, his *being*, when he touched it had gone silent, and in the stillness he felt . . . blank. Did Zeus really expect him to pull this off without his powers? He closed the drawer with a sigh.

"Okay, but don't rush it," said Hermes. "We all know what happens when you do that."

The comment burrowed itself under Eros's skin. Why did everyone think they knew the business of love better than he did? "Yeah, yeah, yeah, point taken, but I wasn't given a strike limit, so why not use it to my advantage? If worse comes to worse, I get a partial hit, but hey, at least the ball starts rolling faster." He shrugged on his way to the door. "Hopefully Psyche's been able to pry open Liz's mind enough for a decent shot at her heart." He gripped the doorknob and turned. "Now let's hope my aim isn't too rusty."

Hermes got up from the loveseat, walking over and clapping Eros on the shoulder. "You got this, matchmaker. Now, I've got to deliver some bad news from Hades to a Central American drug lord." He slid a finger across his throat. "I'll see you tomorrow, bright and—well, I'll see you tomorrow."

"Ha, ha." Eros pushed the door open for Hermes, which allowed him to slip on a pair of mirrored aviator sunglasses as he strolled through.

"See you later, Leo." Hermes waved on his way to the side exit.

Leo stopped typing to give him a bro nod. "Always a pleasure, mate."

Eros pretended to inspect an empty pastry box sitting on the counter in the kitchenette.

One Mount Olympus, two Mount Olympus, three—

"I'm afraid Liz beat you to it," announced Leo, taking the bait.

"Oh, hey, Leo. I didn't see you there." Total lie. Eros's

wings shifted under his dress shirt, pleased he had it in him. He glanced at Liz's empty chair. "Where's Liz?"

Leo shook out his hands. "She and Willa went to Starbucks. Didn't they ask you if you wanted anything?"

"No."

"Join the club."

A wry smile quirked Leo's lips, indicating he wasn't offended in the least. In fact, he seemed a bit wistful.

Which meant his heart strings were prime for the plucking.

Eros couldn't come right out and demand Leo ask Liz out on a date, but he could push him in the right direction. Gently, of course, since mortals were defiant, stubborn creatures. The more that was demanded of them, the less they cooperated. He couldn't afford that. "Well, I'm glad we're alone, because there's something I want to talk about and it's kind of personal."

"Personal for me or personal for you?"

"For you." Eros pulled Liz's empty chair over to Leo's side of the desk and took a seat. "I want to talk about the elephant in the room."

"What elephant?"

"You and Liz."

Leo gave him a quick sideways glance before staring at his computer screen. "I have no idea what you're talking about."

"Look, I've seen it. Willa's noticed. Even Robby has said something. There's a spark there, and I don't blame you, Leo. She's cute, she's witty . . ."

Leo's shoulders fell. "You call it wit, I call it she hates my guts."

"No she doesn't."

"Oh? Then why is she ripping me a new arsehole 99.9% of the time?"

Eros knew the answer—she was terrified—but he couldn't

tell Leo that. "Well, ripped nether regions aside, I want you to know, in case you were wondering, I one hundred percent support a relationship between you two. I know you might think, since I'm your boss and everything, that I'd have a problem with dating someone at the office, but it's quite the opposite, I assure you."

"Hold on a minute, mate. Even if I am interested in Liz, you really think she's going to date a guy like me?"

"What do you mean a guy like you?"

"She's made it clear she's not fond of," Leo paused to rub his neck, "men who are so charming."

"Well, you know what I say? Life is too short." Eros's wings squirmed, laughing at the irony, and he pressed his back into the chair to shut them up. "If you want to ask her out, you should ask her out. If I had to wager, I'd bet she'd say yes." He held his breath. There could be no betting, he'd have to make sure she'd say yes. His life—and hers—depended on it.

"You think so?"

He was about to reassure Leo when the side door burst open, causing them both to jump. Gods *dammit*. Why couldn't Chronos cut him a frigging break on timing?

"What are you two losers talking about?" Liz headed over to the kitchenette to rinse out her empty Starbucks cup and throw it into the recycling bin. Willa winked at him and Leo on her way up front.

Leo raked his fingers through his hair. "Super secret guy stuff. No girls allowed." His grin was hesitant, faltering halfway through, and easily mistaken for dismissive.

It took everything Eros had not to smack a palm to his forehead.

"Well, *pardon me*, Prince Charles." Her curt tone matched her brisk stride to the restroom, and the door slammed shut.

"Are you really that terrible at reading the room? Work

with me, man. I'm trying to help you out here. You always start sincere and then ease in with the humor. You set up the jokes in the beginning, not make them." Eros pushed out of the chair. "Watch and learn, bro. Watch and learn."

When Liz came out of the bathroom, he wheeled the chair over to its usual place at her desk. "Actually, we were talking about all the cool stuff around Seattle Leo hasn't seen yet. Like the Fremont troll."

"How interesting." She cast a sly look over the partition. "I didn't know you had family here, Leo." Her snicker was small, but the grin that followed was huge. And her eyes were bright with something Eros knew well, even if Leo didn't recognize it yet.

Feelings. The wall-crumbling kind.

"It was a joke, get it?" said Liz. "I'm basically saying that you're a troll, but it's ironic because you don't look anything like a . . ."

Leo responded with a silent nod, causing her cheeks to tint red, and she sat down without another word.

Eros surveyed the scene before him. They were on the precipice, all right. Leo was interested and Liz was warming up to the idea. The iron might not be hot yet, but it was on its way, and Eros needed to time his strike accordingly. "You know what? I've got an idea. Let's all go see the troll right now. It'll be fun." Eros shuffled sideways toward the front before either of them could protest and pulled the curtain aside. "Hey, Willa, could you come here for a minute?"

He kept his back to the wall so he could hide the squirming bumps. They were getting bigger, stronger, and more noticeable. He made a mental note to stop by the drug store and pick up an ace bandage. If Liz and Leo only knew the real reason he could never turn his back on them. It would be tragic if they saw his wings moving during one of their fits, which was getting more and more frequent. That would be grounds for medical intervention, or maybe even an exorcism, and would derail the whole shebang.

Psyche glided through the curtains and into the back. "What's up?"

"Lock up the front, we're going on a mandatory field trip. Beers at Fremont Brewery, right after we do a little trolling."

Eros stared at his flight of beer. He preferred red wine, but they were at a brewery. Mortals sure loved their hops. Gods, these small sacrifices were killing him. He glanced up, half-expecting lighting to strike.

Sorry, horrible analogy.

He refocused on Liz and Leo. It was encouraging to see her at least sitting next to him. Eros had wanted to shoot while they were under the overpass checking out the local attraction, but Liz had avoided Leo like they were a couple of middle schoolers.

Now, as the girls chatted, Eros caught Leo's attention before widening his eyes and nodding in Liz's direction.

Leo promptly obeyed his suggestion, silent though it was. "So, Liz, what did you think of the troll?"

She shrugged her shoulders. "Eh, it was cool." The corner of her mouth pushed into a smirk, cementing her nonchalance in place.

Eros took a sip of beer, his knee bouncing.

Poseidon's balls, the Fates weren't playing.

Her fear of abandonment was proving to be quite literally the bane of his existence. A real Sisyphean feat. Eros tossed a quick smile her way nonetheless. She had feelings, he had no doubt about that, but they weren't the issue. It was her walls that were the problem. They were preventing her from taking the risk with her heart. She'd lowered them some, but he needed them down more.

Maybe Psyche and Hermes were right. He was forcing things to move too fast. Perhaps he *should* wait a bit longer. He tugged at the hair along his temple. They were so close, yet still so far away.

Psyche picked up on his declining mood. "Everything okay?"

"Yeah, everything's fine."

Psyche tilted her head. "You sure?"

"Okay, maybe I'm a little tired."

Liz and Leo shot each other a look, both going poker straight in their seats. Ah, the mortal illness they'd diagnosed him with. He felt bad they thought—wait a minute. No . . . he couldn't.

But he might have to.

"Hey, guys?"

"What's up, mate?" Leo dragged his gaze from the small pile of shredded paper that had previously been Liz's napkin.

"I know this might sound like it's coming out of left field, you know, because I'm your boss and everything, but I feel like we're past that employer/employee thing, right?"

"Yeah, Eron, absolutely. We're all," said Liz, her gaze darting over to Leo, "friends."

"Good, because life is too short to not say what's on your mind." Eros said the words for Liz and Leo's benefit, but they also rang true for his. And Psyche's. Not that he wanted to guilt her into taking him back. He didn't want that, but he did want her to know how he felt. "I like you guys more than I ever thought I would. And I know you know." He held up a hand when Liz opened her mouth to say something. "Promise me that neither of you will take life for granted, okay? It's precious, and there's no time to waste one minute of it on anger or fear or . . ." He looked into Psyche's entrancing gold eyes. "Doubt."

CHAPTER FOURTEEN

Dappled shadows danced across the pages of Liz's book. Engines rumbled, horns honked, and sirens wailed in the distance. After growing up in Chicago, the constant hum of Seattle made her feel right at home.

She set her book in her lap and twisted her spine while surveying the Saturday morning scene in front of her. An older couple held hands and talked on a nearby bench. Pedestrians shuffled past, some in a hurry, some not. A city squirrel unearthed acorns in a flowerbed full of blooms ruffled by the breeze.

A child laughed like a maniac.

The sound was contagious, and she couldn't help but grin as she shifted the book from her lap and onto the blanket spread out beneath her. She was living vicariously through that sound, that glorious belly laugh pushed out into the world without a care. Her childhood didn't include much of it.

When she scooted around to have a look, her whole body went rigid. There was Leo, all six lean and muscled feet of him, letting a blond-haired little boy peg him in the back with a Nerf football.

Seriously?

She could handle seeing him at work, even out of work, with Eron and Willa as a security blanket, but outside the confines of their backroom office space? That was different. Not having frosted glass or errands at lunch to hide behind was another. It was too much. And could he be any more adorable playing with that kid?

The way her belly fluttered—like now—and the way her pulse insisted on racing—like now, even with half the park between them—confirmed the effect he had on her was just as strong outside as it was inside those office walls. She thought about him constantly. Worse, she was beginning to like the obnoxious way he called her *love*. Don't even get her started on the cologne he wore or the way it mixed with the chemistry of his skin.

Plus, there was that day in the alley, when that thing happened.

Embarrassment squeezed her chest as she shoved her book into her tote bag. He'd almost kissed her, and she'd *wanted* him to, but then . . . and, oh God, the unsolicited *hugging*. Her arms had wrapped themselves around him without permission, and she'd been powerless to stop them.

She tried coaxing her lungs to stop their pitiful gasping, and her gut to release the lead balloon it held captive, as she shook the dirt and dried bits of grass off the small blanket. The urge to look in his direction while she hurried toward the street, trying to slink away unnoticed, tightened her neck muscles.

"Liz!"

The sound of his voice, the urgency in it, as if begging her to turn around and look at him, pinned her to the spot. She pasted on a smile before turning to him like a moth dive-bombing into a flame. He handed the boy the football and rumpled his hair before jogging over. What would she even say?

Well, here he comes, Weird Liz. Better think of something fast.

"Fancy meeting you here." He sounded out of breath. She couldn't figure out why, because the body under his tight-fitting T-shirt certainly offered zero indication of poor physical health.

"Oh, hi, Leo."

Casual. Sound casual. Ignore the voice . . .

"Yeah, I live right over there." She pointed in the direction of her apartment building—like an idiot.

Give him a chance.

"Brilliant. I live right over there." He motioned in the opposite direction, where the swanky apartments were.

Curse that troublesome British accent.

Give him a chance.

And those eyes she couldn't seem to find her way out of once she looked into them. Damn those, too.

Give. Him. A. Chance.

"We're so close, yeah?" he said with a hesitant smile. "Maybe we should hang out some—"

"You know them?" She peeked around his shoulder at the boy, who'd gone to sit on the bench next to his mother. The subject needed changing, and she wasn't above using perfect strangers to save her ass. It was obvious she couldn't stand there, in a public place, without fumbling for words let alone holding a coherent conversation. Her luck, had he finished his sentence, she'd have jumped on his back and told him to lead the way.

"Oh, that's Claudia and Owen. They live in my apartment building."

Her next question came out unbidden. "Where's his dad? Working or something?"

The memory of her father leaving for another carton of cigarettes bloomed like a poison mushroom cloud in her head. Even now, the smell of stale cigarette smoke left a toxic cocktail of anger and resentment swirling in her gut. It had taken him days, sometimes a week, to find his way home. Like kids desperate for attention do, she'd prayed every night he was gone that it wouldn't be the day he'd decide to disappear for good.

And she still hated herself for it.

"He's not around" said Leo.

She knew she should stop but couldn't. "How do you know? Did you ask?"

Lines creased his forehead but smoothed as he waved to the pair sitting on the bench. "Yes, right after I asked if I could have a look at her bank statements. How daft do you think I am? I've only ever seen those two, no one else."

Bile rose, burning her throat. She knew all too well what it felt like to have a deadbeat for a father, and how their unconscionable actions could scar a kid. She just couldn't figure out what Leo had to gain by inserting himself into this one's life.

Except, perhaps, bagging a lonely single mother.

"Do you think that was the right thing to do? What if he cries himself to sleep tonight because he got a taste of what it's like to have a dad around?" Anger and resentment rose from somewhere deep inside her. "What if he wishes things had turned out different and you just made it worse?" The questions burst out like rockets. She had started out asking them on the boy's behalf, but realized the damaged little girl in her was the one who really wanted to know.

"Whoa, whoa, whoa, Liz, calm down. It was a friendly gesture, that's all. I didn't mean anything by it." His hands found the tops of her shoulders, like they knew the way by heart. The weight and warmth of them comforted her, and the building storm of emotion inside her began to settle.

He bent at the knees so his face was level with hers. "I'm not up to anything, I promise. I know you think I'm capable of dastardly things when it comes to women, but I'm not *that* guy. I know what it's like not having a father around."

"You didn't have one either?" She was referring to herself, but if he thought she was talking about Owen, that was fine by her. Her personal information was on a need to know basis.

He shook his head, a silent answer to her question. His hands slid from her shoulders, resting on her arms for a moment before ending up at his sides. "I would have given anything to have had someone to toss a ball around with, even if it was some foreign bloke. An incredibly handsome foreign bloke, I might add."

Dammit.

He wasn't supposed to have depth. He was supposed to be a self-centered asshole. It would make it easier to walk away after this infatuation she had with him fizzled out.

The lump clogging her throat grew bigger. This was one more thing they had in common. Another sign she had been wrong about him. She leaned closer, wanting to put her arms around him. Again. And she almost did. Until the memory of her father walking away on that last day stopped her.

She had to put an end to this ridiculousness. They could be friends, maybe, but that was it. She would not develop feelings. Because feelings, real feelings, well, that was when the shit usually hit the fan. He would leave, sooner or later, and she'd be back where she started. Alone. So she screamed at her softening heart, commanding it to harden again.

The sudden stabbing pain that lanced the lower right side of her back caused her to stumble forward. She grabbed onto the strong arms that steadied her, yet again. It was infuriating for them to feel that good. That safe.

"Are you okay?" His voice pulled her head up toward his eyes, which were full of concern. The look that was beginning to be her weakness.

"I'm fine." She untangled herself from him.

"Are you sure? You look pale." He regarded her carefully.

"No, I'm okay," she murmured.

"You still seem a bit wonky. Do you regret giving me hell for playing catch in the park with my neighbor's son, is that it? Here, let me feel your forehead." His smile was blinding as he placed the back of his hand on her brow. "No fever, but your hives have made an appearance. Next, you'll be pushing your glasses halfway up your forehead. You do that when you're nervous or angry."

She pushed her glasses into the bridge of her nose. "No I don't."

His laugh was all that was right in the world. "Shall I go by the scowl on your face, then? Because that definitely means you're angry."

She did do that when she was angry, push her glasses up and scowl. A nervous tic she'd developed in the third grade. But she wasn't angry. She had been at first, but now she was only desperate to stop Weird Liz from thinking letting her guard down was an option.

"I'm sorry if I've upset you." He filled the silence with an apology.

But he wasn't at fault her emotional hard drive needed a reboot. "It's okay, I'm not upset. I mean, I was, maybe a little, but I'm not now. I'm fine." She scanned for any feelings of tenderness and pressed delete.

"Well, seeing as your only two emotions seem to be irritation and anger, I figured I had a fifty-fifty chance at getting it right."

A breeze blew, ruffling his hair. She bit the inside of her cheek to stop herself from reaching up and slipping her fingers through it. He was wrong, irritation and anger weren't her only emotions. Not lately.

"Contrary to popular belief, there is nothing I want more than for us to not be at each other's throats constantly." His eyes seemed bluer in the afternoon light. Or maybe it was sincerity that made them shine like that.

Why couldn't she walk away from this man?

"Same." Her heart was sprinting again, annoying the hell out of her. "I guess."

The wattage on his smile increased exponentially. "Brilliant. Now, can we start by me not having to don armor every time we're around each other?"

She dropped her gaze, the discrepancy between her brain and heart making her head spin. "Sure."

"Not the resounding yes I had hoped for, but it will do." He reached out to take her bag. "Here, let me carry that."

"Seriously?" A snort escaped. "You want to carry my bag? What, are we back in the 1950s?"

"Easy." His palms shot up in defense. "I was only trying to bring a bit of chivalry with me from across the pond, yeah? Plus, it looks heavy." He slipped the bag from her shoulder then pretended to drop it. "What the bloody hell is in here?"

She rolled her eyes. Why did a piece of her carefully constructed wall crumble every time he opened his mouth? At this rate, it would be in shambles at her feet within the hour. "I'm not used to guys being nice just to be nice, you know? Especially guys like you."

"Oh, here we go again with the *guys like you*. You sound a tad resentful, you know."

"I'm *not* resentful," she protested. When another smile lit up his face, she abandoned her argument. "All right, fine. I find most of you intolerable once you hit teenager status."

"Let's see if we can't change that then, yeah? Fancy a trip to Starbucks?"

She did fancy one, and not because she needed her iced mocha fix, which she did, but because she didn't want to say goodbye yet. "I do fancy one," she responded in a British accent.

He held out his elbow to her. "Deplorable."

She hooked her arm in his, and her heart started galloping again. But like everything else, she ignored it. They were just friends. Why the skin-on-skin contact succeeded in making her dizzy as they made their way out of the park, she refused to say, but good thing her *friend* was there to help her keep her balance.

CHAPTER FIFTEEN

The strange part about seeing Eron wasn't the way he dove around the corner, but the giant longbow, or whatever a bow that large was called, he'd been carrying. Leo had been in the middle of a debate with Liz over coffee versus tea when a flash of sunlight bounced off its polished surface. He pointed at the intersection a few hundred yards ahead. "Was that Eron up there?"

"Was it? I didn't see anyone. Even if I had, my eyesight can't be trusted from this far away." Liz tapped the plastic frames of her glasses. "Blind as a bat without them, and I need a new prescription."

Another tidbit to add to the collection of things he'd been compiling since the moment they'd met. Coffee, not tea. Purple, just because. Cats, obviously. Blind, as in bat.

Brown eyes he couldn't do justice describing.

He chuckled as he rubbed the underside of his jaw. Perhaps he needed to visit an optometrist himself. "Maybe it was someone that looked like Eron, then, on the way to one of those Cosplay things." He bit his bottom lip and decided not to mention how uncanny the man's likeness had been, misshapen humps and all. Then again, he couldn't be certain there had been anything of the sort with that quiver of arrows strapped to the man's back.

"Maybe we can catch him." Liz tore off down the street, a sudden, spontaneous side of her making an appearance. He rather liked it, these different sides. All the other women had been one-dimensional, too simple compared to her complexity.

When she got to the corner, she shook her head and shrugged. He ticked his shoulders up, too, and as soon as he noticed the way she cocked that one hip and tilted her head as if to say, *"Hurry up, Guy Fawkes, I haven't got all day,"* he forgot all about the man who may or may not have been Eron.

Leo held the door open for Liz as she slipped past him into Starbucks. He'd always liked the scent of ground coffee, but never developed a taste for the resulting liquid. Life could be bitter enough on its own. Why drink it down in a cup every day?

"It's packed. You grab those two seats over there, and I'll stand in line," he said over the whine of the industrial-sized espresso machine.

"You're so bossy," replied Liz, shouting over the hiss of the industrial-sized steamer. "Do you even know what I want?"

He sent a playful shrug her way before heading toward the counter. Did he know what she wanted? Of course he didn't, generally speaking, but he did know how she took her coffee. Baby steps.

He handed her a skinny iced mocha with no whipped cream, and she smiled at him when he plucked the straw resting behind his ear and held it out to her. She was letting more of them slip lately, those smiles, and it made his insides pull tight every time she did.

"So, I guess I was kind of hard on you at the park, huh?" She tapped the straw on the table to liberate it from its paper prison.

He took the lid off his chai tea latte to let it cool. "You're just now coming to this conclusion? I'm not sure if you realize this, but I think it's your life's mission to wound me with words."

She glared at him. God save the Queen, he better be careful. He was only beginning to make progress and seeing as he seemed to have a knack for ruffling every one of her feathers, he might want to keep an eye on his teasing. And his scalding hot tea.

"You?" She leaned over and flicked him in the bicep. Not a hard, angry flick, a soft, teasing one. "The handsome and charming Leo Simmons wounded by words? Inconceivable."

"Aha!" He grabbed her fingers en route back to her side of the table. He almost thanked her for giving him the perfect excuse to touch her. She snorted in surprise, the sound making him grin. "The wee bonny lass finally admits I'm charming. I had a feeling all along you thought I was handsome." He still held onto her fingers. They felt too good to let go.

She pulled them from his grip and curled them around her cup, which was beginning to sweat. He could relate.

"I admit nothing." She caught the straw of her drink between her lips for a quick sip. "With moves like that, I bet you were super popular in high school."

Smiling. Laughing. Bloody hell, even talking. All the things she'd refused to do when they first met. Leo wished he knew what he was doing differently to make her not want to strangle him. He wanted to keep doing it. Because that smile, that warm gaze instead of a chilly glare, was worth the price of admission. "You'd be surprised."

"Oh, come on. With those eyes?" A blush tinted her face.

"I wish, but no. These eyes, ravishing as they are, didn't get me what I wanted most."

"And what was that?"

He'd shared the details before, matter-of-fact and detached, but never the pain. Yet, for some unexplainable reason, he wanted to—*needed to*—share a piece of himself with her. "We found out mum had cancer when I was in primary school. I accompanied my mother to chemo treatments instead of girls to dances my first two years of secondary. Mothers on chemo and dances, both cause for therapy, by the way." He couldn't help but soften the hardness of his reality with humor.

Liz swallowed so hard her throat nearly hit her chin. "So your father . . . ?"

Leo's sadness evaporated, anger seeping in to take its place. Perhaps therapy as a youth would have done him some good. "Was and still is a bastard. He never came to see her once. I suppose his wife wouldn't have liked that very much." Now he was the one scowling.

"Damn," she whispered. "What an asshole." She surveyed the lacquered table with more interest than a piece of furniture deserved. His guess, she was looking for a place to hide.

At least her response had been honest, even if it did imply the worst about him. Her honest reaction was more comforting than the fake sympathy he usually got. "It's all right, love. I've made peace with it." A bloody lie, but he didn't want to talk about his father or the character traits he'd inherited from him. Leo maneuvered back toward a subject he'd rather talk about. Her. "See? It's your life's mission."

She screwed up her face, and he smiled at the way she

glowered at him. He'd grown fond of the the way her neck turned red, letting him know when he'd said something right, but mostly wrong, and to his complete surprise, he wanted more.

"What would you say if I asked you to go to dinner with me tonight?" His gut looped in anticipation. Not his smoothest delivery, but it was out there now and he couldn't take it back.

She met his gaze and held it, motionless. *E*motionless. "I'd probably say no."

His chest deflated, the air releasing from his lungs so completely he thought they might collapse. Bloody hell, maybe she was a cyborg after all. Karma was biting him in the arse right now. Hard. Liz had him eating out of her hand. Wrapped around her cranky little finger.

It was quite uncomfortable, that shoe on the other foot thing.

"You're right." Leo struggled to keep his tone light. "It's a bad idea." He sipped his tea as he quietly tried to puzzle it out. So this was what crushing rejection felt like?

And how was it he still wanted to spend time with someone so unavailable to him? He should have moved on by now. This was too much—she was too much. He liked his life the way it was, no commitment and no one to worry about but himself. So what was he doing?

Something flickered behind her eyes, and her glare softened before she broke eye contact to dig a ChapStick out of the front pocket of her jeans. "I said no because it's too much like a date." She tore off the cap and vigorously applied the balm to her lips before recapping and shoving it back into her pocket. "You're slick with words, Shakespeare, but I'm afraid you're not dating material. Besides, dating is off limits. We work together. Don't you know office romances are a no-no?" She crumpled her straw wrapper into a ball and flicked it at him. It bounced off his chest and into his lap. Per usual, a direct hit. "However, I might be convinced to hang out. You know, if I don't have anything else going on. You're kind of amusing."

Wind filled his sails again, pushing his lips into a grin. He could work with that. "Two admissions in one day?" He flipped his palms up at her. "Careful, love, don't hurt yourself."

"Don't get all up in arms, William Wallace. I said you're *kind of* amusing."

"William Wallace was Scottish."

"Yeah, well, I'm running out of famous British people I know, so I've opened it up to the whole of Western Europe now."

"I see. Your game, your rules. And, for the record, I am so dating material."

Liz unleashed a kitten snort. "Don't get any ideas, because I'm not."

Leo leaned back in his chair. "Don't worry, I wouldn't dare dream of dating you."

But wasn't that exactly what he was doing?

Her smirk disappeared, replaced with something that looked almost like hurt. "Oh, so you think I'm un-dateable? Now who's wounding who with words?"

She might not be dateable, but that didn't stop him from hurtling over the obstacle in his way. "I wouldn't know if you're un-dateable because we're only allowed to hang out, remember? We should at least find out if you're hang-outable, though. How about tomorrow?"

"You're on." Liz tapped his shoe with her foot. "But I'm bringing a few of my best insults along. Someone's got to keep you off your high horse, Sir Lancelot."

CHAPTER SIXTEEN

Leo's gaze dropped to the granules of sugar clinging to the edge of Liz's top lip. He flicked a finger over the corner of his mouth to call attention to the debris on hers. She either didn't notice or was ignoring him. Most likely the latter, but she needed to wipe it away soon, lest he be tempted to take matters into his own hands.

"These mini donuts are to die for." She bit another in half before brushing the sugar away. "We've got to get more of these to bring in to work on Monday. What do you think, a dozen? I can't wait to see Eron go nuts."

The farmer's market in Ballard had been an excellent choice for their first date—hang out. It was only a hang out. Regardless, he wasn't sure he would enjoy it, what with the outside food preparation, people milling about and bumping into him and whatnot. It all seemed so plebeian. But, despite the crowd and dubious food stall setups, he was having a great time. It was only eleven o'clock in the morning. If he played his cards right, and didn't piss her off somehow, they might be able to spend all day together.

He might even get another chance to kiss her.

Not his normal habit, donuts, but he plucked another from the white paper bag and popped it in his mouth. "Quite delicious, indeed. He'd go through a dozen way too fast. Perhaps we should get two."

He accepted her offer for another before she crumpled the top of the paper down and stuffed it in her bag. Donuts safely stowed, she brushed the cinnamon and sugar remnants off the chest of her Smashing Pumpkins T-shirt. The black fabric made the bright colors of her tattoos pop. He almost asked her if they had any significance, but the question remained lodged in his throat. It seemed like something—beeswax, as she would no doubt put it—she might not be ready to share. The last thing he wanted to do was step on a landmine and get blown back to square one.

"You like the Smashing Pumpkins, yeah?" That seemed safe enough, getting confirmation on something he already knew. She'd worn that T-shirt before, under a hoodie most of the time, but he'd seen it enough to guess she was a fan.

"Uh, the Pumpkins are only the best alt rock band ever."

He grinned. He didn't know much about the band other than what Google had revealed, but the brightness in her eyes was spectacular. Breathtaking, even. He wasn't sure, now that he'd seen it, how he'd ever gone without it.

"Plus, they're from Chi-town, so I'm partial. I know what I'm about to say is sacrilegious, but Nirvana never did it for me. The Pumpkins' lyrics are so—"

"Sublime." Like the curve of her throat, where the skin was pale and smooth like porcelain. His eyes found the pulse that jumped just above her collarbone, and he imagined pressing his lips to it. Was her hair as soft as it looked?

Shite. She was staring at him. He suspected for ogling her neck like a ravenous vampire. Also, no doubt, because he held a lock of her hair. How it had gotten there he hadn't a clue, but it was there, soft and curling around his fingers. He gently placed it behind her shoulder. "This length suits you," he said, trying to cover up his apparent black out.

She didn't shy away, or scowl, thank the heavens, but her mouth did fall open. Before she could protest, and, bloody hell, knowing her she would protest, he grabbed her wrist and pulled her to her feet. "Ready for our next stop?"

"Are you sure this isn't a date?" Suspicion laced her words. "This seems too planned for hanging out."

Of course it was planned, but only loosely, in case things got awkward. Like perhaps one of them couldn't help but stare at the other in a lust-filled daze. He hadn't thought he'd be the one doing the staring. She didn't have to know that, though.

He arched an eyebrow. "Trust me, if it was a date, you'd know it."

True to form, she rolled her eyes at him and huffed.

The crowd parted as they made their way toward the main street. Google had revealed another place he thought she might like. He'd never put much thought into where to take women on dates before now. He had a system—nice restaurant, trendy club, or perhaps the theater if there was something good he wanted to see, then back to his place. Farmers markets had never been part of that lineup. It had always been what *he* wanted.

But he was enjoying thinking about someone else for a change. Besides, Liz was turning out not to be just any other woman, and by the time they reached the intersection, he no longer held her wrist. Somehow, their arms had twisted and their hands had connected, and now her fingers were entwined with his. Her touch loose and tentative, the kind that indicated she was considering if holding hands was permissible while hanging out, but there nonetheless.

The red neon rocket at the top of the record shop sign was bright even in the daylight.

"Are you serious, Simmons? Well played. This is one of my favorite places in Seattle. I was actually going to see if you wanted stop in, you know, since we're already out here and everything, but I wasn't sure you'd go for it."

Normally he wouldn't, but the giddy feeling he was currently experiencing seemed to prove that even the most unlikely of things was possible.

He held the door open, executing a discreet, yet perfectly timed inhale as she slipped by. She smelled lovely, not flowery, but sweet like candy. He smiled at the irony. So many things about her seemed at odds, almost as if the woman beneath had been twisted by fate into a harder version of herself in order to keep them apart.

He trailed behind her as she wandered over to the "S" bin, suspecting it was to see if there were any Smashing Pumpkins albums she didn't already own. When she shot him a sideways glance, one that said, *"This isn't a date, weirdo,"* he ventured off toward a bin at the beginning of the alphabet, which seemed like the only self-respecting thing to do.

Real subtle, Elton John.

Bloody hell, she was in his head now.

He flipped through the stack of albums in the "E" bin until he found what he was looking for and held Elton John's *The Legendary Covers Album* up over his face. He assumed a posture that would seamlessly match the sullen, bespectacled face of a leopard print clad Elton John and cleared his throat.

A loud guffaw sounded from over by the "S" bin. He hadn't heard her laugh that hard before. Come to think of it, had he ever heard her laugh at all? The sound electrified him. Every synapse in his brain fired, sending pleasure zipping through him head to toe. He waved in her direction to make the beautiful sound continue, which it did. "Hey there, brash

American, are you laughing at me? Is it because I look constipated? I'll have you know, I am Sir Elton Hercules John, and my constipated arse has sold millions of records."

"You're so stupid."

He dropped the cover in time to see a smile accompany the insult, and the anxiety that corkscrewed through him slowed to a more manageable pace. He returned her smile and dropped the album into the bin. "Why, Liz Johnson, that's the nicest thing you've ever said to me."

He continued to meander through the store, flipping through random records and stealing glances at her. But he never caught her looking back, and he began to wonder if he needed to fire up the old charm machine when, somewhere around the "G" bin, he noticed her tapping on her phone. The corners of his mouth dipped. He'd lost her attention and that just wouldn't do, because having it felt a bit like taking a long swig of water after crossing the Sahara. Highly refreshing.

He pulled out an album featuring the most ridiculous looking cover he could find and held it over his face. "Am I boring you, love?"

"Nothing compares to Elton, he was the pinnacle of your comedic success," she replied, deadpan.

He peeked around the cover, nervous of what he might discover. He'd successfully gotten her to open up, to relax a bit around him, but she had suddenly gone serious. He shrugged, trying to appear unbothered, but his mind raced, already searching for more ways to make her laugh.

She stood by the door, and when a gray sedan pulled up to the curb, she raised her hand to signal to the driver she was the one who'd ordered the Lyft. "Ready for our next stop?"

He gripped the record he was pretending to inspect a little tighter. "Are you sure this isn't a date?"

"If it was a date, you'd know it," she responded,

butchering his accent on purpose before pushing open the door and walking outside.

The urge to toss the album, letting it fall wherever it landed, and run after her unsettled him. Bloody hell, it was worse than he thought. His heart ricocheted around his chest as he walk-ran after her as calmly as his remaining dignity could manage.

He slid into the backseat, as close to her as he could get without making it seem like he thought their afternoon together was a date, and shut the door. The car pulled away from the curb and, finally, she dropped her phone into her lap and looked at him.

"I'm afraid of heights, so you better not laugh at me if I pee my pants. I heard the view is amazing at night, though."

He shot her a look that was supposed to say, *"I guarantee nothing,"* but his sweating palms said something altogether different. He had no idea where she was taking him. Regardless, in that very moment, it was clear that he, consummate bachelor by choice, dashing lady's man by nature, didn't care. To add insult to injury, it was quite obvious that, yes, he would follow wherever she led.

Liz wanted to throw up. She couldn't tell if it was from being in a rotating steel contraption several stories above the ground or because she was in such close proximity to Leo in a small space. Why had she agreed to this again? Oh, right, it had been her idea. Because he'd wanted to ride this frigging deathtrap the day they met and she'd said no.

He'd been such a sport all day, going to places she couldn't imagine he and his Armani Exchange jeans frequented very often, like the farmer's market or her favorite record shop.

They were seated across from each other when the Great

Wheel began its slow and heart palpitation-inducing ascent upward. She was surprised at how relieved she'd been when he came over to sit next to her. She welcomed it so much, in fact, she hadn't said a single word when he cited obstruction of view as the reason. Bullshit. They were in a glass cabin, with a 360-degree view of the harbor and downtown. But she'd take that excuse over having to admit she'd been hoping he'd come to her rescue. Now she was trying to get him to hold her hand through mental telepathy. If it worked, he'd feel her shaking, so never mind that last part.

She wouldn't look down, that's all.

The sun was low in the sky, trying to cast its burnished light over the bay, but the clouds had other ideas. She peered out over the water, keeping her eyes fixed on the pink sky splashed with misty blues. It was beautiful, but it would be even prettier if they were standing on solid ground, or sitting on a beach somewhere. Why hadn't she thought of that instead? She swayed in her seat, trying not to think about the dizzying height at which she was currently floating.

An arm came down around her.

Praise be.

"You okay?" Leo squeezed her shoulder and pulled her into his side. She leaned into him without protest. "You really are scared of heights, aren't you?"

She felt his heartbeat against her arm, pounding almost as furiously as hers. What was *he* afraid of?

To stop herself from wondering, her old friend sarcasm made an appearance. "This is where I would wound you with words, Leo Simmons. And in case you haven't caught on by now, yes, I would be extra mean, just to make you think about the absurdity of that question. But I'm too freaked out right now, so you're going to have to pretend."

A chuckle vibrated his chest, and before she knew what

she was doing, she leaned farther into him, intending to absorb every last reverberation before it ceased. She let a puff of nervous laughter escape. "By the way, what part of I might pee my pants did you not get?"

The patter of raindrops on glass filled the silence that followed. She felt the electricity between them as his chest expanded. Determined to turn the voltage down a notch, she stared at the floor. His slow, smooth exhale, the warm woodsy scent, the damn romantic rhythm of the rain, they all begged her to look at him already.

The butterflies were back, and her untrustworthy heart about burst from her chest when he hooked a finger under her chin and pulled her gaze to meet his. This was *not* supposed to be happening.

But the sunset's indigo streaks had nothing on the dark blue of his eyes, and there was no way the churning gray water below could have as much depth.

His thumb grazed her bottom lip, announcing his intention before he opened his mouth to make her an offer she already knew she couldn't refuse. "Shall I distract you?"

She thought about the alley again, and how badly she'd wanted him to kiss her.

This is a bad idea, Weird Liz. Bad, bad idea.

There were two things she knew to be true. One, Leo Simmons was a player. A charmer. A *that guy*. And, two, she steered clear of guys like him. At all costs. If it were any other guy, she would batten down the hatches and move on. Yet here she was, hatches dangerously loose, and by her own doing no less. The mortar holding the stones in place was in great peril of crumbling, because the record shop, the way he kept trying to get her to laugh, that had to mean something, right?

Plus, the way the man ate donuts. Sweet. Baby. Jesus.

She blinked, and his face came back into focus. The unassuming look in his eyes, nervous and waiting for an answer, made her think that maybe she was different. Maybe she had judged him too soon. "Do you want to distract me?"

His lips tipped up, not into a cocky grin, but a genuine smile. "I've been dying to distract you," he whispered before dropping his gaze to her mouth.

And just like that, she melted. Right there in the rotating steel contraption several stories above the ground. Into a pool of desire for him. It didn't matter that she knew he was on his best behavior, using every charm in the book to get her into his bed. She had to know what it was like to kiss him, and she would deal with the consequences later. Her brain and mouth fell out of sync again, and her answer came out more breathless than she wanted it to. "Distract me, then."

She didn't need to tell him twice.

His fingertips were molten lava as they slid along her jaw, his thumb scorching a path across her cheek. When they settled into the hair at the base of her neck, she thought she might spontaneously combust, leaving him to kiss nothing but a smoking pile of ashes. How was it possible to shiver and burst into flames at the same time?

She was still reveling in the sensation his fingers had burned into her skin when the warmth of his breath on her lips almost burned her alive.

When he finally kissed her, it was soft and slow. Reverent. No feverish rush. No greedy plundering. He took his time, from one corner of her mouth to the other. Coaxing with his lips until hers moved in time. The faint sound of rain hitting the glass in a hard, steady rhythm registered.

Holy shit. I'm kissing in the rain.

The thought dissolved when he brushed his tongue against the seam of her lips, her own meeting his in return, inviting him in. It was by far the sweetest kiss she'd ever had. And she didn't know how they'd go back to work tomorrow the same two people, fighting over coffee versus tea. Because this kiss—this achingly tender, ridiculously perfect kiss—changed everything.

CHAPTER SEVENTEEN

Liz's morning started like any other, with a Starbucks. Except, curiously enough, her beloved iced mocha was no longer the highlight of her day. Coffee and chocolate had competition.

As much as she hated to admit it, ever since the farmer's market and the ride on the giant rotating death trap—ever since that kiss—things were different. They'd shifted, and now a head full of carelessly toss about hair had taken the lead.

This development should displease her more. She could think of a dozen reasons why kissing him had been a huge mistake. The problem was none of those reasons seemed to hold water anymore. In fact, much to Cautious Liz's dismay, the only disappointment she really felt kissing Leo was in herself, for not seeing if his hair felt as good as it looked while she'd had the chance.

Also, maybe she should amend that no dating thing.

Absolutely not.

They were just friends. Who happened to have shared a kiss. Several, actually, if she included the time it took for them to descend from the sky. And the goodnight kiss, okay, two, but who was counting? Now that they had it of their system, they could concentrate on things like . . . whatever things friends did. Catch a movie or go to the record shop or stay home and share mini donuts all night long.

Ah, Christ. See what you've done, Weird Liz?

"So, love, shall we hang out again tonight?" asked Leo, as if he'd heard the entire conversation going on in her head.

She hesitated. "I'm not sure your definition of hanging out is the same as mine."

He stopped typing to peer at her from over the top of his workstation. "I thought you were going to drop the tough girl act? We shared donuts."

"It's not an act. It's an art. And they were small, so technically, it was *one* donut."

One perfect, wonderful donut she wanted to take a bite out of again and again.

"Did you not like it—them?"

She rolled her eyes at him. God, did he really think she hadn't enjoyed kissing him? Oh, she wanted to have hated it, very much so, but that hadn't been the case. And considering she couldn't stop thinking about it, the pretending it didn't happen ship had already sailed.

"I did, but you know what they say about too many donuts between friends."

"No, do tell."

"It leads to guys like you getting to have your cake and eating it, too."

"Sounds splendid. Let's proceed."

Liz groaned. He was getting ideas, and honestly, it was all her fault. "Look, I had a great time, but we got carried away. Maybe we should try a Sounders match or something next time?"

"With no cake afterward?"

"Nope. Now, leave me alone, Mary Berry. You're trying my patience."

"Honestly, love, why are you so impossible? Just admit you want cake."

"Friends don't eat cake together, Leo." She pushed away from her side of their desk.

"Where are you going? You're dodging my question, aren't you?"

"What question? I need to go to the bathroom, you psycho."

"Well, hurry back," he called after her. "I find your constant protestations have grown rather comforting to my soul. Besides, who knows what kind of trouble I could get myself into between now and then."

After several minutes of performing positive affirmations in the mirror that, yes, they were only friends, and, yes, that was the extent of it, because, no, she didn't have proof he was capable of anything more, and, yes, it was better this way, Liz convinced herself she was strong enough to leave the restroom.

She stopped at the kitchenette to buy herself time before breaking the news to Leo. Her lips quirked in satisfaction when she discovered nothing but an empty bag of donuts.

She readjusted her glasses and blew her bangs out of her eyes. She could do this. She could hang out with him again, sans the kissing business. That would only lead to cake. And cake would lead to trouble.

But maybe just one slice wouldn't be so bad.

She left the kitchenette and walked the ten paces over to Leo's side of the desk. "All right, all right, you twisted my arm, maybe just a little more k—"

To her embarrassment, she discovered she'd been flirting with the brick wall. Instead of tapping away at his computer,

Leo was gone. Frowning at his empty chair, she sat down and grabbed her ear buds.

A faint giggle came from up front. Then, that rich, smooth-as-silk voice of Leo's murmured something she couldn't quite make out.

Liz tossed her ear buds onto the desk and made her way toward the heavy curtain that separated the studio from the front. Halfway there, an unfamiliar woman's voice—filled with more seduction than should be legally allowed—stopped her in her tracks. Liz swallowed hard and, sneaking the rest of the way like a 007 agent, leaned against the rough brick and angled an ear toward the inside of the gift shop.

"Laurel branches?" She heard Leo say. The thick curtain muffled his voice, but if she leaned in a little closer . . .

A woman's voice cooed, "Mmm hmm, and you're my last hope. I've been to *every* flower shop in Belltown, even down to Pike Place Market, and *no one* carries them."

Liz pretended to gag at the affected way the woman spoke.

Leo again. "I'm sorry, I'm not sure if we stock laurel branches. Are these what you're looking for?"

The tapping of high heels on tile flooring set Liz's teeth on edge.

"But your website says you specialize in carrying *everything.*" The pout in the woman's voice was annoying, but the clicking noise she made with her tongue nearly launched Liz into the stratosphere. "No, that's not it. Oh, I'm at my wit's end. I have a big event coming up, a *really* huge affair, and I want everything to be absolutely *perfect.*"

Did she really think all that whining was cute?

"Perhaps we'd be able to order some," said Leo, "Willa is our sales expert, however. I'm sure she can help you when she gets back. I'll leave her a note."

"Do you think you could you order them for me? I like

doing business with *you*. You're so *helpful* and that accent is simply *captivating*."

Liz held her breath, blood pounding in her ears while she pictured that handsome, devilish grin of his. The one with which she was currently just friends.

"Why thank you. It's a pleasure doing business with you as well." The flirtatious tone in his voice was unmistakable. Liz knew it well. "But I'm the marketing guy, so I won't be able to order what you need. I can tell you the difference between RFP and ROI, but I wouldn't be able to pick out a laurel branch if you slapped me in the face with it."

He was puffing out his chest by now, Liz was sure of it, showing off that lean, muscular plumage she so desperately tried to ignore. Another round of the woman's laughter grated on her nerves, sending her eyes rolling to the back of her head. His joke wasn't *that* funny.

With each squeal of delight from up front, something more than annoyance tightened her chest until her lungs had trouble expanding. She massaged her jaw, moving and stretching it in order to loosen the tension that had suddenly taken up residence there. Upon further introspection of how her teeth came to be so firmly clenched, a hand flew to her mouth.

She *did* want cake. And she didn't want just one slice. She wanted the whole thing to herself.

Liz pulled back the curtain enough to get a peek at the woman hitting on Leo and immediately regretted it. Her skin was flawless, and even from a distance Liz could see she was a knockout. Her limbs moved with the grace of a prima ballerina and she exuded the effortless charm Liz could only dream of possessing.

"I'm Ashley, by the way. Ashley Woods," said the woman, offering up her hand in a dainty, kiss the ring sort of way.

Leo took the leggy brunette's hand, whose skirt was too

short and her Louboutins too high for a Wednesday afternoon, and for a moment, Liz thought he really was going to kiss it. Instead, he stared at it, mouth agape as if in a trance, and shook it.

Liz fought the urge to stomp up front and smack him in the face with a laurel branch—maybe even the whole tree. She snuck another peek through the curtain. She couldn't help it.

"Leo Simmons," he mumbled, still shaking the woman's hand and staring. By the look of his stupefied gaze, he didn't intend on releasing it any time soon. "Charmed to meet you."

Oh my God, he's not even blinking.

Liz let go of the curtain, disgusted. Whether more at the way he was acting or for being so concerned with whose hand he was holding, she couldn't tell. She ignored the rough brick digging into her back and scrambled to think of what to do next. Cautious Liz would waste no time writing him off, but somewhere between Weird Liz first locking eyes on him and now, something had happened. And it was more than curiosity about what it was like to kiss him.

She hooked a finger into the collar of her T-shirt and pulled. Was it hot in here? Her armpits certainly thought so. The best thing to do, she decided, was to go back to her desk and wait. But would he see the jealousy written all over her face the next time he looked at her? Dumb question. Of course he would, and he'd probably relish the fact that he'd finally broken through.

She shoved away from the wall and made a beeline for the bathroom. She would hide out there until she got a hold of herself, then once he returned to his desk, she'd go back to hers and pretend like she hadn't seen or heard a thing.

The cold water from the faucet cooled her burning face. She fanned her neck, hoping it would help the irritated skin there calm down. This was the last thing she needed. Kiss of her dreams or not, she wasn't about to turn into some possessive madwoman.

After a few minutes, she crept out of the bathroom and stood in the small hallway, listening to the clacking of Leo's keyboard. She needed to get a grip. When she passed the kitchenette for the second time, she decided the whole thing was ridiculous, and by the time she got back to her desk, she resolved to put an end to her foolish behavior once and for all. They'd kissed. So what.

Liz eased back down into her chair, hoping her voice wouldn't crack or shake or whatever voices did when they're totally lying. "Sorry, can't hang out tonight," she said, careful not to look Leo in the eyes. "I've got shit to do."

CHAPTER EIGHTEEN

Eros poured cream into his coffee, then added more sugar. Liz slurped the dregs of her Starbucks as she walked over to her desk. "You're here early." She set the empty cup down and powered up her computer. "Miracles do exist."

He pulled the carafe off the hot plate and added a touch more coffee to his cup. He was going to need it. Progression had slowed to a snail's pace, and it was making him twitchy. Strike two was officially now in progress.

He followed her over to her desk. "A venti instead of your usual grande. What's the occasion?"

He knew the occasion. Her heart was thawing.

"Eh, just because, I guess."

His shoulders scrunched at the memory of the park, and how his arrow had bounced off Liz like she'd had on a suit of armor. He'd been a fraction too late, and time, unfortunately, had become of the essence. He must attempt another strike, and if that meant manufacturing another opportunity to sink an arrow home, so be it.

“Morning, love.” Leo breezed past them both on his way to his side of the desk. “You too, Liz.”

Eros grinned into his coffee at the joke. He glanced over in time to see Liz’s eyes flutter closed as she inhaled the pheromones Leo had left in his wake.

Oh, yeah, it was on.

“Seriously, will you stop calling me that?” Liz protested without warning.

Eros choked on his coffee.

“Someone woke up on the wrong side of the bed,” replied Leo. “Not a good morning, love? Didn’t get all your shite done last night?”

Eros attempted to clear the liquid blocking his airway with a cough and a sputter. He was glad Leo didn’t sound concerned, but the breakfast sandwich Eros had consumed on the way to the office, which now suddenly felt like a cement block in his stomach, wasn’t convinced there wasn’t anything to worry about.

“You okay?” asked Liz. When he nodded, his gasping finally subsiding, she turned on Leo. “I got all my shit done, thank you. I’m just not sure I like it when you call me ‘love.’ It sounds too *familiar*.” She stared at him, gauging his reaction.

“All right, love, calm down—oh, sorry.”

She slammed her bag down, emptying its contents onto her desk with a scowl. “Don’t tell me to calm down.”

Eros could spot a lovers’ quarrel from a mile away. Before he could fully take stock of the situation, however, the curtains rustled. Liz and Leo stopped their bickering long enough to notice the whispering that accompanied it.

Liz shot Eros a look of suspicion. “What’s going on?”

Before he could explain, Hermes and Psyche came through the curtain, Hermes clutching a vase full of white roses and Psyche holding her phone in the air. Prince’s 1999 played on full blast, and the duo were lip-syncing and dancing in a Congo line.

You've got to be kidding me. I say make an entrance and this is what you two come up with?

"What's going on here?" snapped Liz.

Hermes handed her the flowers. "It's your birthday."

She buried her nose into one of the blooms and sniffed, the corners of her mouth still holding a faint smile when she set them on her desk. "Thanks for the flowers, but my birthday isn't for another two and a half weeks." Her smile dropped. "How do you even know when my birthday is, anyway?

"It's on your application" said Eros. It wasn't, but it was on the paperwork stuffed inside the Johnson/Simmons folder on his desk. Before Liz had a chance to think about whether she'd filled out an application or not, he elbowed Hermes in the ribs. "And I love birthdays, don't I, Robby?"

Hermes corroborated his story with a nod. "You sure do."

"He really does." Psyche tucked her phone into the back pocket of her skinny jeans.

"Anyway, I'm tired of waiting for something big to happen around here," continued Eros. "You never know what tomorrow brings, so we're going to celebrate tonight, at Some Random Bar."

"Oh no we're not," grumbled Liz.

Hermes did an obscene dance move befitting of a Prince concert. "Come on! You deserve it. *We* deserve it. We've all been working our butts off. It's time to let loose a little."

"Yeah, come on, Liz," said Psyche. "It'll be fun. And you did promise not to take life for granted."

Liz glanced at Leo, who had pulled out a box of chocolate covered strawberries. "Happy early birthday." He held them out to her. "Come out with us, yeah?"

"Fine, but I'm only having *one* drink, you losers." She

grabbed the box of strawberries, took out the biggest one and bit into it. "How'd you know chocolate covered strawberries are my favorite?" She covered her mouth to shield the shards of dark chocolate from flying out as she spoke.

Eros couldn't help but smile. He'd been right on the money, and asking Leo to help convince Liz to go out had been an excellent idea. So had suggesting chocolate be a symbol of romantic gestures a couple centuries ago.

"I had a feeling." Leo met Eros's eyes for a split second.

"Of course you did, Cadbury," she replied, her tongue and teeth searching around her lips for more stray chocolate.

CHAPTER NINETEEN

Leo's palm rested on the small of her back as they walked into Some Random Bar. The urge to grab his hand and never let go, claiming him for her own while snarling, *"He's mine,"* to every human being within a ten-foot radius, rattled the padlocked chains around her heart.

Cool it, Weird Liz.

The DJ played awful pop music, and the bar was packed, but Liz was cautiously optimistic about having a good time. As if by the will of God, two tables near the front window cleared. Their group headed over and pushed them together, and once they settled in, a waitress came by to take their drink orders.

She focused her attention on Robby first, clearly impressed with the way his dress shirt stretched across his broad chest. "What can I get you?"

"Gin and tonic, please." Robby flashed a perfect smile at her.

The curvy waitress reluctantly tore her gaze from Robby, and when it landed on Leo, her eyebrows shot up in delight.

Liz had to force herself to stop glaring up at the woman. Of course the waitress had heart eyes for Leo. Why wouldn't she? He was hot.

"Johnny Walker, neat," said Leo.

"Oh, and an accent, too." The waitress lowered her falsies before opening her eyes wide.

Seriously? That was supposed to be seductive? It looked more like she had something in her eye. Something in her eye, all right. Leo.

With a much less flirtatious tone, Betty Boop turned toward Liz. "And what can I get you?"

"Rum and Coke." Liz's words were flat. Like this woman was going to be if she didn't stop ogling Leo.

"Glass of red wine for me," said Eron.

"Red, huh? Let me guess, you're a hopeless romantic." The waitress leaned on one hip, tilting her head.

"You have no idea."

"I'll have a red wine, too," said Willa, glancing at Eron, who lifted his brows.

Liz bit her lip to suppress a smile, wondering if they might be indulging in a bit of cake again.

Once everyone had their drinks, they were all content to people watch. Some of those people actually had skills on the dance floor, while others simply flailed their limbs to the beat, but they all looked as though they were having fun. Surprised, Liz found she was glad she'd agreed to go out. It would seem she'd been fairly successful at making friends.

She enjoyed the comfortable silence through her first rum and Coke. By her second, Robby had wandered off toward the bar, and when her third arrived, the plan to have one had not only gone out the window, but was lying on a beach somewhere in Jamaica.

When the DJ started playing slow songs, Eron held his hand out to Willa. The conflicted look on her face urged Liz to nod encouragement. Willa took Eron's hand and followed him out onto the dance floor. Leo leaned in his chair with a slouch and watched them go, one arm rested on the table, fingers tracing imaginary circles, while the other rested on the back of Liz's chair.

She took a sip of her drink, trying to distract herself from the butterflies at it again. "I hope those two end up back together."

Leo turned to look at her, a smile lifting one corner of his mouth. "Liz Johnson, am I getting another peek at the softer side of you?"

"What? No!" She shouted over the music, her heart leaping and twirling on a mountaintop like that nanny in the Sound of Music before she could get it under control. And that was from half a smile. How much damage could a full one do at this point? "But, I mean, look at them. Doesn't it seem like they were just meant to be together?"

"Careful, love. You might overtax that shriveled heart of yours."

She elbowed him in the ribs.

"Seriously, though. Why is your heart the size of a raisin?"

"Why do you ask?" said Liz, the room suddenly vacant of enough air. "Are you concerned about my heart?"

Leo cocked half a grin up again. "Maybe."

"I'm supposed to divulge all my secrets to you because you *may* be concerned?" She hoped she was doing a passable job of keeping a calm facade, but her curiosity was making it difficult to concentrate. So was her shallow breathing.

"Sure, why not," shrugged Leo.

Disappointment, heavy and brooding, knocked her down a few notches. More than a few, actually.

"Sure, why not?" scoffed Liz, all trace of the warm fuzzy feeling she'd felt a second ago gone. He'd managed to ruin one of her elusive good moods with three words. "Boy, you're really proving my *that guy* theory correct right now."

Leo pressed his lips together, the steel blue of his eyes now storm cloud gray. "You're impossible, do you know that?" He pulled his arm from behind her, the legs of his chair screeching loudly across the floor as he adjusted his body forward. "Of course you do." He clasped his hands together and stared straight ahead. "I'm about ready to give up."

"Give up?" Liz softened, realizing she'd gone too far and hurt his feelings.

Did he even have feelings to hurt?

"Being so nice to you." Leo drained the last of his whisky.

The dizziness in Liz's head grew worse, and for once she didn't know what to say. Even though her heart was screaming at her to say she was sorry, her mouth, insolent, refused to form the words. Not knowing how to deal with the awful silence, she lifted her glass and shook the ice cubes.

"It's because I've been burned before." She set her drink down and fiddled with the edge of the napkin underneath it.

Confusion took over his face. "In a past relationship? Is that why you're so closed—?"

"No, I mean literally." She couldn't bear to hear him say it. Yes, she was closed off. She knew it. He knew it. Everyone knew it. She glanced up at him. "I've been burned before."

Oh my God, am I really going to do this?

Leo's forehead wrinkled as his brows drew closer together, so she rolled up one of her sleeves to reveal an ornately inked sun and moon surrounded by bright yellow stars. Yep, her and her liquid courage were going to do this. "This was the first one."

Eager, Leo leaned in for a closer look. "Your first tattoo? It's lovely."

"No, my first burn."

Leo stared at her, still not grasping her meaning. She grabbed his hand and ran his finger back and forth over a scar. The feeling sent a jolt of electricity crackling up her arm. "Cigarette burn. Compliments of dear old dad." She positioned his finger over another scar, this one hidden under the wings of a raven.

"My God, Liz. I'm so sorry."

"Yeah, well, there you have it. Reason *numero uno* why Liz Johnson is damaged goods."

"That's awful." He took one of her hands, his thumb caressing her knuckles. "But your scars do not make you damaged goods."

Liz picked up her glass of melting ice cubes with her free hand, leaving the one Leo was holding right where it was. She wanted to believe she wasn't as damaged as she thought, but she refused, because what if she was wrong?

"I don't even know why I'm telling you this because . . ." She took a sip, trying to buy more time before the words left her mouth. She'd never said it out loud before. "They're ugly and they remind me of that asshole every time I think about them."

"But you covered them up with something beautiful, yeah?"

Liz nodded, trying to swallow the aching lump in her throat. She removed her hand from his and began to pull down her sleeve, but Leo stopped her.

"Can I see the others? Tattoos, I mean, not scars."

She let him, but willed herself to ignore the hope swelling in her chest that she was someone special. People were either appalled or curious when it came to her tattoos.

Liz held stock-still as he examined her arm, steeling her heart against the belief his interest was anything more than curiosity. The ring of armor sliding into place was still echoing when a sharp pain lanced her lower back. Hand flying around to clutch the spot, she gasped before the intensity stole her breath.

"Are you all right?" Leo placed one hand on her shoulder blade. Leaning over, he tucked a loose strand of hair behind her ear with the other.

A random muscle cramp was all. Stress did weird things to the body. She took a deep breath, nodding as she pulled down her sleeve the rest of the way. The rum made her head spin, that and the fact she had just shared way too much information. She slipped off her chair. "I'll be right back."

"Where are you going?"

The look on his face told her he didn't want her to go anywhere, but the moment was too intense. She'd completely blown her carefully constructed facade to bits. A minute or two to collect the pieces was in order. Now if only she could manage a smile. No, manage wasn't the right word. She didn't have to force them anymore. Her lips edged up. "To the ladies' room, Whereabouts Police."

Liz squeezed her way into the bathroom. Waiting for a stall to open up, she checked her phone. One voicemail, but it was from her mom. She contemplated listening to it when an obnoxious round of braying assaulted her eardrums.

She turned toward the two women standing in line behind her, laughing and carrying on like schoolgirls, and shot them an irritated look. She'd shown Leo her scars, something she'd never done with any other guy before. It was big. Maybe even groundbreaking in the forgiveness and healing departments, and all this cackling, way louder than necessary, was ruining her emotional high. She didn't get many.

Well, she hadn't until recently.

"Ohmigod, Anastasia, he so cute!" said a short blonde with the smoothest, tannest skin Liz had ever seen.

Giggle.

Liz rolled her eyes and turned back around.

"I know, right?" Anastasia was much taller, with chocolate eyes, caramel skin and honey highlights. Liz wasn't sure about what kind of surprise was under the wrapper, but the packaging on this girl was delicious.

Giggle.

The blonde further interrogated her friend. "Are you going to ask him out?"

More giggling.

Liz stepped inside an open stall, but she, and the rest of the women in the ladies' room, she presumed, could still hear the conversation.

"What? Oh my God, Taylor, no! I don't even know if he's interested. Besides, we're just friends."

Even more giggling.

Seriously, Taylor, stop with the giggling.

"Just friends? No way! You should definitely ask him out. What have you got to lose?"

"What if I ask him out and he says no?"

"What if he says yes?

She's got a point, Anastasia. What if he says yes?

Liz washed and dried her hands slowly, not wanting to miss Anastasia's final decision. The consensus was that she would ask him out, which led to more giggling as the women left the restroom.

Liz pretended to fuss with her phone. She wasn't ready to face facts yet. There was something about Leo that drew her to him, she couldn't deny it. But how that was possible, she didn't know. She'd spent years hardening her heart, roughing up her exterior. So she wouldn't be caught in a situation like this, a place where she was actually starting to have feelings. Because, known fact, feelings were terrifying. They only led to trouble. And someone pretending to love you, then squandering every last bit of your hope they loved you back before skipping town was the most treacherous feeling of all.

But he was out there waiting for her. She'd seen the look in his eyes, felt his nervousness before they'd kissed. The constant fluttering in her belly, and the incessant hammering in her chest. The way just thinking of him sometimes made her want to . . . giggle.

She stared at herself in one of the mirrors as she reached inside the front pocket of her jeans. Uncapping the tube of her newest drugstore purchase, she swiped the berry-colored pigment across her lips. The hair knotted on top of her head tumbled down around her shoulders as she looped the hair tie around her wrist.

The woman in the mirror was flushed, and her eyes were so bright they sparkled. She was even smiling. Clearly, she wanted to be more than friends with Leo. And it seemed as though, if he wanted her to be that kind of girl, she was willing to try.

There, she'd admitted it. She wanted more. It was nonsensical, and she might be certifiably insane for thinking there was a chance, but mirrors don't lie.

Fine, Weird Liz. Have it your way.

She glanced around the now empty restroom before leaning in to check her lipstick. Of course it was all over her teeth. No wonder she never bothered with the shit. She wiped a finger across her front teeth before cocking her head at the woman gazing back at her. "But I'm warning you. If this doesn't work out, you're never seeing the light of day again. Ever."

CHAPTER TWENTY

Leo scrubbed a hand over his chin. He knew Donny boy was a horrible human being, but what kind of sick bastard puts cigarettes out on a child's arm? His heart wrenched so hard it hurt. He knew how terrible the pain of losing a parent was, but enduring physical abuse from one? One who was supposed to love and protect you? There was a special place in hell for people like that.

He slid his fingers over the back of his neck. No wonder she'd been hard to reach. The walls were too high. Now he understood why she wore sarcasm like armor and wielded words like weapons. There was too much hurt behind the fortress she'd built for anything less. He could relate.

Except, his weapon had been charm.

If he thought her tattoos were interesting before, now that he knew what they meant, the self worth and control they'd given back to her, they were amazing. Everything about her was. And his desire to be with her, and not in just a physical way, was beyond his control at this point.

He'd known it even before she showed him her tattoos. When she'd hit a nerve earlier and Monster Leo, confused and irritated at being desperate for her to want him back, reared his ugly head. He'd known.

He peered out onto the dance floor, then over to the bar where he caught sight of Willa and Eron embracing. Liz was right, they did look like they were meant to be together. She was also right about another thing. Eron glowed. Leo squinted, as if it would somehow sharpen his twenty-twenty vision. Willa, too?

Perhaps he'd had one too many drinks.

He didn't notice the waitress approach, and when she set another glass of whisky in front of him, he winced in surprise. "You look like you could use one more."

He blinked a few times, testing his ability to see straight before taking a sip of the rich, amber-colored liquid. "I shouldn't, but I will. Thank you."

When she didn't leave he reached for his billfold, but she waved him off. "It's on me." She sucked her cherry-red bottom lip into her mouth. Her gaze roved over him, and he was certain by the look she was wearing, his shirt was somewhere on the floor in her mind.

Bloody hell, not now.

Monster Leo knew what kind of proposition that look held. *He* would have jumped at the chance, but not this Leo, the good guy Leo. This Leo couldn't stop thinking about a certain foul-mouthed woman with the most beautiful sun, moon and stars inked across her arm.

"Forgive me if I'm being presumptuous here, but I think that look means you're interested. I'm flattered, but I'm afraid I would be thinking about someone else the entire time. I'm sorry."

The waitress stiffened, her face nearly the same shade as her lipstick. He hadn't meant to embarrass the poor girl. "What I'm trying to say is don't settle for guys like me. Wait for someone special. It'll be worth it."

She turned on her heel and walked away. He couldn't blame her. He sounded like someone's father. At least she hadn't thrown the drink she'd bought him in his face. He'd take an eye roll over that any day.

Speaking of worth the wait, where in the bloody hell was Liz? He'd give it another few minutes before he'd go into the ladies' room and beg her to come out. The minutes ticking by without a barrage of insults from her were starting to feel unnatural.

He took another sip of his whisky and replayed their kiss in his mind. Her lips had been softer than he'd thought possible, and the way her skin had felt beneath his fingers . . . He could kick himself in the arse for not kissing more of it. If he ever got another chance, he would.

If she'd let him, because it was possible friendship was as good as he was going to get. And if he was being completely honest, he didn't know if that would be enough. But did he see himself with her for the long haul? A two-story house surrounded by a white picket fence?

No, she was a city girl. She'd want a brownstone with a large stoop. There would have to be a park nearby, so they could take their two, maybe three, little girls, all with their mother's brown eyes, to play. The girls would gang up on him, sass in triplicate, but he didn't care. He'd even go for the bloody dog if they wanted.

A burst of adrenaline popped in his chest, accompanied by a sharp intake of breath when he realized that, as long as she took to come around, he'd wait.

And then a voice hijacked his thoughts.

"Hey there, handsome." The woman from the shop the other day helped herself to the chair next to him.

"Ashley, right?" He glanced at her, hoping she would get up and go away. The woman he wanted to talk to would be coming back soon, and there was so much he wanted to say. He couldn't very well do it with an audience.

"That's right." She flipped her long, dark curls over her shoulder. "I was walking by and saw you were alone. I thought you could use some company."

"I'm not alone, actually." Rudeness wasn't in his repertoire, but he'd use it if he had to. Right now, he wanted her to get lost.

She rolled her head from side to side, exaggerating the movement. "Oh? You look alone to me. So alone, in fact, it would have been silly of me to pass up such a perfect opportunity." She pushed her lips into a pout, her nebulous eyes flashing.

The moment they focused on him, his line of vision shrank and black shadows crept in on every side until all he saw was her hair snaking around her face and down her shoulders. Eyes a bit too large, yet somehow fitting with the odd contours of the high, sharp ridges of her cheekbones.

She crossed her long, lean legs and hooked a slim ankle around his calf. The contact sent tendrils of stinging nettles up his leg, growing stronger as they inched their way up.

Amidst the pins and needles, a thick fog blanketed his brain and numbed his senses. The only feeling he registered now was the pulsing in his temples—and the throbbing elsewhere. He could still feel that.

Pressure on his knee. A hand? Yes, her hand was on his knee, her strange eyes locked on his, smoldering and burning away any other thought save for her. She caressed her way up his thigh, lazy strokes with purpose.

Not . . . now.

He fought for control, struggled to concentrate, but her roaming hands suffocated his thoughts. He could no longer form coherent words, let alone stop the bulge in his trousers from growing. Mind of its own, indeed.

"Do you feel that, Leo?" she whispered, her voice hissing like dead leaves blown by the wind.

He nodded, something between a sigh and a groan escaping as his lust pumped harder, thicker. Images of her straddling him with those long legs, breasts bouncing above him, projected onto his brain like a movie.

But there was something else. Someone else. Another face flickered into view, until it was no longer Ashley. He reached out in his vision and pushed the golden-brown hair aside . . .

The pinch to his inner thigh wrenched him back.

Ashley's jaw was set with anger. She leaned in, practically falling out of her chair to press whatever part of her body she could against him, and guided his arm around her waist. Then she proceeded to nip his earlobe with her teeth, flicking at it with her tongue.

Another vision, wavy around the edges like a mirage, but otherwise crystal clear. Mirage Ashley looked up at him from where she knelt before him, his lust on full display, and he felt his knees go weak when her lips parted . . . her eyes trained on his . . .

"There's more where that came from." Real Ashley's voice rasped, the soft tickle of breath on his skin ending the vision as it slashed the last of his will to shreds. "Spend the night with me and I'll show you."

He waded through the murky blackness of what was left of his consciousness, searching for a reason to stay. The heaviness in his heart and the ache in his chest called to him, trying to pull him back, but he couldn't hear it above the hungry growling in Monster Leo's head.

He needed to take this woman home. It'd been a while, and if the pressure threatening to burst the front seam of his pants was any indication, it was about time he christened his new flat.

CHAPTER TWENTY-ONE

The smile that pushed up the corners of Liz's tinted lips dropped, and she rubbed at the itchy spots sprouting under the collar of her T-shirt. Sidled up to Leo was the woman who had come into the shop looking for laurel branches.

The long-legged brunette was exactly one toss of luxurious, shiny hair—and two lacy push up cups—away from being a Victoria's Secret model. Except, this woman, with her glossy, plump lips and ridiculous fake laugh, didn't even need the damned bra.

Liz wiped off her lipstick with the back of her hand. She hadn't noticed she'd come to a complete stop right in the middle of where the staff picked up their drink orders. Not until the waitress shot her an irritated look as she weaved around her.

Even though Liz shuffled forward, the thought of turning around and heading back to the bathroom tugged at her. It would be what Cautious Liz would do, hands down, walk straight the hell out of here without giving him a chance to explain. But Weird Liz urged her to go on. Too much had happened for her to walk away now.

Besides, maybe this was good. Not that having competition was ideal, especially *that* kind of competition, but it might prove how Leo felt about her. If the kiss they'd shared had meant anything, or if he was biding his time until someone better came along.

Someone taller, like Vickie's Secret over there.

Her shaky legs carried her toward the table. Benefit of the doubt, don't jump to conclusions and all that playing on repeat in her head. It wasn't his fault he looked like he belonged in one of those ripped firemen holding a baby animal calendars, or half-naked men wearing nothing but six packs and kilts. Only, he'd be in a sexy businessmen calendar, where they were all in—or out of—suits and ties.

When she reached the table, she sat down opposite Leo and . . . *her*. Even though Liz's smile wasn't genuine, the woman who'd stolen her chair didn't make any attempt to reciprocate the gesture.

The heat consuming her chest and neck inched up to her ears, and the silence between the three of them grew awkward. Leo didn't know she'd seen this woman before, eavesdropped on them if one were to get technical, and when he failed to introduce them, she took matters into her own hands.

"I don't think we've met before. I'm Liz."

The woman leaned an elbow on the table, wiggling in her seat for a better angle toward Leo than she already had, and shrugged a bony shoulder at her. "Ashley."

Liz ground her teeth. That's it? No handshake? No hello, it's a pleasure to meet you? Not even a wave? She was trying, really trying, to be the bigger person, but this woman was making it difficult to keep her shit intact. Where was her other hand, by the way? And why wouldn't Leo look at her?

If the tightness in her muscles didn't confirm her jealousy, the seething in her being did. She looked at Leo, and the memory of his lips, the way they felt on hers, made her heart thunder.

She pulled in a calming breath, her anger softening at the thought of how tender he'd kissed her. How he'd stirred feelings in her she could no longer ignore. He'd felt it, too, right?

Why did the universe always throw a wrench in things? What had she done in a past life that meant she couldn't have nice things in this one? Like a dad who'd stuck around, or a man who wasn't capable of destroying her on every level with one kiss.

That kiss urged her to set her jealousy aside, for the time being at least. Maybe Ashley was shy, or socially awkward. "You came into Follow Your Heart the other day. Did you ever find what you were looking for?" Liz gnawed on her bottom lip. How would she have known that? Thank God neither of them seemed to notice.

Ashley gave Leo a sideways glance. "I did find what I was looking for, thanks."

Liz heard the *pat, pat* of the woman's hand on his knee, even over the chatter of the bar, confirming her suspicion about where it had been—and still was—all this time. Nope. Her first impression had been spot on. This woman wasn't shy or awkward. And she wasn't there to make friends either.

Game on.

Liz willed Leo to look at her, but his eyes remained fixed on Ashley. Two heaving parts of Ashley, and the razor-sharp edge of hurt stabbed into Liz's chest, slashing her open.

Don't be that *guy. Please . . .*

She swallowed the words humming like angry wasps in her mouth, hell bent on stinging the offending intruder to death. She didn't want to make this precarious situation worse, and unleashing the army could mean losing the tug of war. She needed to wait, so he could explain.

She hesitated, giving Leo the chance to prove Cautious Liz wrong, but his callous behavior poked at the nest. It also worried and confused her, leaving her with the very thing she'd been trying to avoid: Gut-twisting doubt, and worst of the bunch as far as she was concerned, painful rejection. She wanted to reach out and touch him, make sure they were okay, but he was miles away.

Maybe all he needed to snap out of this, whatever *this* happened to be, was to hear her voice. "So, Leo, do you want to hang out again tomorrow?"

He tried looking at her, but his movements were slow, like he was swimming in a pool of drying cement. Labored. Struggling. Almost out of breath. "Uh, maybe?"

Her throat tightened, and the back of her eyes stung. She was losing this game. It had been a loaded question, she knew, but she'd been so confident her strategy would work. Wrong. And the fact he didn't have the decency to look at her, but at Ashley instead, as if *she'd* asked the question, made it worse. So much for being nice.

"It's a yes or no question, Einstein."

She didn't know if it was what she'd said or how loud she'd said it, but his gaze jerked toward hers, the last word knocking a tiny grin out of him.

That's right, Simmons, he's technically not British, is he?

He opened his mouth to say something, but Ashley cut him off before he could utter a single word. "Drat, I was hoping you could show me around Seattle this weekend. I'm new here and haven't had a chance to get out much. You know, because I've been so *busy* with this *event* and all."

Drat? Who even says that?

"I don't see any reason why you couldn't tag along," said Leo.

He did not say that. Lord in heaven above, he did not just invite this barracuda to hang out with them. No way in hell was Liz spending one minute with this grabby-ass succubus. If she couldn't keep her hands off him now, Liz couldn't imagine the woman would be able to go an entire day without feeling him up. Having to witness that car crash, one in which her heart was in the passenger seat without a seat belt or an air bag? No.

Time to leave. Her composure was almost gone, and she'd be damned if she'd give either of them the satisfaction of a complete meltdown. "That's okay. You and Mary Poppins have a nice time. We'll hang out another day."

That's it, Cautious Liz. Act like it's no big deal. Now throw in a kick to the nuts.

"If I feel like it."

When he didn't respond, she pushed away from the table, making as much noise as possible. Whatever she thought was starting between them had been all in her head. She should have known better, but she had to hand it to him, he really did know how to use that charm of his. Because she'd almost fallen for it. Better she found out now rather than later their kiss had meant nothing. "Okay, I'm out. See you losers later."

She looked into his eyes before she turned to go, trying to find some semblance of the man he'd been not even twenty minutes ago, but, like a total dick, he was staring at Ashley.

CHAPTER TWENTY-TWO

Eros stared at the glass of wine the bartender set in front of him and contemplated asking for the whole bottle. Psyche stood next to him, wrangling the trendy fashion backpack she'd taken up carrying around onto her shoulders. The sequins sewn into the shape of a butterfly flashed when they hit the overhead lighting just right.

"It's okay. You've still got time."

A puff of air blew past his lips. They'd snuck off the dance floor, hid in a closet marked "Employees Only" and used her magic to veil him, just to be on the safe side. Thank the gods no one but her had witnessed his horrible marksmanship. Unless Hera happened to be in the viewing room. If that was the case, then she'd seen it, too, and had probably cackled with delight at the sight of his arrow bouncing off the concrete surrounding Liz's heart.

He'd handed his gilded bow and arrows to Psyche afterward and sulked back to the closet without a word. She'd refrained from saying anything when she'd entered the cramped space filled with cleaning supplies a moment later. She remained quiet when she shrank his bow, along with his quiver of arrows, and stuffed them into her backpack. As soon as she'd unveiled him, he went straight to the bar and ordered a drink.

Now, here he sat, pathetic and drowning his sorrows in fermented grapes. Granted, he'd been closer this time around than he'd been at the park, but unless her heart was next to her kidney, there was no denying he'd missed. Again.

"It's unnatural the way she switches back and forth so fast. One minute her defenses are down, and I think I've got a decent shot, the next her walls are locked up tight again." He snapped his fingers. "Just like that!"

"You've still got a couple more weeks."

His head sank under the weight of his failure, and he felt like whacking it on the bar top. Two weeks might as well be two days. Psyche's slender fingers toyed with the curls at the back of his neck and he exhaled, soothed by her touch.

He didn't question it when she pulled him to her, but simply swiveled on the stool and buried his face into her neck. She smelled like wildflowers. Like summer breezes and happiness. Like home. He wrapped his arms around her, sliding them under the backpack, and hugged her tight, soaking in her warmth and clinging to the comfort it offered. The thought of never holding her again tore at his heart.

Then, like a gift from the gods above, most likely his mother, the music slowed. He looked up at Psyche. "One more dance? You know, in case . . ."

She untangled her fingers from his hair and stepped back. "You're not going to be demoted, okay?"

He followed her out onto the dance floor where he guided her into his arms, determined not to take the moment for granted, and held her as close as he could without crushing her bedazzled backpack, or the gauzy, whisper-thin wings she was hiding beneath her shirt. They turned in a small, intimate circle as he rested his cheek on the top of her head.

Somewhere around the fifth full rotation, he caught a glimpse of Hermes talking to an uncommonly tall woman with perfect, long blonde waves, the colored lights giving them the appearance of sea foam. He lifted his head to get a better look, but there were too many people obstructing his view. No matter, the only woman he wanted to pay any attention to was already in his arms. For how much longer, he didn't know.

Yes, he did. Two weeks.

"Hermes says he likes being single, but look at him." He nodded in the direction of where he'd seen Hermes, but both he and the woman were gone.

Psyche cocked her head up at him, and he shrugged his shoulders. Gods, he wanted to kiss her, but now wasn't the time. He should go check on Liz and Leo, make sure everything was still on track, but he couldn't help himself.

If he didn't make it out of this alive, she had to know how he felt about her. How he would always feel about her. He pulled back, his hands cradling the sides of her neck, thumbs caressing her cheeks. "If Hera wins, butterfly, just remember I'll always love you."

She gazed up at him, her finger stopping any more confessions from coming out of his mouth. "Don't talk like that."

He looked into those soulful eyes of hers, the power they held over him lit from within, and the lights, the crowd, the fact there was a deadline looming on his life, all faded away. And at that moment, nothing else mattered but kissing her.

He wrapped a hand around hers, moving it from his lips to his heart, and tilted his head down, his eyes closing right before he pressed his lips to hers. They held firm for an instant, torn between yes and no, before yielding and the beating in his chest took over.

Thump . . . thump . . . thump.

His whole body shook, the pounding so strong he lurched forward with each beat.

Thump, thump, thump.

It continued to slam, in the distinct shape of a large hand, and in the region right between his flattened-with-an-Ace-bandage-and-hopefully-now-better-hidden wings.

Hermes smacked the middle of his back a few more times. "Dude!"

Eros spun around and glared at him. The kiss had barely started before being interrupted. Was Hermes *trying* to ruin the moment? It took another ten seconds for Eros to register the alarmed look on his best friend's face. "What is it? What's wrong?"

"I think we might have ourselves a little problem." The tension in Hermes' voice pulled tighter. "Liz is gone."

Psyche's grip on his arms tightened, her fingers digging in hard, and all three gods craned their heads toward the front.

She gasped. "Who in Hades' Realm is *that*?"

Eros peered over the heads in his way. Leo was still there, except, where Liz should have been was a leggy bombshell with hair the color of sin. His heart started pounding again, but now it was for a different reason.

Son of a Titan. Why did I think a bar was the right place for intimacy? How could I have been so stupid?

He hadn't been thinking, or paying attention, and it was going to cost him.

Psyche was the first to take off, pulling him through the crowd. He clutched her hand tight, in sync with her every move as they weaved through the mortals slow dancing. Despite the weight of impending doom crushing the air from his lungs, it wasn't lost on him how well their hands fit together.

"Leo, where's Liz?" Psyche asked as soon as they reached the table. She pressed her lips into the thinnest line he'd seen in decades. Eros knew she was trying not to choke the man.

Leo fixated on the woman sitting next to him, his speech slow and unsure. "Huh? Oh, she . . ."

The odd way Leo searched for approval from the woman sitting next to him caused Eros to direct his attention toward her. The tension in the air grew thicker at the way the woman stared back. Was that a look of triumph on her face?

The woman shrugged her shoulders. "The girl with all those *frightful* tattoos? She left."

Her tone was matter of fact, bordering on careless and approaching arrogant. Whoever this woman was, she didn't have a confidence problem.

"I'm Ashley, by the way. Leo's friend."

The woman addressed them with a cheerful wave, but Eros noticed the subtle way the muscles in her face worried over jawbone, and it dug at him. Also noted, if she moved any closer to Leo, she'd be in his lap.

There was something about this woman, something familiar, but Eros couldn't quite put his finger on it. "Nice to meet you. I'm Eron. This is Robby and Willa." He tried not to sound concerned, pretending like everything was under control. What was the term? Fake it until you make it? "I own the flower shop up the street. Follow Your Heart Flowers & Gifts." His wings twitched. If they were asking questions, he should be, too. "I'm sorry but you look familiar. Have we met?"

"I just got here, but what a small world. I met this handsome guy when I went into your shop a few days ago . . . or was it this morning? Time moves so quickly! Anyway, I was looking for L—some adornments for centerpieces." The words dripped out of her mouth like honey. More like saccharin, sweet but deadly. "I'm an event planner. I make things happen." She eyed Eros with a bravado that seemed out of place for someone who planned parties for a living.

"Hmm, I don't remember seeing you in the shop the other day. Was I out?" Psyche asked Leo, but Ashley answered.

"Yes, I do believe you were. Leo was kind enough to help me in your absence and I'm *so* glad he did."

Nervous energy ricocheted through Eros's body, his muscles twitching and jerking as it sought an outlet. It found two. He tapped his fingers on his thigh to detract from the movement happening on his back, and pressed his wings flat, holding them there. He bit the inside of his cheek and looked at Psyche. They needed to contain the situation. The crowded bar was noisy, but he heard her without an ounce of trouble when her voice entered his mind.

Your wings are about to bust through your shirt. Why don't you take Leo outside? See if you can find out what happened while Hermes and I distract her.

Panic flashed across Ashley's face, her gaze flicking between Hermes, Psyche and him. Was this mortal somehow attuned to their otherworldly power? Well, Psyche and Hermes' power. Eros wasn't radiating anything but stone-cold panic at the moment.

Without wasting another second, Hermes flanked the side of Ashley that wasn't hermetically sealed to Leo. "So, you're new to Belltown, then?"

The color in her high cheekbones deepened, her chin jutting farther into the air. "Yes, I'm new to Belltown."

"In that case, welcome. It's nice to meet you." Psyche pulled Leo up out of his chair and away from the woman's clutches. "Where is it you said you were originally from? And what sort of event planning do you do?" One of Ashley's eyes ticked, but the rest of her face remained placid when Psyche handed Leo off to Eros. "I think Eron wants to have a word with you outside, Leo."

Leo shook his head hard and fast. "Yes. Yes, of course."

Eros clapped him on the back lightly. "There's something important I want to discuss with you, in private if you don't mind." He looked at Ashley. "Please excuse us."

"Don't worry. Robby and I will keep her company. Won't we, Robby?" Psyche sat down in the vacant chair next to Ashley, blocking her in.

Eros nodded his thanks before ushering Leo out onto the sidewalk. Ashley craned her neck at them through the window, forcing him to position Leo so that his back was to her. Good gods, she was persistent.

"Who is that woman?"

Leo unrolled a sleeve of his button-down shirt only to reroll it as he spoke. "She came into the shop looking for some sort of foliage or branches or some such thing. She stopped in tonight to say hello, that's all."

"Really? Because you two looked pretty cozy in there." Too cozy for this stage of the game, and since he hadn't been able to rely on his aim this evening, he was going to have to correct his mistake another way. With the power of subliminal messaging. "I thought you and Liz were *hanging out*?"

"We are," said Leo, attacking his other sleeve. The first drops of rain left wide, dark splotches on the cement.

"Let me guess, she left because she was upset you were canoodling with Ashley?"

"I wasn't canoodling. I was . . ." Leo rubbed the back of his neck so hard Eros thought he might rip the skin clean off his spine.

"Canoodling," finished Eros.

Leo stuffed his hands into his pockets, guilty as charged.

"For the love of sweet Persephone, no wonder she left."

The tips of Leo's ears blazed red, his shoulders sagging

under the weight of his transgression. "I don't know what the bloody hell happened, okay? One minute I'm waiting for her to come out of the loo, the next thing I know Ashley is draped all over me and Liz is stomping off in that way of hers. Now I'm out here with you trying to piece together the last half hour!"

"It's all right, man. Calm down." Eros's wings jerked to life again, trying to break free of their bonds. He arched his back in warning.

I. Got. This.

"See that 7-Eleven over there? You're going to go in there and you're going to buy a rose. They should be up near the cash register, by the hotdog roaster. Are you listening to me, Leo?"

"Yeah, mate, I'm listening, but she doesn't like flowers."

"Think of something else, then, but you need to bring a peace offering, something from the heart. Trust me on this."

"All right. Then what?"

"You're going to march yourself straight to her apartment and apologize."

Leo's hand found the back of his neck again. "I'm not sure I know how. I've never done it before."

Eros pinched the bridge of his nose. Herding cats. Getting these two together was like herding cats. An impossible task he wasn't sure he could manage much longer. He looked into the night sky, rain falling from it in steady drops. Even though he knew he wouldn't see any of his fellow gods there, he prayed one of them might take pity on him anyway and talk Zeus into cutting him some slack.

CHAPTER TWENTY-THREE

Liz pressed her fingers into her temples. What was he doing here? He'd already made it clear he was into women like Ashley. With the way he'd been looking at her, completely enraptured, shouldn't the two of them be rounding third base by now?

She stood on the balls of her feet and looked out the peephole a second time, just to make sure he wasn't a figment of her imagination. After the way he'd acted, she hadn't expected him to come knocking on her door, so he very well could be an apparition Weird Liz had conjured. But it was Leo, all right. Tall, dark-haired and rained on. Plus, no one in the universe had eyes that color of steel ringed in blue.

"Liz? I know it's late, but can we talk?" Peephole Leo's shoulders were drawn up, holding something behind his back.

She set her heels on the ground, folded her arms and shook her head. He couldn't say more than two words to her an hour ago, and now he was standing in the hallway outside her apartment door asking to talk?

"*Liz.* I know you're home. Can I please come in?"

The urgency in his voice sent her mind racing almost as fast as her heart. She needed to make a decision. Did she want to give him the benefit of the doubt or turn him away? Would she get an explanation, a pitiful excuse, or both?

She hiked herself up on tiptoe to look out the peephole again. He was a mess. A damn fine one, with his hair askew and his shirt dotted with raindrops. He looked good in blue.

Assholes usually did.

"Please."

Fuck. Her iron will melted like butter when he sounded like that. Against her better judgment, and also because her hands, yet again, seemed to have a mind of their own, she opened the door a crack. She peered out at him, trying to determine if his anguish was real or fake, if she could trust him or not. She was leaning toward hell no, but she should at least hear what he had to say . . . right?

"I don't know what we need to talk about, seeing as your boner made your feelings on event planners abundantly clear." With trembling fingers, she slid the chain off its hook and opened the door all the way. "You've got five minutes."

He handed her a grande iced mocha with no whipped cream. "I thought you might like one of these."

Her lips struggled to climb into a smile, but she wrenched them down. The iced mocha helped, but he still had some major explaining to do.

Neither of them spoke as she led him down the short hallway into the tiny living room adjacent to the even tinier kitchen. His head swiveled from one side of her apartment to the other. No pictures on the walls, no personal effects. She didn't even own a television. She did, however, own a box full of stolen office supplies and the book of Edgar Allen Poe and his macabre poems and short stories laying on the scratched up old end table next to the recliner.

"I see you have no design sense, love."

She turned and walked into the kitchen. "Yeah, well, at least I make up for it with common sense. What are you doing here, Leo?" So far, he was doing a shit job using his time to any kind of advantage.

"Sorry," he said, shaking his head regretfully at his previous comment. "I needed to see you." He followed her, as if she might try and run out of her own apartment to get away from him. It wasn't a bad idea.

She set her coffee in the fridge for later, when she could actually enjoy it. "And why is that?" She tugged at the bottom of her sweatshirt as she made her way around him and over to the recliner. She half sat, half stood on its arm and watched his every move like a hawk.

He sat down on the sofa and patted the empty cushion beside him. "I won't bite, love."

Classic diversion tactic if she ever saw one. And she should know. "I can't guarantee the same. Trust me, after tonight, it'll be safer if I stay over here." And by safer, she meant *she* would be safer. With her emotions on high alert, she needed the distance right now. Depending on what he had to say, maybe forever.

Yet, she was drawn to him, even when she was angry enough to spit nails, she wanted to put her arms around him. Press her lips to his. Run her fingers through that thick hair. "Well?" She snapped, shoving away the thoughts. He needed to get on with it.

Leo bent his head and rubbed the back of his neck, and Liz braced herself for the *"It was fun while it lasted, love, but you're just not my type"* conversation. The collar of his shirt fell open, and her gaze dropped to the smooth skin there. She forced it away, back up to his face.

"Look, I know you're angry with me, and you have every right to be, but—"

So it was going to be an excuse. Well, news flash, unless

it was an apology, she wasn't sure she wanted to hear it. "Tell me about it. Because I was under the impression we were having a perfectly good time without Ms. Victoria's Secret."

"I didn't ask her to come, and I certainly didn't invite her to sit down. To be quite honest, I don't even really know what happened." His forearms rested on his thighs, hands clasped together in the space between his knees.

"I'll tell you what happened, your penis. It was like you were under some witch's spell or something." She wiggled her fingers at him, wishing she could cast a spell. A hex more like it, one that would make Ashley disappear forever. "You acted like an asshole."

He sat up and rubbed his hands across the thighs of his jeans. "I did, and I'm sorry. Things are so bloody confusing when she's around."

Liz's teeth clenched at his audacity. "Confusing? Is that what we're calling it now? A man gets a hard-on over a pretty girl, and it's *confusing*?"

He dropped his gaze. Was he preparing for an argument? Another excuse?

"I don't expect you'll believe me, but there's something not right about that woman. Besides, she's not my type."

The hives on her chest itched, pleading for attention. She wouldn't scratch, wouldn't so much as move a muscle if it gave him satisfaction in any way. "Oh, tall *and* gorgeous, that's not your type?"

He pursed his lips and dragged his gaze toward the ceiling, sighing loudly before answering, "Contrary to popular belief, some men prefer short and irresistibly cranky. I mean, I don't. I only kiss *that* kind of women because I feel sorry for them. Not because I can't quite find the words to accurately describe the color of their eyes or how my stomach does this annoying flipping thing . . . or how I feel like I've known them forever."

Heat flared high on her cheeks, the taste of her own medicine bitter. He'd disarmed her with the truth. Also because he'd put into words exactly how she felt.

"And not because I can't stop thinking about them, either," he continued, "even though they're incredibly hurtful and quite challenging to be around a *significant* portion of the time."

She wrung her hands, which, thankfully, were stuffed inside the front pocket of her sweatshirt. The tough girl act was necessary, to protect what little of her heart she had left, why couldn't he see that? "Look, guys like you don't like girls like me, remember? So that means, you're free to date all the hot event planners you want, and it's totally your business, not mine."

He stared at her through those long lashes of his, lips still pursed. "Have you not grasped the meaning of a single word I've said to you this entire time? I don't want to date Ashley."

"Does *she* know that?" Liz couldn't help herself. The words just slipped out.

"I shall repeat myself, more slowly this time. I don't. Want to date. Ashley." He jabbed a finger in the air. "In fact, the truth of the matter is I must be a glutton for punishment, because I would much prefer to date a woman who insists on shredding me to pieces every chance she gets." He threw his hands in the air before grabbing the back his neck again. This time he added in a squeezing motion while looking down at his Italian leather boots.

Oh boy, he rubbed his neck when he was nervous, she knew that, but what did the squeezing mean? He was nervous and what? Telling the complete and utter truth?

"Look, I get it," said Leo. "I messed up. But I've already said I'm sorry. If you don't believe me, that's fine. I won't waste any more of your time. We can go back to being just friends."

The long pause made it impossible for Liz to sit still. "We were more than friends?" she said, fidgeting from trying to keep her trusty old friend sarcasm at bay.

He peered up at her, eyebrows drawn together. "I thought so, but I must have been mistaken."

The weight of his stare—his words—hung heavy in the air. She wanted to take back every mean thing she'd ever said about him, *to him*, but all she could do was stare into his eyes, even though doing so could very well lead to her demise.

"You thought we were more?"

He moved his long fingers from the back of his neck to his jaw, darkened by stubble. "Christ, love, I don't know how I can be more clear on the matter. I thought it was just . . . but it turns out . . ." he stammered, the difficulty in finding the right words obvious. "It kills me to think that I've hurt you."

"It does?"

"Yes." He answered without hesitation.

For once, she was speechless. He hadn't exactly confessed undying love for her, but he had admitted that he cared about her, about her feelings. And he didn't like it when she was upset. *Her*. Liz Johnson, the prickliest woman on Earth.

CHAPTER TWENTY-FOUR

That feeling, knowing him for an eternity or whatever, the one he knew all about, pulled her up from the chair. Her heart was back at it, gaining speed even though it felt like she was wading through a waist-high pit of mud.

She sat down next to him and angled herself so her knee just barely rested against his thigh. It was a small touch, but it made the butterflies come rushing back, and with them the confirmation that somehow, despite her best effort not to, she was falling for him.

Hook. Line. And mother-effing sinker.

Remorse drove her to inspect the cuffs of her sweatshirt. "I like spending time with you, too." He'd chosen her, not Ashley, and she hadn't trusted he would. "I know it doesn't seem like it most of the time, but I do."

Leo closed his eyes and sighed, the corners of his mouth lifting. "This is new to me. I've never been this . . ." He cleared his throat. "Involved."

"Ditto." She slid to the back of the couch. Leo lifted his arm for her and when it came down to rest around her shoulders, she felt like she did when they were in the Great Wheel. Dizzy. She nudged him with an elbow. "Let's be honest, though. You're not surprised, are you?"

He grinned down at her and shook his head. And then he had that look on his face, the one that made it hard to remember to breathe.

"So what happens next?" She rested her head on his chest. This admitting your feelings business was exhausting.

"Marriage, kids, 401(k)s?"

"Let's not get ahead of ourselves, Matthew Hussey."

"You're assuming I know as much about women as *that* guy?"

"Well, you sure act like you do."

"Fine, we'll skip the financial planning for now. In the meantime, shall we get to the part where we kiss again?"

The room tilted, and she circled an arm around his ribs in an attempt to straighten it out. He was talking about their future together. And more kissing. "Maybe."

He reached over and tucked the rogue strands of hair that had fallen out of what was surely a rat's nest by now behind her ear. His fingers continued along her jaw until they stopped under her chin.

She was helium, lighter than air, and she anchored a hand against him to keep from floating away. Or was it to brace herself for what was coming next? The muscle beneath her palm flexed as he moved toward her.

"You forgive me, then? For acting like a daft prick?" He murmured the question into her lips, making her own muscular system malfunction.

He was with her because he wanted to be, and it made her confidence unfurl, blossoming so full she couldn't keep the huskiness out of her voice. "Not yet. It's going to take a lot less talking and a lot more tongue before I let you off the hook."

"So crass." He lifted her glasses off her face. She felt naked without them, but she let him set them on the coffee table.

"But now I can't see you," she half-heartedly protested.

"Don't worry about seeing me." He brought his mouth to hers again with agonizing slowness. "Just feel me, yeah?"

The man had a point. Sight wasn't the only sense she had at her disposal. Anyway, she didn't need her glasses to see that his eyes were hooded, darkened with desire, and looking as though he was about to devour her like a piece of cake.

Yes, please.

He brushed his lips over hers, the tip of his tongue flashed feather-light, and suddenly she understood why women acted like blubbering idiots around guys like him.

She ran a hand along his arm, feeling each dip and ridge, relishing every hard curve. A living work of art, and if appreciating him while half-blind but still fully clothed made the organ in her chest, the one she thought couldn't beat any faster or harder, pound against her ribs like a jackhammer, she could only imagine what was going to happen when his clothes were off.

Because if it was up to her, his clothes were coming off. And the sooner, the better.

His fingers worked their way into her hair, lightly stroking the back of her head. The feeling was divine. Heavenly would work, too. Maybe even spiritual, but none of those words seemed adequate. There had never been anyone else who'd made her feel this way, want so much, and she was having a rather difficult time finding an ounce of self control at the moment, let alone the right words.

After what wasn't nearly long enough, he pulled back. "How was that?"

"Good," she whispered.

What a dumb thing to say. It was more than good. She

might as well be a puddle of goo on the floor. She swallowed hard, a little embarrassed she couldn't seem to look anywhere but those magical lips of his. She thought her head might explode, or her heart. That was a strong possibility, as well.

"Do it again."

He chuckled, a short burst of amusement that sparkled like champagne, and it made her tipsy. When he obliged her request, the warmth pooling low in her belly spread, gathering strength and heat until there was nothing left to do but let it catch fire and burn out of control.

She pinned his shoulders into the back of the couch and slowly dragged a knee across his thighs before settling onto his lap. The hiss of his breath, coupled with the hard line of him pushing against her, incinerated the last of her will to resist, and she pressed into him until his hips rose to meet hers.

It was her doing the kissing now.

She slipped her fingers into his hair. God, how long had she been waiting to do that? It felt as good as she imagined. Better. It was thick and luscious and a total crime for it to belong to a man.

The stubble on his face tickled, and when she couldn't take another second of the delicious torture, she bent down to nibble at the smooth ridge of collarbone she'd wanted to take a bite out of earlier. She breathed him in. Then, unbuttoning the top button of his shirt, she inhaled deeper still, drawing in more of his scent. Not his cologne, but *him*.

The next thing she did with her mouth should have surprised her, but somehow it felt like the most natural thing in the world.

"I want you . . . to want me. I mean, really want me. Scars and all."

He stopped kissing her neck to look into her eyes. She

promptly closed them, expecting him to say some smart ass, braggadocios remark and ruin the moment.

"Look at me, love." He stroked both temples with his thumbs, and when she opened her eyes to meet his, she would have bet her life those endless pools were promising her forever. "I do want you. All of you, but only if you want to give it to me."

She did, she just wasn't sure how much. The only thing she knew for certain was, right now, it was her body she wanted to give him, so she answered him with a kiss.

It didn't register they were moving, that he'd lifted her off the couch in one strong movement and carried her down the short hallway, until her back was pressed against the wall with her legs wrapped around him like a vice grip.

The two doors on either side of them were closed, which meant she'd have to stop kissing him long enough to give directions to the bedroom. "To the left."

He was carrying her again, one arm leaving her waist only long enough to open the door. It returned not a moment too soon, and he cradled her back as he placed a palm on the bed, his teeth refusing to release their hold on her bottom lip even while easing her down. He hadn't needed to, because her arms were latched around his neck like a steel trap. She was going nowhere.

He planted kisses under her ear, trailing them down her neck and darting his tongue across her skin when she least expected it. And he hadn't done that sooner, why?

She didn't know who'd taken off her sweatshirt—her or him—but it was long gone, flung into a corner of her bedroom. And her yoga pants? What were those? His hands roamed the curves of her body, his mouth not far behind.

When he stood up and began to unbutton the rest of his shirt without taking his eyes off her, she thought she would die on the spot. How on Earth could there be a more beautiful man? There couldn't, and watching him undress was agony, so she climbed onto her knees and undid the bottom buttons while he finished the top.

Teamwork.

She ran her hands over his chest, having a finite answer to her theory that it was as solid as it looked. Her fingertips danced across his ribs, exploring as she pressed her lips to his skin. He stroked the nape of her neck before pulling her to him for yet another kiss. Her hands continued to roam and, discovering the waistband of his jeans, ventured inside. She smiled when his breath hitched, but when his long, nimble fingers returned the favor, she bit her bottom lip. She undid the zipper and pushed them down until they dropped onto the floor.

His boxer briefs went next.

And did she say a work of art? She meant a goddamn natural wonder.

She was about to test another theory, but he had other ideas. Her bra landed next to his jeans, and he brushed a thumb over a sensitive peak as he bent down to draw the other into his mouth. When he finally shifted on top of her, she arched her neck, her back, anything that would bend, to make contact with his smooth, warm skin.

He spread a hand over her ribs, dragging a palm along her side and following the curve of her hip. Then down he went, dropping magical kisses like breadcrumbs, her stomach fluttering with each one.

He slid off the last article of clothing between them and tossed it onto the floor with the rest. When he hooked his arms under her thighs and grabbed ahold of her hips, she gripped the bed sheets tight.

She peeked down at the top of his head. The dark mass of tousled hair was blurry, but holy hell the *mmm* that vibrated the inside of her thigh made his intention crystal clear. The streak of pleasure that bolted through her sent her knees dropping in opposite directions.

She gasped when the first kiss landed. The rush of hot breath from his satisfied laugh made her whimper. When the second kiss lingered, she sucked all the air in the room in through her teeth.

"Like that?"

Had she been able to form words just then, she would have told him how he'd been right—she didn't need to see him—but with every kiss that followed, her ability to communicate diminished.

He had taken the time to ask, so she dragged herself to the surface just long enough to give him an answer. "Exactly like that."

The exquisite pressure built, the tiny sparks gathering strength until they lit into electric flames that licked higher and higher, harder and faster until she could no longer contain them. The last kiss made her cry out, and the dazzling burst of brilliance that followed blew her apart from the inside.

Fireworks. And he'd stayed for the whole show.

He caressed the tops of her thighs, the backs, the insides, until they stopped shaking. Only when her breathing was somewhat under control did he start nipping and pecking his way back up the breadcrumb trail. "Do you have anything?" he asked when he reached the top.

She blinked at him. Did she have any of what?

Oh, right. He's thinking with the head on his shoulders.

She ran her fingers over the smooth skin of his back. "No, but I'm really hoping this is one of those times you're *that* guy."

He dropped kisses on the corner of her mouth, over her cheek and up to her temple. His breath tickled her ear. "I hope you don't think me presumptuous, but I'm always prepared. Since you're calling the shots, though, I thought I'd ask."

Her insides fluttered when he slid his fingertips over the slope of her stomach, toward the place where the dynamite was sparking again. She lifted her hips, arching into his touch, every stroke slow and light. Christ, had she ever wanted something, *someone,* so badly before?

"Oh God, Leo, please."

Goose bumps broke out across her skin when he got up, leaving her to writhe in her need for him until his body covered hers again.

He shuffled around in his jeans for his billfold, and when she heard a small tearing noise, every part of her responded.

He came to the side of the bed, and she reached out for him, pulling him to her and burying her face into his chest. She willed herself to remember this moment forever, because this was it. If he broke her heart, she would stop breathing. Cease to exist. There was nothing more clear or simple in the universe than that.

The walls that had been protecting her lowered, and as he moved to kiss her again his steel eyes pierced through her, to the *real* her. To the woman who, way down deep, believed in love.

His need for someone had never been this urgent. Ever. Nor had his desire to give pleasure instead of receive it been this strong. Despite his eagerness to continue to do both, Leo willed himself to wait for permission.

Thankfully, it didn't take long. Liz grabbed a handful of his hair and kissed him. It was slow, but urgent, and he couldn't help but moan when she guided him in.

But he still didn't move. Not yet.

He propped himself on his elbows and rested his forehead

on hers. He wanted to savor the way their bodies fit. Just as perfect with her on top, he imagined. He'd know for sure soon enough, but for now, he simply wanted to admire the way her pale skin glowed in the moonlight.

Impatient, she tugged at his hips, to which he proceeded to trap first one, then both of her arms above her head. "We've got all night, love." He smiled when she pouted, silencing her protests with his mouth.

He fought not to come undone, but her face, with its perfect kiss-swollen lips, and her hair rippling like the finest silk across the pillow, made it a most difficult task.

He'd always prided himself on being a good lover, on knowing how to please a woman. When to stop, when to go, he'd always been the one in control. Now look at him, on the verge of losing his ever-loving mind.

He looked into her eyes as he finally began to move. How could he show her this wasn't just sex? He brushed a thumb over one of her hips, gently setting the pace. She complied, but for how long, he didn't know. To be honest, he wasn't sure how long he'd last either.

He tried to keep it steady, but it wasn't long before she was pulling at his hips again. So he let her go. If he had his way, this would not be their only time together.

When their rhythm went from slow and rolling to quick and urgent, she twisted their bodies so that she was in control. He wrapped his hands around her delicate wrists, supporting her as she rocked above him, taking more of him each time they crashed into each other. Her breathy sighs, and the way she flushed with desire, pushed him closer to the brink of his madness for her.

He would give her whatever she wanted, over and over, for as long as she wanted. He would go to the ends of the Earth to make her happy, because it was different this time. It wasn't about him anymore. If she'd have him, his days of dodging commitment were over. It was a terrifying thought, caring for someone other than himself, but it was nothing compared to the alternative.

She was the real deal, the one who could finally make it happen. Liz Johnson was the woman who could vanquish Monster Leo forever. And so he closed his eyes and held on tight as they both tumbled over the edge. Together.

CHAPTER TWENTY-FIVE

Leo sprawled across her bed, every glorious inch of him looking like a god with the way the morning sun cast its light over his body. The shadows it created weren't half bad either.

He hadn't left her side the whole weekend, except to dash home for a change of clothes and pick up carry out. The fact that he wanted to spend so much time together had Cautious Liz on high alert. Weird Liz, on the other hand, was walking on effing sunshine.

Being wanted felt even better than she'd imagined it would.

Although, her luck if she wasn't careful, if she let her guard down too much, too soon, the other shoe would knock her out cold when it dropped.

Leo tucked his arms behind his head and crossed his long legs at the ankle, the strong muscles in his thighs calling her name. As it turned out, they one hundred percent could hold 125 pounds against a wall during a fit of passion.

"So, love, I'm dying to know. Am I God's gift to women?"

He rocked his foot back and forth, a telltale sign he was eager for the verdict.

Liz let her gaze linger on his hipbones, and the skin hidden beneath the rumpled corner of her bedding, which was just barely keeping his God's gift from being exposed. How proper, but didn't he know modesty no longer mattered? Not now, and not when she had already memorized every inch of his body. Her favorite? His collarbones. Then it was a toss up between the hollow of his throat and the dimples on his lower back.

There was no rule stating she couldn't enjoy herself while she waited for a more concrete sign, like that bolt of lightning, for instance, to confirm Leo truly was the one. It was obvious they were compatible between her clearance sale sheets, but there was still some small part of her that wasn't convinced Leo would, or *could* for that matter, commit. Not during the light of day, anyway, and as much as Weird Liz swore up and down he could, that he was exhibiting all the signs Homo sapiens did when they were ready and willing, Cautious Liz was still preparing for the worst.

But she really hoped the worst wouldn't come.

"Well, you're certainly something. I'll give you that." She pushed her fears aside to better admire the fine cut of his arms and the deliriously perfect stack of abs that accompanied them as she tied her robe shut. "God's gift, though?" She squinted, rocking her hand in a *so-so* motion. "The jury's still out on that one. I might need more proof."

She walked over to his side of the bed and leaned down to nip at his bottom lip before kissing him. "A lot more proof."

"So you mean to tell me an entire weekend of deliberation wasn't enough?" His fingers trailed down the inside of her arm and over her palm as she got up from the bed. "I'd like to direct the jury's attention to exhibit A, your honor." He swept both hands from the top of his head down the length of his torso, ending outstretched toward his feet.

"I demand a retrial," he called after her as she slipped around the corner on her way to the bathroom.

She doubled back, popping her head into the room to give him the verdict. "Yes, Leo, you're an excellent lover. Are you happy now?"

"Immensely, and I'm very proud of you for having the courage to finally admit it. My gifts are bloody well exhausted." He reached over to quiet his buzzing phone.

Doubt dropped like an anvil into her belly. Did she say anvil? She meant anchor. One of those Titanic-sized deals, with a whole mess of slimy barnacles attached to it. She swallowed around the swelling that had suddenly formed in her throat as she adjusted her glasses.

Don't do it, Liz. Don't ask. Trust him.

"What are you doing over there, anyway? Come back." He patted the bed next to him, buzzing phone forgotten. "I've gotten my second wind. Or should I say third?"

"Oh you have, have you?" His easy smile assured her she had nothing to worry about, side chick-wise. As far as she knew, he hadn't seen or talked to Ashley since the night at Some Random Bar.

She thought about sliding back under the covers and wrapping herself around his perfect body. There was nothing more she wanted to do than stay in bed with him all day, gathering more evidence, but there was rent to pay and ChapSticks to buy.

She went into the bathroom and grabbed the extra toothbrush she'd made him bring, chucking it when she got back into the bedroom so it landed on his chest.

"What's this?" he scoffed. "Are you trying to tell me something?"

She tilted her head and planted her hands on her hips. "In

America, we call it good oral hygiene. And, yeah, I'm telling you to get your fine, God's-gift-to-women ass up or else we'll both be late for work."

"You're no fun."

"You knew that going in, lover boy, now get in the shower."

Damn, how had this happened? How was he here, in her bed, with *her*? She untied her robe, deciding not to question the universe, at least for the moment, and let it fall to the floor as she turned to walk back into the bathroom. "Court is now in session."

If Leo was forced to be completely honest, the longest he'd ever gone without getting tired of a woman was a week. Two on rare occasions, when his lover had been of particular use breaking into London's most vapid social circles, but that was pushing it.

He'd kept them around for longer than a week, of course, because even though he had no intention of committing for the long term, he didn't like spending his nights alone.

It had been double that, going on triple since they'd officially started dating, and he *still* wasn't tired of Liz. In fact, if he had to swear the whole truth and nothing but the truth, he didn't think he ever would be. He'd even amended his strict no overnight stay policy. It seemed only logical, given that his single days were over. A fact he was okay with. Even more than okay.

Monster Leo wasn't so happy about it, but considering he'd had some of the best sex of his life in her tiny decor-less apartment, he couldn't say much.

Leo's phone vibrated, and he stopped typing to delete the text. He peeked over the partition at Liz. If she ever saw they were from Ashley, she'd flip. He shuddered at the thought.

That night after the bar, the first night he'd spent making love to Liz, he'd ignored every call and deleted every text from the woman. He was off limits. But she wasn't getting it.

His phone buzzed again, which made text number five—so far. The day wasn't even half over yet. It had been a mistake giving her his mobile number, he knew that now. Honestly, what in the bloody hell had he been thinking?

He hadn't been, that was the problem. Nothing felt right when it came to Ashley. Not like it did when he was with Liz. That felt right. He was sure. He *knew*. With Ashley, he felt strange and unsettled. Only one thing dominated his thoughts, and it was maddening because it wasn't her he wanted. He wanted Liz.

He rubbed at the hair on the nape of his neck when he thought about how he'd tried telling Ashley to bugger off, multiple times. But she continued to leap over his boundaries, calling him constantly and sending multiple texts per day. He knew he should block her, but he was afraid she'd show up somewhere else uninvited instead. God help him if she decided to pay him a visit at work.

If telling Ashley he wasn't interested face-to-face was the only conceivable way of getting it through her rather thick skull, then so be it. He just hoped he didn't have to be an arsehole—and not a charming arsehole, a real one—but if being a prick one last time was what it was going to take to keep his chance with Liz safe, he would.

"We going to Saffron Spice for lunch today?"

Her voice jolted him out of his thoughts. Shite. What excuse could he use without setting off alarm bells? "I have a special errand to run today, love," he said, the answer hitting him suddenly. "You don't mind going without me, do you?"

"I do mind, but I'll live. You better not be getting me a birthday present, either."

Of course he was getting her a present. A man couldn't

very well take the woman he was dating to dinner for her birthday and not have a present. That was just uncouth. Besides, better to let Liz think he was spending his lunch picking out a gift than being anywhere near a woman she despised. That wouldn't go over well. "What do you have against birthday presents?"

"Nothing, I just don't want to be greedy."

"And how would getting a present on your birthday from a handsome British gentleman be greedy?"

"Because you already gave me one, remember?"

An instant chat message popped up on his screen.

LJohnson: God's gift

He smiled as he typed out his reply. A true statement he'd live by if she gave him the chance, because LJohnson was everything he never knew he wanted and more. He'd have to thank her somehow for helping him on his way to becoming the man his mother knew he could be.

LSimmons: The gift that keeps on giving

CHAPTER TWENTY-SIX

Hermes settled himself onto the love seat in Eros's office and crossed an ankle over a knee. "Good news. Leo's taking Liz out to dinner tonight for her birthday."

Eros inhaled sharply. It was down to the wire, only eight hours to make this happen. They were all on edge, but he was hanging on by his fingernails. Or what was left of them, anyway.

He'd decided to let Liz and Leo's relationship progress naturally over the last two and a half weeks, to ensure a better shot—his last shot. It had been a calculated risk on his part, and if things didn't add up in the end, he'd be out a job. Forever. On the other hand, if it paid off, he'd be back in the business of love before midnight.

He drummed his fingers on the top of his desk. Maybe he should get it over with and do it after lunch. Liz was close enough, right? Her defenses were the weakest they'd ever been. He could pierce through them as long as his aim was tight, couldn't he?

Eros rubbed his forehead. He'd tried that song and dance

before. Timing was everything. "Gods dammit, this is stressful."

"I know, but it's all good," said Hermes. "I was just out there. She's ready, matchmaker. You're going to have a perfect shot during dinner, easy."

A red, heart-shaped stress ball materialized in the palm of Hermes' hand and he tossed it. Eros plucked it out of the air before showing it no mercy. "I know it's cutting it close, but I really think they needed to bond on their own a little bit first, you know? You and Psyche were right. I was rushing it. Now that they're officially dating, and bonding in more—*ahem*—passionate ways, that target on her back will be one I can't miss."

"As they say, fingers crossed." Hermes hooked both forefingers around their longer neighbors. "Psyche and I will keep an eye out to make sure Ashley doesn't come slinking around again, too."

"She does have a knack for that, doesn't she?"

"She sure does," replied Hermes, screwing his mouth up.

It still bothered Eros, the Ashley thing, and his wheels began to turn. "It's almost like whenever she shows up, that's when Leo acts like a complete idiot."

"By the way, totally off topic . . ." Hermes stretched. "But don't Liz and Leo kind of remind you of Apollo and Daphne?"

Eros worked the squishy heart even harder. Apollo and Daphne's messed up relationship was mostly his doing. It was also the last thing he wanted to think about.

"I mean, they've got that whole love-hate thing going on, and come to think of it, Leo kind of looks a bit like Apollo. Like a demigod half-brother, or a mortal god of sun and light but with more charm."

Eros froze, mid-squeeze. "That's it, Herm."

"What? Leo's a demigod?"

"No, he's mortal, but *she's* one of us. Ashley." He tossed the heart to Hermes. "I can't believe it took me so long to realize it."

Hermes threw the ball up and it froze, suspending in mid-air. "She can't be a major one of us, though. Is she a minor goddess?" The ball disappeared with a wave of his hand.

"Remember when I shot Daphne with the leaden arrow and Apollo with the golden arrow? And he fell in love but she didn't, blah, blah, blah?"

Gods, what an ordeal that had been—still was.

The foam heart reappeared in Hermes' hand. "Yeah, but what does that have to do with Ashley or whoever she is?"

"Ashley's the other nymph. Orea is her real name, I think," said Eros. "There was a rumor floating around that she was with Daphne in the woods when Apollo and I were duking it out. I didn't know there were two nymphs there, I just shot the first one I saw."

"Which was Daphne. Is she still hiding from Apollo disguised as a tree, by the way?"

The foam heart sailed through the air toward Eros again. "Yes and yes. Why do you think Apollo is such a dick to me?"

"So do you think he sent her, to get back at you? Does he know about you having to close the Johnson/Simmons account?"

Eros sighed. "If Leto knows, everyone knows."

"Fellow gods love her, but that goddess cannot keep her mouth shut for anything."

"The problem is, Apollo isn't up for the job. Hera was clear on that. Plus, I don't think he even knows who Orea is. Once I hit him with that golden arrow, it was all Daphne, all the time."

"Then what is Orea, a.k.a. Ashley, doing messing with our man Leo?"

"I don't know. I guess it's possible she still hates me enough to want to see me demoted."

"I suppose, but how did she even get down here?" said Hermes. "She had to have gotten approval from somewhere. She's a nymph. She can't pose as a mortal without permission from a major god or goddess."

The answer clicked at the same time, and Hermes sprang to his feet the moment Eros slammed a closed fist down on his desk. "Hera." His nostrils flared, and his wings strained against his dress shirt.

"Holy shit, it makes so much sense now." Hermes nodded, swiping a hand over his face. He began to pace. "We've got some serious damage control to do. Who knows what kind of permissions Hera gave her. We need to get Oreashley out of the picture, like, right now."

If she was working for Hera, it was guaranteed she'd show up at dinner tonight, and that complication was the last thing Eros needed. "Son of a Titan." He walked over to the credenza and punched it. It hurt like Hades' Realm, but felt good to hit something, to give his anger an outlet. Gods damn her. He should have known she'd interfere. Because when had Hera ever played by the rules?

Never.

"You have that the-god-of-war-is-my-father look in your eyes, matchmaker. What's going on?"

"I'm going to pay Hera a visit."

"Now?" Hermes gaped at him. "Do you think that's a good idea? Shit blows up whenever Hera's involved. There's too much at stake."

"It's utter crap, Hermes, and you know it. I can't let her get away with this. This is my life she's toying with. And not just my life, but my mom's . . . Psyche's." His voice cracked under the weight of his emotion.

There was a single knock on the door before it swung

open. Psyche rushed in, not bothering to close the door behind her. "What's all the yelling about? You two are lucky they're both out to lunch—" Her eyes went to his knuckles, which were red and felt as sore as they looked. "What happened to your hand?"

"Nothing. It's fine." He tried to shake out the throbbing. "Ashley was sent by Hera. She's Orea, the nymph who's in love with Apollo."

Psyche's eyes widened. "I *knew* something wasn't right when she wouldn't look me in the eyes. Her mortal shell is strong. I didn't detect a divine aura at all."

"No wonder Leo acted like Liz didn't exist whenever she was around. Ash—Orea had him enchanted," said Eros.

"It's probably why she's always groping him, too," added Hermes.

Of course, the staring, the touching. That's how she was controlling Leo.

Eros balled his fists, and his wings shook with rage. He'd been working his ass off for months down here, with no power, under less than ideal circumstances. He couldn't let Hera get away with this. She was going to call off her dog, and he'd go all the way to the top if he had to.

He reached one hand up, calling his powers to him. They shot down from the heavens in a blinding flash of light. The fabric of his shirt tore, and his wings, now close to a foot long, popped free as he began to fade.

"Be careful, Eros. Time down here moves faster than you think." Psyche reached for him, but he was already halfway gone.

"Don't worry. I'll be right back." His voice dimmed then disappeared with the rest of him.

CHAPTER TWENTY-SEVEN

Eros pushed open the door of *Hera & Associates* just as Hebe, Hera's daughter with Zeus, came around a large potted palm clutching an oversized watering can to her chest. "Oh, hello, Eros."

Her slender figure was draped in a flowing chiton and the smattering of freckles on her nose accentuated her youthful appearance. Dark auburn curls spiraled down her back and her large green eyes sparkled. Unlike Hera's ever-present scowl, Hebe's smile was bright. How she could stand to work in the same office as her eternally abysmal mother and keep such a positive mental attitude, he'd never know.

"Hi, Hebe." He managed to tamp down his anger enough to pass as cheerful. "I just stopped by to talk to Hera. Is she around?" He lifted the heavy container out of her hands.

"Thank you. What a gentleman you are!" Hebe flashed another brilliant smile at him as he set the canister on the waist-high ledge surrounding her desk.

"Let me make sure she's in today." She went to consult her calendar. Not only did she work in the same office as Hera, she worked *for* Hera. The only associate accommodating enough to withstand the notoriously snarly Marriage Manager. It didn't surprise him, really, since serving others—usually cups of ambrosia—was the mild-mannered Hebe's specialty.

Without realizing it, he began tapping his fingers on the ledge as she checked. Her gaze flicked up toward his quickly moving extremities then back down at her calendar, causing him to stop mid-tap.

Don't give yourself away before you even get in there, genius.

Even though he wanted nothing more than to fly straight into Hera's office and let her have it, getting past her first line of defense against unwanted visitors was priority one. He also wanted the element of surprise in his back pocket.

"She's in." Hebe reached for the phone. "Let me just call her and make sure—"

His impatience surfaced. "That won't be necessary." It was difficult keeping his anger at a simmer, and he wasn't sure how much longer he had before it boiled over. He cleared his throat, gave her his best lopsided grin and started over.

"She's expecting me." His grin turned into a smile, dazzling enough, he hoped, to convince her. "It won't take but a minute or two. Please hold her calls, okay?"

"Oh, okay." A blush deepened her rosy complexion. "Go on through then."

"Thanks, Hebe."

Perfect. Now if only he could be as convincing in front of Hera.

"Good luck," she whispered as he hurried away.

His footsteps resounded through the mosaic-tiled and marbled hall as he headed toward Hera's office. He had no idea what he was going to say, but whatever it was, he wasn't going to come off as calm as Hebe. Here he was, forced to play this little game of Hera's, and she wasn't even playing fair or square. He was done with her complete lack of professionalism.

Without knocking, he threw open the door. He was momentarily stunned at how homey her office was, how *cozy* it felt, with the warm glow of lamps and an actual fire burning in a brick fireplace surrounded by a carved mantel. How in Hades' Realm it felt so inviting was beyond his comprehension, especially with such a cold-hearted, nine-headed hydra occupying the room.

She waited a few beats before looking up from her paperwork. His sudden entrance hadn't surprised her at all. Of course she had been expecting him.

"Stop trying to sabotage me." His voice was even, but his hands clenched and unclenched at his sides. He caught himself and stopped. Although he was furious, beyond furious even, maintaining a poker face was essential in this game of divine chess. He needed to take the queen with wit and strategy. Brute force would only engage a battle he couldn't win.

"I have no idea what you're talking about." She sighed while gathering a handful of papers and tapping them on top of her anally-retentive neat and orderly desk. He wasn't surprised when they fell into line like obedient little soldiers.

"You're lying." His voice rose to a decibel that would surely pierce mortal eardrums, an otherworldly growl rumbling through the words as he spoke. "If you're going to try and get rid of me, at least have the decency to admit it."

What he really wanted to say was don't be such a bitch-on-wheels, a snake in the grass, an ugly, jealous harpy, any one of those would do, but there wasn't enough time. He couldn't resort to name calling, not if he wanted to have any chance at walking out unscathed.

"I know you sent Orea," he continued through gritted teeth.

"Orea? Why would I send her?" Hera leaned back in her chair, nonplussed. "Isn't she that woodland nymph pining away in the Sacred Forest for Apollo?"

"You know exactly who she is, and you know why she'd want to take me down. She hates me for shooting Daphne instead of her. It infuriates her that Daphne gets all of Apollo's attention, and she refuses to believe that if I'd shot her instead, she'd hate him just as much as Daphne does. Using her resentment against me? It's pretty clever, I must admit."

"Really, Eros, you think I'm scheming against you? I mean, look at all this paperwork." She gestured toward an extensive system of file holders. "Honestly, where would I find the time?"

"We all know how you operate, Hera, and sending a nymph to do your dirty work is *exactly* the kind of scheming you'd find all the time on Mount Olympus to do."

"My, my, I think your incompetency has finally sent you over the edge." She shook her head and clicked her tongue. "Truly off the deep end."

He'd admit he wasn't the strongest of gods, but suggesting he was insane? Nonsense. *Dionysus* was the crazy one, not him.

Eros walked over to her desk and planted his hands down before leaning in and staring her square in her green snake eyes. "Nice try, but your plan isn't going to work. Your plan is going to fail. Do you want to know why?" He threw caution to the wind and let loose. "Because love wins, Hera. Love always wins."

He stood, pushing away from the desk, unable to stand touching it one moment longer. "It's not just love either, it's *mad* love. The purest, most driven kind of love there is. It's unstoppable. I'm unstoppable. Because I'm not mad, Hera, I'm *pissed*."

He stomped over to the fireplace, and with a twist of his

wrist, a burst of light turned the flickering flames into a solid wall of fire. It felt good to use his magic, to stretch his muscles and display his power. He had missed it, and if this all worked out in the end, he was never going to take it for granted again.

An image flickered across the wall of flames. Orea and Dionysus sitting together on a blanket, in their natural state, which was pretty much naked, indulging in wine, feeding each other grapes and laughing with sheer, blissful happiness.

Hera's nostrils flared and her eyes narrowed to tiny slits, her mouth twisting into an ugly sneer.

"Orea's had a change of heart," said Eros. "She's not working for you anymore. She's decided to pursue something a little more rewarding, like love instead of hate. Just thought you'd be interested to know."

"How did you manage that without your powers?" Hera's upper lip curled like a dead spider, and her eyes turned an inky black.

He hadn't. It was a ruse. An alternate reality he'd conjured to trick her.

"So you admit it."

"I admit nothing." Her voice was tight, the effort to keep her composure making her aura glow a venomous green, but she reeled her anger in enough to continue. "I am rather curious. Do tell me the secret to accomplishing so much in so little time . . . with such tiny wings."

"It's no secret, Hera. You should try love sometime. Maybe then you could start using your power for good. Maybe that way, more marriages wouldn't end up in the dumps. And your divorce rates wouldn't be so high."

He walked toward the door and swung it open. He was suddenly weary of fighting. Exhausted from defending himself, trying to convince someone who was determined not to see the good in the work he'd done so far—or ever.

He'd have to do this the hard way.

Before leaving, he turned to face her one last time. "If that doesn't convince you to call off your nymph, then maybe a formal complaint to the Fates will."

Head snapping back in surprise, her face elongated, features going serpentine, and her eyes shined with malice. "You wouldn't dare," she hissed, baring wicked sharp fangs. It didn't take a genius to see he'd found a weak spot. She was terrified of the Fates, like everyone else.

Finally, he had her where he wanted her.

But would his threat hold long enough for him to hit his mark?

"I'm headed to Fates Incorporated right now. Would you like me to tell them you say hello?"

The stricken look on her face morphed into pure delight, and a chuckle issued from deep within her as she called his bluff. "Go ahead, waste more of your precious time."

The air squirmed like bugs on his skin when the power shifted back into her hands. He tightened his fists in an attempt to control his temper. Whatever verbal assault she was about to unleash on him, he wouldn't take the bait. He couldn't let her get to him, not when so much was at stake.

"We both know it takes ages to get a meeting with the Fates, but, by all means, tell them I say hello. But you do know it won't matter, don't you? Because you've already lost." Her sneer was ugly, and he knew her words would be cruel. "Did you really think I wouldn't be able to see right through that lie you conjured?" Her laughter bubbled out.

She's going to try and break your spirit.

"The Fates are preparing to cut that pitiful mortal's life short *as we speak*. Her demise is in motion, Eros, and so is yours. I've seen your pathetic attempts at landing your arrow and binding their hearts. Did you actually try binding them at a *bar*? It was quite comical, I assure you. The hardest I've laughed in decades."

Stay strong . . . Don't listen to her . . .

His body trembled, the feathers on his wings ruffling, quite literally.

"I've got to hand it to you, though, you really did try your best," she continued, "Too bad you're weak. You've always been, and you always will be. I'm not even sure what Aphrodite and Ares were thinking when they made you."

Okay, that hurt.

He tasted blood when his teeth sliced through the inside of his cheek. He wanted to flip something. Smash it to bits. A table, a chair, the desk. Her face. Anything. Because hadn't that always been his struggle? Love and hate had united to create, what, a big-hearted baby with a bad temper? A flawed deity possessing the best of his mother's intentions and the worst of his father's knack for destroying things.

His wings fell, curling in on themselves for protection as every insecurity he ever had poked at him, taunting and laughing at the sensitive side of his soul.

You're not strong enough.

Breathing grew difficult, yet the churning in his gut made his knees weaken easily.

You're not good enough . . . give up.

Eros stood there, numb, all fight gone. His will evaporated, and hope faded, dimming slowly before blinking out. She'd done it. She'd known what buttons to push, which ones would snuff out his light and leave him in darkness. Hera would finally have her revenge.

"Oh, and since you're here I might as well tell you, you should have listened to your darling Psyche and stayed down on Earth instead of coming up here and trying to put me in my place. As you know, Orea is an expert at using her body as a weapon." She lifted a hand toward the fireplace. "Tick tock, lover boy."

A wall of flames leapt up from the hearth. Another image, but this time it was in the form of the mortal map, a magical global positioning system that allowed them to keep tabs on every mortal soul on Earth. His mouth went dry, and his shoulders sank low as she splayed her fingers wide, zooming in on the three dots labeled Leo, Liz and Orea. Leo's dot showed him at Some Random Bar. Orea's dot hovered practically on top of his. And Liz's dot? Her dot was on a crash course toward the other two.

He'd come hoping to at least force Hera into a stalemate. But after all he had said and she had done, one thing was abundantly clear. This game of chess was over.

CHAPTER TWENTY-EIGHT

Leo checked the time on his phone. The sooner he got this over with, the better. He'd much rather be buying a birthday present for someone who would most likely reject it. Instead, he had to break up with someone he wasn't even dating. How, in God's name, did he manage to get himself into these predicaments?

The waiter shot him a confused look when he waved him off. If all went according to plan, he wouldn't be here long and there would be no need for food or drinks. Best to keep the table sans liquid. He'd learned that lesson.

He removed the salt and pepper shakers, along with everything else that was breakable, from the table, and checked his phone again. What if Ashley still didn't get it? What would he do, sic Liz on her? That might be amusing, until Liz turned on *him* for not having disclosed vital information. Like why he'd given Ashley his number in the first place. It was a vicious circle, a deadly roundabout he had somehow gotten on and was now trying to make it off alive.

"Hi, handsome."

How in the bloody hell did she do that? Sneak up on him

so thoroughly it was as if she appeared out of nowhere. "Ashley." He greeted her with a curt nod as she sat across from him in the booth, his gaze flicking up at her before looking back down at his phone. He'd look her in the eye at the absolute last moment, when he told her he was about ready to report her for stalking. He'd pin her with a look so deadly serious it would prove he wasn't messing around anymore. "We need to talk."

"Of course. What would you like to talk about?" She rubbed a stiletto against the side of his leg.

Irritation coursed through him. He'd met some persistent women in his day, but she was taking stamina to a whole other level. He set his phone on the table, face down, before turning his full attention on her and drilling holes into her soul. If she even had one.

He'd tried doing this the easy way, the charming way, but now it was time to play hardball. "Stop calling me. And don't text me anymore. I'm not interested, do you understand?"

She said nothing, but her eyes narrowed. He froze, helpless against the fog pulling him under. Her pupils grew wider until they were two black pits. "I thought you might be hard to convince, but this love business is getting on my last nerve. Let's see if this will do the trick."

"I should have kept my eyes on my phone," was his last lucid thought before the pins and needles started. It wasn't long before his whole body pricked with the painful static, and for the hair on his arms to stand. His surroundings dimmed, fading away as the movie being projected in his head came to life.

His hands gripping the curves of her waist . . . her long curls splayed across her back.

"Listen here, Leo Simmons. I have a job to do, and I'm going to do it, do *you* understand *me*?"

He wasn't sure how or when it had happened, but now

she was sitting next to him, one hand trailing across his shoulder to the other. The hair on his neck rose, as if by command, and her other hand turned his face toward hers. His limbs grew heavy, and the body cradling him felt too soft and luscious for him to care. He closed his eyes when she pressed her lips to his, and the whole world went black when she slid her tongue into his mouth.

Liz wasn't one to gawk. She had never felt the urge to peer into windows, staring in at people enjoying each other's company. It had always reminded her that she was on the outside. So why had she done it now?

She'd been on her way to Starbucks when she'd been compelled to turn her head and look through *this* window. Whatever it was—curiosity, the fact that she finally felt wanted, sheer stupidity—she wished she hadn't, because then she wouldn't be standing in the middle of the sidewalk with her world blown apart and scattered at her feet.

At the exact moment she had peered through the vinyl lettering that spelled out "Some Random Bar," the couple sitting in the back had come into focus. She'd recognize that tousled hair from miles away.

She felt the blood drain from her face as her brain tried to make sense of what she was seeing. Leo. Ashley. Their lips pressed together in a kiss.

On the verge of hyperventilating, she stood rooted to the spot, wanting to run away as far as possible but unable to move. Scenes of her mother, crying and begging her father not to go, flashed uninvited through her mind. Dammit, why wouldn't her legs *move*?

They'd betrayed her then, too.

Although in a different way, she'd felt the wound as deeply as her mother did when her father walked out the door for good. Not that she wasn't glad to see him go, she hated the son of a bitch, but seeing how much her mother still wanted him—*needed* him—even after all the pain and suffering he'd caused, something inside her had broken.

She wondered if her mother would have felt differently if she'd told her the man she loved so much put cigarettes out on their kid. Maybe she should have, but she couldn't risk being abandoned by her mother, too. So she wore long sleeves until her eighteenth birthday, when she was old enough to cover them up without permission.

Her stomach turned, nausea on the verge of ruining her Converse sneakers. She stared at the concrete and focused on a large crack in the sidewalk as she began the laborious process of pushing her emotions back down where they belonged, from where she should have never let them have been in the first place. She stood immobilized, fists balled tight, grimacing as she gulped down the pain and swallowed the heartache. The taste of betrayal was a thousand times worse than sweet relish, but she had to shove it down, or she wouldn't find the strength to go on. And she needed to go on.

Move on.

How could he do this to her? She should have listened to her gut, all those times his phone buzzed. She should have questioned every ring. But she hadn't wanted to be *that girl.* She thought she could trust him, because she actually believed there had been a chance. Turns out she was stupid, after all. So, so stupid.

Déjà vu washed over her, drowning her in the notion that he had done this before, more than once. She dug her fingers into her temples as the anger tore at her throat first then ripped through her chest.

How is this even happening?

A lightning bolt of anger ignited her fury, causing it to

explode like a powder keg. The sheer force of it drove her back through the people on the street, pushing and shoving as she went. Birthday present her ass. After stepping inside, she stomped past the patrons waiting to be seated.

"Hey!" a bearded man dressed head-to-toe in the latest hipster fashion shouted at her.

"Relax," she shouted back. "I'm not going to be here that long. Trust me."

The man didn't continue challenging her motives. Good. There was no time to be arrested for assault and battery. Not when she could very well be charged for murder in a few minutes.

She moved through the bar like a five-foot-four freight train, muscling her way over to Leo and Ashley until she stood over them trembling with anger.

"Leo."

No answer.

Her hand slammed down on the table. "*Leo!*"

He turned his head and blinked up at her. "Hello."

Is he seriously pretending he barely knows me?

"Oh, hi," said Ashley through a fake smile. "Liz, is it?"

"You know who I am," Liz spat the words at Ashley before rolling her eyes over to Leo. "I have news."

Leo squinted at her, his gaze darting over her face as though he was trying to place where he'd seen her before. She watched in horror as any trace of feelings he may have had for her, any memory of their last few weeks together, faded from his eyes and his crooked brow straightened. "I'm glad you stopped in, love." Methodical. "Won't you join us?" Calculating.

Like a man afraid of commitment.

"What's wrong with you? You're acting weird. Or maybe you're just acting like yourself, an asshole." She let the angry wasps fly before glaring at him. Let's see how he dealt with *that* bit of constructive criticism.

To her amazement, he ignored it.

"What's the news, love? Have you found out what those bloody humps—?"

"Fuck Eron's bloody humps! I'm leaving."

Stars. Red. Anything and everything a person sees when they're in a blind rage. She had been willing to give him a chance, to let him explain what was happening—yet again—but seeing as he was determined to keep messing with her heart, his chance was over.

"What?" He looked as though he was trying to do trigonometry in his head. She could see the wheels turning, his surprise and confusion so evident she half-expected smoke to come pouring out of his ears.

"Yeah, I've been offered another job." It was a lie. But there was no way she was going to continue working with him, not after this. "I'm going back to Chicago."

"Congratulations! When do you leave?" Ashley didn't even try to curb her enthusiasm, and Liz pictured punching her right in her lipsticked mouth.

"Tonight." She refused to look at the woman. Instead, she focused her attention on Leo. "Today was my last day at Follow Your Heart."

"But we have dinner plans . . . it's your birth . . . Liz, why didn't you tell me?"

Was it possible for one's heart to soar and plummet at the same time? The old Leo—*her* Leo, not this callous imposter—was making an appearance, giving her hope. And in the same breath, he was acting like she meant nothing to him.

Once was bad enough. She couldn't live through it twice.

"I just did." She was careful not to give any indication of the storm raging inside her, hammering away at her resolve to hold firm. "Besides, I didn't think you'd care all that much anyway. Seeing as you were just making out with an event planner."

Ashley pursed her lips, her irritation evident.

Liz couldn't have cared less.

"Of course I do . . . we're . . . because I'm . . ." He rubbed at his forehead before running his fingers through his hair. Opening and closing his mouth—the old fish out of water thing again. One touch from Ashley's hand and his face went blank.

Just what the hell kind of power over him does this woman possess?

She fought the urge to punch something. His knee, her face, whatever was closest.

"Oh, how adorable. You're going to miss your little friend, aren't you?" Ashley feigned sympathy as she caressed Leo's shoulder.

Liz wanted to remove her hand, and if all five slender, manicured fingers attached to it were mangled beyond recognition in the process, then, oh well.

"You guys *are* just friends, right?" Ashley searched out Leo's gaze. When she found it, she held it firmly, staring into his eyes as if she were shooting laser beams straight into his soul. He blinked a few times, the sharp steel gray of his eyes going dull.

Ashley stared at him, concentrating.

Liz held her breath, waiting.

"Yeah, we're just friends," he muttered, nodding. "Congratulations, Liz."

The world was suddenly devoid of air as Liz watched Ashley take possession of her trophy by placing her hand over Leo's. It's a wonder she didn't raise it above her head in triumph.

"Thanks." It was all Liz could say. Her throat ached. Her

tears welled. She turned away so neither of them would see and left without saying another word.

The rage drained out of her, slipping away and leaving what was left of her mangled heart to throb painfully in her chest. She should have known better. This was exactly why she never let her guard down. Why she refused to lower those impenetrable walls she'd built, to keep her heart safe from the torturous pain of love.

"Goodbye, Liz," Ashley called after her, waving and carrying on. "Best of luck in Chicago!"

Any hope Liz had this was all a mistake, that it was happening to someone else, was gone. "Screw you, Ashley."

Screw you, too, Leo.

Even though she hated him, even after everything he'd done, she wanted him to stop her. Turn her around and beg her to stay. She walked slower, in case there was a small chance he would. After saying they were nothing more than friends, she still imagined him rushing after her, pushing through the crowd, turning her around by the shoulders and asking—*begging*—her to stay.

She was as pitiful as her mother.

Because her father didn't do any of those things, and neither did Leo. Before she knew it, her legs had carried her back out onto the sidewalk. They hadn't moved when she wanted them to, and now, when she wanted to stay, they worked perfectly fine.

She wiped an errant tear before it could make its way down her cheek and pulled out her cell phone. She dialed as she hurried down the pavement in the direction of her apartment. It was time to get out of Seattle, and she would, as soon as humanly possible. But first, she needed to quit her job for real.

CHAPTER TWENTY-NINE

In the blink of an eye, the serene gardens of the atrium surrounded Eros. He knew he should go back down to Earth, but he couldn't quite find the energy. Perhaps the word he was looking for was dignity, since he wasn't sure he'd be able to face Psyche and Hermes. A quick walk around one of his favorite places in the universe—aside from Psyche's arms—might help him muster the courage to deal with the loose ends he still needed to tie up.

Very loose ends, since his hard work had surely been blown to bits by this point. Any thought of a successful shot was beyond all hope by now.

He replayed the confrontation with Hera in his head as he veered down a stone path. Charging into her office and threatening to report her to the Fates might have seemed like a good idea at the time, but now that his passion-fueled outburst was over, he wasn't sure it had been the smartest.

Several sculptures, including one of himself as a child curled up and sleeping on a large rock, lined a cobblestone path branching off the main walkway. The lush greenery thickened on either side of the path, and he followed it until he came to a mass of hanging vines concealing the entryway to a small clearing. He pushed aside the long, leafy tendrils and slipped inside.

An assortment of butterflies fluttered about as sunlight filtered through the trees surrounding the opening. In the center of the clearing, the biggest ray illuminated a sculpture of two figures entwined, one with a glorious set of wings fanned out behind. It was his favorite sculpture in the gardens—he and Psyche entwined in a lover's embrace.

There were benches surrounding the statue, but he didn't sit. How could he? He'd just had a shouting match with Hera. Partner at Life Industries. His boss's wife.

The most powerful goddess in his existence.

A monarch fluttered past him. Not being able to resist its beauty, he reached out, extending his forefinger, and the butterfly clasped on.

"I knew I'd find you here." The voice was as soft and gentle as a breeze.

Eros whirled around, his heart jumping in his chest. The butterfly, startled by the jolt, flew away to join the others in their swirling waltz through the air.

Psyche, who'd been sitting at the base of the statue tucked out of sight, got to her feet. "It didn't go well, did it?"

He slid his hands, now free of his little friend, into his pockets and shook his head. "How did you know I'd come here?"

"Because you always do when you're upset. As soon as you left, I came here and waited. Did you at least get her to call off the nymph?"

He shook his head a second time, avoiding her eyes. "Of course not. I don't even know why I thought I could. Doesn't matter anyway. She's already won."

"What do you mean she's already won?"

"I saw the mortal map." His gut clenched, and the rest of

his words came out a stammering mess. "Orea and Leo . . . Liz . . . she was about to see them together."

He braced himself for what he knew was coming next. Psyche might have held her tongue after he missed his second shot, but there wasn't a snowball's chance she was going to do that now.

"Then what are you doing here? We need to go back." She pointed toward the ground. "You need to be down there, not up here."

Fear and doubt tore through him, shredding the last of any faith he had left in himself to pieces. Defeated, he answered with a question, "Why? It's over. There's no way to bind them now, there's no time. I don't even know if I have the strength to go back. I'll have Hermes close down the shop and be done with it." Hera was right. So was Apollo. He was infantile and weak. Inferior. "I might as well send word to Zeus it's over. Eighty years, give or take a few. That's a good deal, right?"

She came at him fast, pushing his chest with both palms. Her eyes darkened, and her lips all but disappeared from pinching them together so hard. She looked like she wanted to do more than shove him. "So that's it? You're giving up? What in Hades' Realm, Eros? You've still got five hours."

"I can't do it. There's no way. Even if time wasn't an issue, which it is, her walls are probably sky-high and rock-hard by now."

"Then find another way." She gripped his arms, imparting one quick jerk to make sure he was listening. "And if that doesn't work, try something else. That's what I did."

She's going to bring up the time I left her.

He was sorry for losing his temper that night so long ago, when she'd decided to sneak into his room even though he had asked her not to. He knew veiling himself and letting her believe he was a beast would complicate their relationship, but he'd only done so because he'd wanted her to love him for his heart, not his face.

"What if I would have given up after you left? Huh?"

Yep, here we go. I looked all over for you.

"I looked all over for you. When that didn't work . . ."

I did the unthinkable.

"I did the unthinkable. I went to your mother—who hated my guts at the time—and asked her for help. Then I went down to Hades' Realm and back, Eros. For you. Do you remember that? Do you even know how impossible it was to complete those tasks? She gave me four of them!" Psyche held four fingers up before throwing her arms out, palms up and fingers spread in exasperation. "But I never gave up. Because I would have rather died trying to find you than never have the opportunity to tell you how sorry I was to your face."

Eros hung his head, not knowing whether to laugh or cry. She meant well, and was trying to give him the push he needed to go on, but her words made him feel so much worse. No, she hadn't given up. That's because her will was stronger than his. It always had been, and that fact crushed him. He was weak, and when it came right down to it, he didn't have a lick of fire in his breast for battle like his father did. He hated confrontation. He loathed fighting. He wasn't strong, he was an embarrassment. The butt of Apollo's jokes. The laughing stock of Mount Olympus.

He didn't deserve to be the god of anything, let alone love.

"No, they're right." He shook his head. It seemed like the only thing he could do with any amount of success lately. "I should just stop pretending like I make a difference."

"Who's right?"

"Hera and Apollo."

She clicked her tongue. "Oh please. Are you really going

to listen to those pompous assholes? Come here." She led him to one of the stone benches and sat down next to him, both of her small hands clutching one of his. "What's the one thing everyone needs? The one thing no one can live without, even the gods?"

He closed his eyes. He didn't want her to see how filled with emotion they were. "I don't even know anymore."

"You. The world can't exist without *you.* We've all witnessed your power. Countless souls have felt it. Love takes strength. It takes courage. It's hard sometimes, but it's the most beautiful, wonderful feeling in the world. The most imperfectly perfect thing that exists. And it's worth fighting for. You're worth fighting for, Eros."

She leaned over and rested her forehead on his temple. A tingle rippled between his shoulder blades as her voice floated through is mind.

Please don't give up. Please. The world needs you in it. I need you in it, too.

She pulled back, her hand guiding his face to look at her. "If you won't do it for yourself, can you at least do it for me?"

He was terrified of failure, but she was even more terrified of losing him. He could hear it in her words, feel it in the way she clung to him, the way his wings stretched and grew another several inches right there on the spot. It made hope trickle back into his broken heart.

She still has faith. After everything, she still believes in me.

He squeezed his eyes shut. He was about to say something he couldn't ever remember saying before, but knew he needed to say it now. And this time he wanted to say it, out loud, because then maybe he would actually believed it for once. Anything was worth a try at this point. "The world needs me."

"Yes, it does. And so do I." Her thumb brushed across his

lips, before giving him a small kiss. "Have faith in your power."

Her words filled the cracks in his heart, mending the broken pieces Hera had shattered back together. He finally understood. Psyche had never stopped loving him, and he must do everything in what little power he had left to make sure their love story never ended.

He couldn't let everything they'd overcome in the name of love be for nothing.

He waved his hand behind his back to repair the torn dress shirt. "Fine, but I hear the power of love has shitty aim." With a snap of his fingers two suit coats materialized on his godly form.

"Well, it found its way to *my* heart." She circled her arms around him and squeezed, resting her head on his shoulder.

The ringing from his cell phone was shrill, and half the butterflies gathered near them flitted away in bunches. He ignored it. The moment felt too good. He wanted to savor it, even if it would only last a few minutes before he had to go back.

His phone continued to ring, and he kept ignoring it. After a moment of silence, it rang again. With a grumble, he pulled it from his pocket and glanced at the number on the caller ID. His heart lurched when he saw who it was, and Psyche bit her lip when he showed her the number.

Dread burned through him like wildfire, but he slid the accept call button and pressed the phone to his ear anyway. "Hello, this is Eron."

The person on the other line was so loud the butterflies circling overhead darted away in alarm.

"Eron, it's Liz. I quit."

CHAPTER THIRTY

Willa seemed to move in slow motion, even though she was barreling toward the table at a high rate of speed. "*What* in Hades' Realm is going on here?"

Leo tried to will the world back to normal, but it was no use. He sat helpless, weighed down by an invisible anchor until the woman clinging to his side detached herself and took the heaviness with her. He sucked in a deep breath, rolling his neck first then his shoulders, pleased his muscles were in working order once again.

"What in Hades' Realm is going on here?" The question echoed through his head. Indeed, what *was* going on here? One minute he'd been in the process of telling Ashley to leave him alone, the next, Willa was standing over them looking like she was about to thoroughly choke the life out of him.

A glimpse of Liz stomping away, the blonde tipped tresses he adored trailing down her back, flashed through his mind. But before he could figure out where they'd been when the memory had been formed, or why it was popping up now, Eron stepped around Willa and grabbed hold of Ashley.

"It's over, Orea," said Eron, tugging her to the end of the vinyl bench as if she weighed nothing. "It's time to go back."

Leo slid to the end of the booth, panic rising like a geyser. This did not look good, he and Ashley alone here together. Not at all, and he needed to explain.

"Get your hands off of me before I call the authorities." Ashley's elbow missed Leo's nose by a hair when she wrenched free from Eron's grasp. "And my name is *Ashley*."

Leo leaned back to avoid any further chance of sustaining injury and waited for a break in the action to clear things up.

"Oh, come off it," said Willa, planting her hands on her hips. "We know who you're working for and why you're here."

Ashley was an event planner. Didn't she work for herself? Leo shook his head and stood. It didn't matter. They could call the woman whatever they wanted.

"Look at me," commanded Willa.

He froze, but relaxed when he realized Willa wasn't talking to him. She wasn't even looking at him. She was too busy staring at Ashley.

"No." Ashley turned her head away.

"We can either do this the hard way." Willa grabbed her by the shoulders. "Or you can get it over with and look me in the eyes. Your call, sister."

Leo's face grew hot, bile creeping up as another vision flashed. The frantic look in Liz's eyes as she said, *"I've been offered another job,"* made him wince.

He swallowed, his gaze desperate for a place to land. The table, the floor, the back of that guy's head two booths away. He needed to find Liz. Make sure . . .

He took off for the door, but before he could make it ten steps, Robby came rushing toward him, appearing as though he'd materialized out of thin air. Before he could say anything

—what it would be, he didn't know—Robby swiveled him around and ushered him back toward the scene of the crime.

"I got your message," Robby informed Eron, still holding Leo's arm. His gaze darted sideways before releasing his grip. "It's not good. You've got to move on this, fast."

An icy dread filled Leo as labored panting came from behind Eron, who stepped out of the way to reveal an epic battle of wills ensuing between Willa and Ashley. The tendons in Ashley's neck stood out, trembling. She gritted her teeth, and a louder, longer grunt escaped. Right before her head finally snapped toward Willa, she closed her eyes.

"Open your eyes, Orea. Or I'm getting the Fates involved."

Ashley's sigh turned into a drawn-out groan, but she opened her eyes. Once she and Willa connected, her shoulders went slack, and she stood there silently swaying on her feet like a balloon tied to a chair.

Leo rubbed the back of his neck. None of this made sense. Not how Robby wasn't there and then suddenly was. Not the weirdness between Ashley and Willa. And definitely not the feeling that something was very, very wrong where Liz was concerned. "What the bloody hell is going on?"

He looked to Eron for answers, but the man only dropped one shoulder and twisted his spine, all the while trying not to wince. The tumors, they must hurt.

Leo knew the feeling. Each minute that ticked by, knowing, but not knowing for sure, was excruciating, except it wasn't his back that was in pain. It was his heart.

The uneasy looks from Robby and Eron made his skin prickle, and the temperature in the room shot up an unbearable number of degrees. "If no one's going to tell me what's going on, then get out of my way."

Robby put his hands up, urging Leo to remain were he stood. "Liz booked a flight back to Chicago. It leaves in a couple of hours." He turned toward Eron. "And if she gets on that plane . . ." He made a diving gesture, followed by a flick of all ten fingers. The universal sign for explosion.

Eron's face paled. "Thanks for the reminder." He nodded at Ashley. "Liz saw you in here with her, Leo."

The sweat Leo had going on turned cold, drenching him. He gulped down air to stop from heaving as the visions—the memories—came rushing back all at once, finally fitting together and forming the complete picture.

Ashley and her tongue in his mouth.

"No."

Liz standing there, refusing to cry. *"I'm going back to Chicago."*

"No, no, no. Not again."

Leo rubbed his eyes, trying to scrub away the image, but the voice he knew so well still echoed inside his head.

"Today was my last day at Follow Your Heart."

Her lips had thinned, pressed together with disgust. No, not disgust. Anger. Hurt.

Regret.

Eron steadied him. "I'm afraid so, buddy, but I can fix it. Come back to the office with me. I want to show you something. Something I think will help. But we don't have a lot of time, so we need to go *now*."

Guilt tore open Leo's chest, gripping his heart and squeezing. There was nothing that could repair this damage. He'd bloody done it again. Except, this time it was so much worse. She'd finally let him in, given a piece of her heart to him, and what had he given her in return? More hurt. More pain. There was no way she would forgive him.

Willa kept her eyes on Ashley as she spoke to Eron. "Go. I'll take her back up. You get him to the office, and I'll meet you there in a couple of minutes. Don't do anything rash, okay?"

Unable to make heads or tails of Willa's words, Leo dialed Liz's work extension.

Please, let her pick up. Please.

It rang until the call forwarded to voicemail. He pressed the end call button with his thumb and tried to keep his cool. "She probably went to get a Starbucks. You know how she loves her iced mochas."

He dialed her cell. Straight to voicemail. Robby and Eron looked at him, sympathy tilting their heads. Willa and Ashley remained locked in their odd staring contest. His stomach dropped, and without a word he made for the door, Eron right behind him when he burst out onto the street.

Their footsteps pounded out the same rhythm as they made their way back to the flower shop. He refused to believe things were that bad. She might be furious with him, but she wouldn't do something as crazy as getting on a plane and never talking to him . . .

Then again, it was Liz.

To hell with walking, he broke out into a run. What a bloody idiot he had been. He should have just told her straight away, so they could have dealt with the Ashley situation together. That's what relationships were about. Fixing problems together. Instead, he'd hid it. He'd messed up again, and it didn't matter that his intentions had been good, he'd kept it from her and now he and his machismo would pay the price.

Leo ran, ducking around pedestrians while trying to envision finding her at the office, scowling at him the moment he got there, perhaps even saying, *"What's the hurry, Mo Farah?"*

But all he could picture was an empty chair.

He cursed the day he'd gone up front and tried to be helpful, because this was his worst nightmare. Like the day he found out his mum was terminal. Or the day she passed, and every other day after that for years. Even some days still.

This was why he had never looked—so he would never find. Because he couldn't bear the pain of losing someone else he loved.

He stopped running, the thought punching him in the gut. He loved Liz, but that wasn't the problem. The problem was could he love her without hurting her?

Eron stopped beside him, panting hard and sweating profusely. "What's wrong? We're almost to the office. Let's go."

"It doesn't matter." Leo grabbed two fistfuls of his hair and pulled before raking his fingers through. "Even if she does forgive me, which, let's be honest, she won't. I'll just mess it up again." His arms dropped to his sides, hanging there, as useless as he felt. "I really am that guy."

"Oh, no you don't." Eron shoved him into motion. "You're not quitting on me now. Let's get to the office. I've got to show you something, remember? Something that might solve both our problems."

CHAPTER THIRTY-ONE

Liz hurried up the stairs that led to her apartment. Done. She was so done. There was nothing left to keep her here. No way was she sticking around for a failed relationship that would try and charm her back into its arms. She didn't want to have to look at the reflection staring at her from the glass partition five days a week, reminding her she was never going to be good enough for a guy like Leo. She'd rather go back home and live with her mother than subject herself to that.

Halfway up the stairs, the door to the stairwell swung open with such force she expected the Hulk to walk through. She groaned when she saw it was the superintendent, Bill the buzzard, his fingers reaching out after her, pointing and shaking like a doddering geriatric telling the neighborhood kids to stay off the grass. Had he been chasing her this whole time, through the Borealis Apartments courtyard *and* the lobby? Enough was enough.

"Save it, Bill." She scrunched up her forehead at the dramatic way he jumped backward before flattening himself against the wall. "I'm leaving anyway."

"What do you mean you're leaving? You're breaking your lease?" he said, his tone haughtier than normal.

"So what if I am?"

"But you signed a contract with Borealis Apartments. You can't just leave."

What was his deal? In fact, what was the universe's problem? All she wanted was to get to her apartment. Why was the cosmos insisting on making her life such a living hell?

The stairwell door opened midway through Liz's existential crisis, and a little girl, who looked around nine or ten, slipped through. Her backpack barely cleared the frame before the door slammed shut. She grinned when she saw Bill, and her crooked smile revealed a mouthful of equally crooked teeth.

"You almost done working?"

Bill shot Liz a nervous sideways glance instead of answering the girl.

She scanned Liz up and down with the scrutiny only kids can get away with before turning back toward Bill, who still hadn't said a word. "Talk to me, Goose!" she commanded. "Do we have permission for a flyby?"

Liz noticed the girl had the same wiry frame and hooked nose as the Borealis Apartments superintendent, only on a smaller scale.

"Affirmative Ghost Rider." In an instant, he'd settled into their routine despite Liz's presence. "One last MiG 28 to take care of and then I'll be up, okay? Your snack is on the counter."

"Roger that. See you back at base." She started up the stairs, and Liz moved out of the way. "Hi," the girl said as she squeezed past.

"Hi." Liz tilted her head, lifting her chin. She inquired with her eyes, and the girl picked up on the subtle question without trouble.

"Kendall. But everyone calls me Kenny. I'm eleven."

"It's nice to meet you, Kenny." Liz offered her hand. "Liz. I'm twenty-four—five. Today's my birthday."

"Happy birthday," said Kenny, shaking hands. "You wouldn't be the Liz my dad's always complaining about, would you?"

Liz smiled, satisfied to have made an impression. "The one and only."

Kenny leaned in and whispered. "Look, his bark is worse than his bite. My mom ditched us. Thing is, she made all the dough. My uncle owns the building, so we get to live here rent free. As long as everyone else pays up." She rubbed two fingers and her thumb together when she said it.

Liz's heart swelled until she thought it might burst. "Gotcha"

The girl reminded her of herself when she was younger. Protecting a wounded heart. It was all too familiar. Except, the circumstances were reversed. It appeared as though it had been the little girl's *father* who'd stayed. Liz had gotten the short end of the stick when it came to hers, but maybe all dads weren't so bad.

Kenny continued up the stairs. After a couple of steps, she turned. "Go easy on my wingman. He's the only one I got."

A smile broke out across Liz's face, no doubt in her mind that, for an eleven-year-old, Kenny had a handle on life. Which was more than she could say for herself right now.

"Roger that, Maverick." Liz saluted. The girl beamed down at her, offering a salute of her own, and sang the rest of the way up the stairs. "*Hiiiighwaaaay toooo the danger zone . . . Gonna take ya riiiight iiiintooo the danger zone.*"

Bill stepped forward to explain. "She loves Tom Cruise, and before you yell at me, I do *not* let her watch the love scene."

"Hey, even if you did—your kid, your rules." She held up

her hands, vaguely aware Leo had said something similar, back when she didn't hate him. "She's not missing anything anyway. Ruins the whole movie if you ask me."

"Well—"

"Look, Bill, I get it now." She wasn't about to get into it with him whether the love scene in *Top Gun* made the movie or not, but she did feel bad she'd given him a hard time. "You're just doing your job. If Borealis doesn't make money, you're out on the street. I know you've got responsibilities, but check your papers. I signed a month-to-month, and I can't stay, so I'm leaving. I'm sure you'll be hounding someone else about rent in no time."

He sighed. "Well, as long as you're not breaking your lease."

"I'm not breaking any leases."

Or hearts. Nope, that would be Leo.

She patted him on the shoulder. "You seem like a real good dad. Keep it up." She turned to finish making her way up the stairs.

"Out of curiosity, where are you moving to?" asked Bill.

Too mentally exhausted to tell him it was none of his beeswax, she muttered while continuing up the stairs to her apartment, "Back to Chicago . . . and out of the goddamned danger zone."

Her hands shook as she fumbled with the keys. When she finally got the door unlocked, she sprinted to her room. Time was of the essence. Her plane left at eight.

She hauled her suitcase out from under her bed and tossed it up onto the wrinkled sheets. Washed, unwashed, didn't matter, she stuffed her clothes into the case. She didn't have one ounce of wherewithal to arrange them into neat stacks. Maybe her new friend, Bill, could arrange to have what didn't fit sent to Chicago.

Or maybe she didn't care.

She snatched a framed picture of her mother and her from the dresser and tucked it between a sweatshirt and pair of jeans. Thank God she hadn't mentioned Leo to her mom yet. She'd come close, though. Several times.

"Goddamn it. I knew this was going to happen." She swiped a duffel bag from the closet and stomped into the bathroom. The drawer squeaked when she yanked it open, and she plucked out her toothbrush plus the half full tube of toothpaste and stuffed them into the bag. A second later, the toothpaste and extra toothbrush Leo had been using landed in the trash with a light *thunk*. She wouldn't make it through security with that much toothpaste.

And the toothbrush could stay in the trash where it belonged.

She scanned her room for anything else she could take with her. The sight of the rumpled bed sheets made the lump in her throat expand, and she fought the urge to bury her face into one of the pillows, which probably still smelled like him, and scream. How many times had they made love there? Enough to make it count.

She rushed out of her bedroom before any more memories could gang up on her. Duffel bag in hand, she went to the living room to collect what few possessions she owned.

She headed toward a pile of paperbacks on the floor and stubbed her toe on the foot of the couch in the process. The same couch where Leo had held her in his arms. Where she'd finally given him a chance, like the voice said she should.

"Ouch! Stupid fucking couch!"

The back of her eyes stung, and she squeezed them shut to keep the burning hot tears from falling. After rubbing the pain out of her battered pinky toe, she stuffed the books into her duffle bag and crawled over to the other end of the coffee table. Kneeling, she rubbed her fingers over the cover of the faux leather-bound book resting there. It was thick, over a thousand pages. The leather was a deep indigo and *The Complete Tales and Poems of Edgar Allan Poe* was printed on the front in gold foil letters. Ironic how it was the most precious thing she owned considering it had been a gift from her father. He'd tossed it at her head on her sixth birthday.

"Here, you can have this. I don't want it. I don't know why your mother would buy me this shit anyway. She knows I don't read books. Reading's for assholes."

She'd never forget the words that had accompanied the first and last birthday gift her father had ever given her. How could she? Joy and sorrow had joined forces to create a pain so powerful she would never forget it as long as she lived. Pain she vowed to never feel again.

And she had broken that promise.

Liz placed Poe into her bag. "You'll never let me down, will you, Edgar?"

She shouldn't have kept the stupid book. Especially when the memory of how it was given to her was so tragic. But it was a reminder to never let her guard down. You never knew what life was going to throw at you, so duck.

She also couldn't resist a good dark and twisted tale.

Liz stood up and parked her hands in the pockets of her hoodie, looking around for more things to pack. Dishes? Nope. Pots, pans, plates? Not hers. Even the silverware and cooking utensils belonged to Borealis Apartments. The box from her old job? She would leave that. She'd only stolen the stapler because she'd been angry, not because she'd really needed it.

"Seriously? Everything I own fits in a suitcase and two bags? Well, isn't that splendid. You're not dysfunctional *at all*,

Liz. You're totally fucking *normal*," she yelled into the empty space around her.

She collapsed onto the couch. Her throat ached from holding back the tears mobbing and assaulting her at every turn. She slid her hands under her glasses and tried to scrub away all trace of emotion. Why couldn't she go back to being devoid of it?

Her glasses fell off and landed in her lap when she pressed her palms over her eyes. She sat like that for a few minutes, jamming them into the sockets so hard she saw pops and flashes of light in the dark. Not only was she trying to force the tears into staying put, she was also trying to fight the realization that she'd been robbed. Leo had picked the lock to her heart, stolen the carefully guarded contents and left her with nothing but a gaping, black hole.

Hadn't it been her fault, though? She'd been the one to invite the thief in, after all.

Her head pounded from clenching her teeth, and her neck and shoulders were in tight, twisted knots. She picked up her glasses and returned them to their rightful place before digging her fingers into her temples, searching for the pressure point she prayed would bring relief from the migraine gathering strength. After a futile attempt at solace, she pressed her knuckles to her mouth. Anything to stop the angry screams from escaping.

She would not scream. She would not cry. Because if she did, it meant she had been nothing short of the damned fool she swore she'd never be.

CHAPTER THIRTY-TWO

Eros stared at the wood grain of his desk. His hands were tied. There was one option left. The truth. He wasn't only trying to save his job, his marriage—his immortality—he was invested in Liz and Leo's future together.

His head snapped up when Leo burst into his office. He'd been waiting for him to see for himself that Liz wasn't there.

"She's really leaving?" Leo's thumbs flew across the keyboard on his phone. "Is Robby sure? How does he know? Did she tell him? I'm going to go see if she's at her apartment."

Eros motioned for Leo to sit in one of the two chairs at the front of his desk. "Please. I only need a few minutes."

Leo sighed impatiently but took a seat.

"Brace yourself," said Eros. "You're going to find what I have to tell you hard to believe, but I've run out of time. I think the easiest thing to do, under the circumstances, is to tell you the truth. Actually, I think I need to show you." Without further ado, Eros stood up and pulled his shirt loose from his pants.

Leo rubbed his forehead when Eros began to unbutton his

collar. "Eron, mate, I know about the tumors. I'm sorry, I really am, and I don't mean to be insensitive, but can we talk about this later? I really need to find Liz."

His hands shot up when Leo stood, preparing to leave. "Wait, it's not what you think. It's something else. Please, let me show you." He quickly undid the rest of the buttons.

Leo's face went pale when Eros sent him a shy smile. "Look, Eron, you're a very attractive man, and I'm sure anyone would be lucky to—"

Eros shook his head. "I'm not coming on to you, and it's not tumors I'm hiding." He peeled off his shirt and turned around to show Leo the feathered wings pressed against his back. He looked over his shoulder. "My name is Eros, not Eron. I'm the god of love you've read about in books."

Leo recoiled, his drawn brows accentuating the incredulous look on his face. "Have you gone mad? What sort of trickery is this?"

The sharp edge to his voice made Eros cringe. It was a lot for mortal minds to take in, he knew. "It's no trick. I'm the god of love." He faced Leo again, all those donuts he'd stress-eaten making him want to pick his shirt up off the desk and use it to hide his unremarkable abs.

Leo's anger wavered on full-blown rage. "Okay, mate. Whatever you're doing right now, it's not funny. You really are ill. Do you know that? Mentally ill."

"I'm not trying to be funny . . . or ill. This is real, Leo. I'm real. The gods exist. All of us."

He fanned out his wings, holding his hands up in front of him to prove he wasn't pulling any strings or pressing any remote-controlled buttons. His wingspan had grown over the last few months, to a couple of feet on either side, although still small in comparison to their former grand and sweeping selves.

Leo shot out of his chair, the force toppling it over. Eros

felt sorry for messing with his head, but the truth was the only foreseeable way of moving things along.

Leo inched his way toward him. "How did you do that? Some kind of mechanical contraption, yeah?" When he was close enough, his hand latched onto one of Eros's wings and tugged.

"Hey, easy! They're still growing out." Eros slapped Leo's wrist. "For the love of Zeus, you can't just go manhandling a brother's wings, you know."

Oh gods, I'm beginning to sound like Hermes.

Leo lifted a feather, inspecting it with more care. "You're putting me on."

"I'm not."

"You're . . . you're really . . . ?" Leo let go of the feather.

"Yes, the god of love in the flesh. Also known as Eros. Commonly referred to as Cupid. Although, I will say Eron Hartman is really starting to grow on me."

"I don't believe you." Leo shook his head. "It's impossible."

"Highly unlikely, but not impossible. It's true, Leo." He slipped on his shirt and walked over to the credenza. Pulling open the top drawer, he grabbed his quiver of arrows.

"What do you plan on doing with those?" Leo's voice climbed higher with every word.

"Never mind that for now." Eros pressed his wings flat and ducked through the strap. "Let's talk about Liz. You love her, correct?" He wiggled his shoulders so that the quiver settled comfortably between his wings.

"Yes."

"Good, because we don't have time to waste. If she gets on that plane, it's over. You need to stop her. You need to tell her that you love her, then keep her still so I can get a good shot."

"A good shot?" Leo's mouth dropped open.

"Yes." Eros reached around and pulled an arrow out of the quiver, sparkly love dust trailing behind the fletching. "With one of these."

He watched as any hope Leo had that the conversation was simply all his imagination vanished with the shimmering sparkles.

"I've never been able to get a good shot. She's had that heart of hers on lockdown for a good long while. I suppose if I had just sunk the damned thing in the first place . . . Then again, you haven't been very much help."

Leo's brow collapsed. "What do you mean I haven't been very much help?"

"You had a bit of an overbearing mother in your first life. Still not sure what happened in the second."

"My first life?"

"Yes, I've been trying to hook you two up for ages, and believe me when I say ages. Now, don't move. Not that I think it will take much, but I need to get rid of any residual doubt left over from Orea's enchantment."

Leo nodded his head in agreement at the suggestion he had lived past lives, but immediately began to shake it when Eros picked up his bow. "Orea?" Leo backed away from him.

"Ashley." Eros took a step forward. "She was sent by Hera to try and stop me from closing your account."

"Hera? My account? My God, none of this makes sense." Leo took another step back, pinching the bridge of his nose.

Eros closed the distance and put one hand on Leo's shoulder. "You mean oh my *gods*. And no one said love was easy to understand, my friend."

A moment later, the door opened and Psyche poked her head in. "Everything okay in here? Eros? How's it going?"

Leo stared at her. "Did you say Eron or Eros?"

She smiled. "Eros, with an S."

"So she knows who you are?" Leo's gaze darted between them.

"She sure does. And *she* is my wife." He tossed his bow in Psyche's direction, and she caught it in one hand with ease.

He grabbed Leo by the shoulders and spun him so his chest faced her. An instant later, an arrow flew toward the bow, drawn together by an ancient and powerful force as old as time. Psyche beamed from ear to ear, and without another moment's hesitation, pulled back, took aim and shot the arrow directly into Leo's heart.

A twinkling cloud enveloped Leo as he staggered backward into Eros, who'd moved closer to steady him. Leo leaned on him for support, alternately gasping for breath and coughing up shiny particles of passion. When he was finally able to stand of his own accord, he rubbed the place where his heart beat hard and steady in his chest.

Eros never got tired of seeing the transformation. He loved how the doubt slipped away, like bindings cut loose, and the fear dissolved, replaced with knowing and certainty. It was one of the best parts of his job. But he didn't get much of a show, since, as suspected, there hadn't been much of the enchantment left.

One down, one to go.

He smiled at Psyche over Leo's shoulder and gave her a thumbs up. Her aura surged, making her shine an effervescent orange.

"She told me she was leaving." Leo hung his head. "Why didn't I stop her?

Psyche handed Eros his bow before walking over to Leo. "Don't be so hard on yourself. There were greater forces at work here. What's important now is that Orea's out of the picture and your judgment is no longer clouded. You can focus on Liz. You can tell her you want her to stay.

Eros gripped his bow tight, anticipation twitching his fingers. "Psyche's right."

"Psyche? You're a god, too?" said Leo, dumbfounded.

"God*dess*. But, yes, I'm no longer mortal."

"You were mortal once?" Leo looked positively shaken when she nodded her head.

Eros raised his eyebrows at Psyche, asking for forgiveness in advance as he set his bow on his desk "It's a great love story, but it's a long one," he said, shrugging off his quiver and placing it next to his bow, both dwarfing the piece of office furniture. "Not that it isn't important, but we've got more urgent things to consider. Let's not forget, there's a certain heartbroken someone we need to stop from leaving Seattle before time runs out. We need to get to the airport before Atropos has a chance to make sure we lose her for good."

Leo groped around for a place to sit. Finding purchase on the love seat, he lowered himself onto a silken cushion. "Who's Atropos?"

Eros tried not to sound ominous. "She's one of the Fates. The deadliest one."

"There's more than one?"

"There are three of them," said Psyche. "Clotho spins the thread of life, Lachesis measures it and Atropos . . ."

"Atropos cuts it." Eros made a snipping gesture with his fingers. "She's the Fate who rules death."

Leo reeled, his mouth falling open in horror as he tried to make sense of the new and disconcerting information. He was breathing so hard Eros thought the poor man might start hyperventilating.

Sorry, buddy, I wish there could have been another way.

It took a few seconds, but Leo finally wrangled his breathing under control. "So when you say lose her for good, you mean something is going to happen to her. Something bad." He gripped the arm of the love seat and front edge of the cushion until his knuckles were white.

Eros drew in a deep breath. "Yes, and if you—we—don't get to her in time, she'll die."

"And so will Eros." Psyche sat down next to Leo on the love seat.

Eros forced the words out. "I'll have about eighty or so years, but yes, I'll die, too."

"How . . . why?" Leo looked between Eros and Psyche for an answer. None came. "I suppose that's a long story, too, then, yeah?"

Eros and Psyche answered in unison. "Yes."

"Then I've bloody well got to stop her." Resolve gave Leo's voice a hard, sharp edge. He bolted off the love seat, the office door banging against the wall as he made a dramatic exit. "I've got to stop her! I can't let her leave!"

"It's go time." Eros grabbed Psyche's hand and pulled her out the door with him. He'd managed to get rid of Orea, but now he was in a race against time to stop the love of Leo's life from coming face-to-face with the worst fate of them all.

Atropos.

CHAPTER THIRTY-THREE

Liz hoisted her suitcase into the back seat of her Lyft before the driver could even get out to help. She grunted, the duffle bag and carry-on careening through the open door next. It took all she had not to let that grunt turn into a howl of frustration.

The driver, an older woman with gray frizz for hair, checked the information on the phone mounted to the dashboard. She sounded like she'd quit smoking a pack a day mere minutes before. "You still going to Sea-Tac?"

"Yep." Liz slammed the door shut and settled in.

The driver pulled away from the curb and out onto the street, then turned right at an intersection. Liz hadn't lived in Seattle for long, but she could say with certainty she did know her way around Belltown. Turning right wasn't going to get her to the airport. Like running up the fare by taking the least direct route wasn't going to get this driver a tip.

"You're going the wrong way." She stared at the back of the woman's head. "You need to go left to get on 99."

"Ah, shit, you're right. Takes a while to get use to these damned GPS things." The driver jabbed a finger at the screen.

"Got sick of my accounting job, couldn't stand one more minute of it. Up and quit a couple weeks ago. It was like a higher power telling me to throw caution to the wind, you know? Ah, there we go." The correct directions popped up and she adjusted her wire-rimmed glasses before glancing at Liz in the rearview mirror. "I only drive during the day, mind you, because, you know, Seattle's full of crazies. You're not crazy, are you? Anyway, this thing tells me I can make a couple of lefts up here. That should get us back on track."

"Good, because I'm kind of in a hurry." Liz looked out the window at the buildings as they passed. One last look at the city she'd grown so fond of, the place she'd leave her useless heart behind.

"My name is Lorraine, by the way." The woman raised a wizened hand, the left turn signal clicking rhythmically as she waited for the light to turn green.

Liz bit back a smart remark about not being in the mood for small talk, but she rather liked Lorraine. She was rough around the edges, and Liz could relate. "Nice to meet you, Lorraine." Plus, the woman may have a smoker's hack and a problem with over-sharing, but she didn't do anything to get her head bitten off. "I'm Liz."

Lorraine peered at her through the rearview mirror again. "Nice to meet you. You seem upset."

"I am." Liz didn't have the energy left to deny it.

She turned her head away from the window when they drove by Some Random Bar. In the process, she noticed Lorraine studying her. Silent and calm, like a therapist waiting for a patient to spill their guts. Well, it worked, because Liz suddenly wanted to tell this practical stranger every lurid detail of the past twenty-four hours. Because saying it out loud would prove it was real, and that running away was the right thing to do. What the hell, she'd never see this woman again.

"I was dating this guy at work."

"Oh, yeah, I love office romances. Let me guess, it was love at first sight." The enthusiasm in Lorraine's voice was evident. Liz suspected it was because the woman was having a conversation with someone other than her ten cats.

"Sort of," said Liz dryly, knowing full well it had been. "Things were going pretty good, you know, considering I make it a point not to date."

"Same here," snorted Lorraine.

Make that twelve cats.

Liz adjusted her glasses. After this, she'd probably have a cat or two herself in a few months. "If you don't date, you can't get hurt, right?"

"Amen to that." Lorraine's cackle devolved into a fit of coughing.

Liz grimaced during the woman's ordeal, waiting until she could breathe again to continue. "Anyway, against my better judgment, I started dating Leo—did I mention he's British?" Her bruised and battered heart ached, but for the life of her she couldn't stop talking. Former accountant? The woman should have been a shrink.

"Don't beat yourself up over it, kid. Statistically speaking, women are more drawn to men with foreign accents. So technically, it wasn't your fault."

Okay, maybe she could see why Lorraine had worked as a number cruncher.

"Yeah, well, it was a lot more than the accent. I really felt like I knew him, you know? Like, from another life or something. And it was going good until Ashley ruined everything. Turns out he was seeing her on the side."

Shut up! What the hell is wrong with you?

"Did you deck the bitch?"

"No, but I really wanted to."

"You're probably doing the right thing by leaving, then. He sounds like a real self-important bastard."

And I love—loved him, with all my shriveled-up raisin of a heart.

"Yeah, it's for the best." Liz blinked, warding off tears. Nope, she wasn't going to do it. She was not going to cry. "How much longer to the air—watch out!"

Lorraine slammed on the brakes, cursing the entire time, and Liz flew forward, held in place by the lap restraint. Lorraine had managed to stop in time to avoid doing any real damage, but still clipped the back wheel of the courier's bike, causing him to go ass over apple cart.

"Dammit!" Lorraine's hands came down hard on the steering wheel. She turned in her seat to face Liz, concern pinching her weathered face. "You okay?"

Liz unbuckled her seatbelt and rubbed her sore gut. "Yeah, I'm fine, but I'm not sure the guy on the bike is so lucky."

More curses flew out of Lorraine's mouth as she pushed open the driver's side door. She tottered around to the front of the car where the courier was inspecting a bad case of road rash on his arm.

"Well hell's bells, son, you know you shouldn't be riding your bike on the road like that, you could get killed!"

Liz pressed the button to roll down the window so she could eavesdrop. Not exactly how she would have approached someone who had as much right to the road, but hey, she had to give Lorraine points for confidence.

"How about you watch where the hell you're going." The biker winced when he reached for his messenger bag.

"Hey, I'm trying to get this nice young lady to the airport." Lorraine pointed at Liz.

"Well, good for you. I'm trying to deliver a message, so I'm going to go with my original statement. Watch where the hell you're going." He unzipped the front of his bag and pulled out a cell phone. "Nice. My screen is cracked." He dialed. "You're going to pay for a new one, you know."

A sense of foreboding suddenly pressed down on Liz and she tensed. Deliver a message? Was this a sign she should stay? She had never had a premonition before, but something tugged at her, and she began to feel like maybe she shouldn't go through with getting on the plane.

Nonsense. It was just Weird Liz being desperate.

She shook the heaviness loose and watched Lorraine peel off an undeterminable amount of money from a wad of cash she'd pulled out of her pocket. Liz rubbed her forehead. Only her. This shit only happened to her. She rolled up the window, wanting no part of Lorraine's seedy dealings, and watched the guy give Lorraine a look that said, *"Are you serious?"* After several more minutes of back and forth, he took the stack of bills, got back on his bike and peddled away.

Lorraine slid into the front seat. "Sorry about that."

"I take it he's okay?"

The woman sighed. "He'll be fine. Damned bike messengers. Streets are riddled with 'em. Always slowing me down. A few free Lyfts and a couple hundred bucks for a new screen is all it takes to keep 'em happy, though. Buckle up kid, we've got to get you to the airport before the universe throws another wrench into your plans."

Five minutes later, they were cruising down Seattle's Pacific Highway, making excellent time. In fact, by some strange twist of fate, Liz was actually ahead of schedule.

CHAPTER THIRTY-FOUR

The gate was teaming with people. Noisy people. Exhausted and disheveled and grumpy-from-traveling people. But most annoying of all, happy people, with the gall to show everyone just how happy they were by having the audacity to *smile*.

Surrounded, yet never more alone in her life, Liz let her anger propel her forward, toward a life without Leo.

Someone bumped into her bag, knocking her off kilter as she paused to make sure she was at the right gate. The jerk didn't even apologize. She should have given him a piece of her mind.

But what would be the point? She didn't need to get herself any more riled up. In an hour, she'd be in the air, rum and coke on her seat-back tray, calmly pretending her brush with love never happened. Why waste her energy? Especially when she'd need all she had left to forget that Leo Simmons even existed.

Because when I get on that plane it's over, Weird Liz. Do you hear me?

She stuffed her phone into her pocket and walked into the

waiting area to find a seat. The sooner she left this place behind, along with the memory of the man who nearly destroyed her, the better. She settled into a hard, molded plastic chair and waited for boarding to begin.

"Good evening ladies and gentlemen," the counter attendant announced, "we are now boarding priority seating for Delta Flight 90107 from Seattle to Chicago. Once again, priority seating ticket holders on our flight from Seattle to Chicago may now board."

Liz slipped off the ear buds hanging around her neck and tossed them into her bag. Heart pounding, she scanned her surroundings. Maybe there was a chance Leo would . . .

Stop it, loser. There's no fairy tale ending. It's just you and a one-way ticket.

"So stupid," she muttered under her breath.

A bedraggled mother threw her a dirty look, all three of her children crying, while trying to fish out whatever it was her toddler had stuffed into his mouth from the floor. "Excuse me?"

They were right across from her, so it wasn't hard to guess the woman thought her comment was directed at her and her children.

The desk attendant came over the loud speaker again. "We are now boarding zones one and two, ladies and gentlemen. If you are in zones one and two, you are free to board."

"I didn't mean you," said Liz once the announcement was over. When one of the woman's older children whacked her in the thigh hard enough to raise the stern eyebrow of a disapproving octogenarian nearby, Liz's heart went out to her. "Is there anything I can do to help?"

The woman's gaze flicked down at her tattoos then up to her nose ring. After another loud cry from the five-year-old now clinging to her side as she tried to pry her toddler and his beloved new choking hazard apart, she sighed. "Here."

She scooped up the toddler and handed him to her. "See if he'll give it to you. I need to find our boarding passes."

"Sure." She didn't feel as confident as she sounded but reached for the boy anyway.

The woman started digging through the bags hanging on the stroller, and the child in Liz's arms stopped crying, but only to study her with waterlogged eyes and tear-stained cheeks.

"Can I have that?" She referred to the penny the boy was clutching in his fist. She scrunched up her nose and shook her head. "Yucky."

After a moment of staring at each other, the boy handed over the coin. As soon as she stuffed it into her pocket, his face crumpled, and he drew in as much air as his tiny lungs could hold. She braced herself for another round of wailing, trying to think of a distraction.

"It's okay, love." She wiped away the boy's tears and began to bounce him in her arms. "Everything's going to be all right."

With a small whimper, the boy fell onto her chest, throwing his arms around her and resting his head on her shoulder. She smoothed down the curls that had sprung to life from the sweat he'd worked up and rubbed his back. She had no idea she was capable of comforting such a tiny human being, especially to this sort of degree. It was a strange feeling knowing she could.

Now, if only she could make herself feel better, too.

"Thank you." The woman transferred her son into her arms.

"No problem." Liz imagined what her and Leo's little boy might have looked like. Would his eyes have been brown like hers, or that amazing steel blue?

The attendant's announcement that zone three was boarding scattered her thoughts. She passed her phone over the scanner, and the reader buzzed red instead of beeping green. She passed it over again. Same thing.

Denied.

The attendant took her phone and tried it, but held the phone back out to Liz when she got the same buzzing red light.

"Try it one more time, will you?" She shoved the woman's hand—and her phone—back toward the scanner. She wanted on that plane, had to get on that plane, even if she had to force her way onto it.

Denied.

The woman set Liz's phone on the edge of the counter before unleashing her nimble fingers on a keyboard. The light coming off the computer screen tinged her face blue. "Elizabeth Johnson?"

"That's me."

"Our system says your life has been revised."

Liz's heart picked up. The woman's blonde hair was swept into a haphazard ponytail, and her name tag was crooked. Not to be judgmental, but she looked a bit harried, and Liz wasn't sure she hadn't just come of a drinking bender that afternoon. "Did you say my life has been revised?"

"Flight," the desk attendant snapped. "I said your flight has been delayed."

Jesus, okay.

Liz took her phone back and tapped through the flight information to make sure the woman was right. Her teeth pinched the inside of her cheek. Yep. Her flight was delayed another thirty minutes.

The attendant picked up the mouthpiece for the loudspeaker. "On behalf of Delta Airlines, I do apologize, ladies and gentlemen, but Delta Flight 90107 Seattle to Chicago has been delayed. We will now be departing at 8:33 p.m."

"Can I wait on the plane?" asked Liz as politely as she could manage.

"No ma'am. You'll have to take a seat." The woman glared at her before giving her a slow blink, her lips pursed. "Thank you for your patience."

Annoyance spiked through Liz, but before a rude remark could make it out of her mouth, a wave of goose bumps rippled her skin so hard it *hurt*. The tiny hairs on the back of her neck flew up, as if pulled by an invisible string, and her head all but snapped clean off as it craned over one shoulder.

She turned in time to see a pilot breeze past. Another round of prickling raced through her body, tiny daggers stabbing down her arms until they settled in her hands, the numbness causing her to loosen the ferocious grip she had on her bag. It landed on the floor next to her with a *thud* as a strange sense of foreboding threatened to take her knees out from under her.

Don't get on the plane.

She gasped at the voice in her head. It sounded exactly like . . . Willa?

The attendant cleared her throat. "Please take a seat, miss."

Liz picked up her bag and stepped aside. Her chest itched, her old friends wasting no time in making an unwelcome appearance, and she felt like she'd had a few too many cocktails at the airport bar. If this was what mediums or psychics or whatever felt like when they received messages, count her out.

In an effort to collect herself she scanned the long line of passengers grumbling at the delay. Her gaze stopped on a man with his nose buried in a book sporting mirrored aviator sunglasses. The brim of his Michigan University baseball cap practically rested on the top rim of his shades. He was also wearing the longest, most out of date khaki trench coat she'd ever seen in her twenty-four years on Earth. Make that twenty-five. Of all the days for her life to come crashing down around her, of course it had to be today. Was it really any surprise? She didn't exactly have the best track record with birthdays.

She blew her bangs out of her face. Hell, even the guy in the Inspector Gadget getup seemed to be having a better day than she was. By the look of it, he was really enjoying that book. He didn't just find out the hard way the person he loved was a liar, almost witness a pedestrian hit and run on the way to the airport, or discover his flight was delayed when all he wanted to do was get on a damned plane and fly away.

Nope, that was all her.

CHAPTER THIRTY-FIVE

Leo handed over his credit card to the Delta Airlines ticket agent. "I need a flight to Chicago." Eron and Willa—Eros and Psyche, whoever the bloody hell they were now—stood behind him, nodding in agreement.

The middle-aged man at the counter leaned an ear forward, as if he'd heard wrong. "What now? You need all four flights to Chicago?"

"No, I only need one."

"Well, thank you for choosing to fly Delta. One moment while I pull up all available flights."

Leo tapped his fingers on the counter. He didn't have one moment.

"Okie dokie, let's see. We've got a red eye leaving at 10:58 p.m. and one leaving in a half an hour, oh, but that one's full."

Psyche stepped up to the counter. "I'm sorry, sir, but we have a dire situation on our hands. I'm afraid we'll have to speed this up." She peered into the man's eyes. As soon as she had him in her sights, his mouth dropped open. "He'll take whatever flight he can get on, full or not."

"Yes . . . that sounds like an excellent idea, miss," he murmured. "May I have the passenger's name, please?"

"His name is Leo Simmons."

The man keyed the information into his computer. "Oh, I see you've flown with us before. London to Seattle. Perfect. I'll use your previous booking information." More tapping, then a moment later he rattled off the flight information. "There we go, I have you on Delta flight 90107, departing at 8:33 p.m. Gate C17."

He didn't care what bloody flight it was. All he cared about was getting through security and stopping the love of his life from getting on a plane.

The man handed over the printed boarding pass, Psyche's gaze still locked on him. "Here you go, Mr. Simmons. Have a nice flight."

She patted the man's hand. "Thank you, and remember, Gerald, nothing out of the ordinary happened. This nice young gentleman bought a ticket from you and now we're going to walk away. There's absolutely no reason to call security. Thank you, Gerry, you have a wonderful night."

Eros clapped Leo on the back before grabbing Psyche's hand and heading toward the line to go through security. Once they got to the entrance, they stopped.

"Okay, this is the end of the line for us," said Eros.

"Wait, where are you going?"

"We've got to veil ourselves," answered Psyche. "We'll still be here, but you won't see us. We'll be waiting for you on the other side."

Gods, nymphs, wings. All figments of the imagination, weren't they? The hard pounding in his chest urged him to contemplate the thought later. Right now, he needed to concentrate on what—and who—was real. "How will I know where you're at if I can't see you?"

Listen for the voice inside your head.

Her lips didn't move, but it was definitely her. In his head.

Bloody hell.

Eros nudged Psyche.

Oh, and follow the love in your heart.

Leo nodded, about to break the tension with a cheeky joke about seeing them on the other side, when Psyche squeezed her eyes shut and her fingers flew to one temple. Her bottom lip disappeared between her teeth. "She's trying to board."

Leo's heart jumped into his throat. He knew whom Willa was referring to, but he couldn't stop the barrage of questions. "Who's trying to board? Liz? How do you know?"

"Yes." Both hands pressed into her scalp now. "I've still got a connection with her. It's faint, but I think she'll still be able to hear me."

"Tell her not to get on the plane!" said Eros, the back of his shirt jerking wildly.

Leo flinched. This wings having minds of their own thing was going to take some getting used to.

Psyche's nose scrunched and her forehead crumpled. "Okay, done. I think she heard. Now let's hope the woman listens for once." She grabbed Leo by the shoulders. "Run directly to gate C17. We'll catch up to you."

He was going to look stark raving mad running through the airport and babbling, but he rushed through the line that snaked up to the security podiums anyway. By some miracle of God—gods—it was nearly empty.

Other than the TSA employee who looked him up and down with a wink and a smile, Leo made it through security in record time. No carry-on had its perks.

His lungs yanked in air that seemed too thin while he pulled his shoes back on. But it wasn't the thought of running through an airport trying to stop a woman from boarding a plane that made it hard to breathe. That honor belonged to the fact he might lose her forever.

Again, apparently.

He entered the terminal and looked around for a map. His gaze searched as frantically as his heart leapt around in his chest. "Which way do I go? Which way!" He looked around positive people were staring at him, but they shuffled past, in their own little worlds and barely paying attention.

Go right.

He took off, ducking and weaving between people. "What do I need to do so he can get the shot?"

Eros says just tell her you love her.

He could do that. The hard part would be getting her to believe it. "Any bright ideas how to convince her true love is real?"

Perhaps he would regret the decision to use his wings later, but right now, Eros didn't care. His window of opportunity to save his job, his life . . . and the curmudgeon of a mortal he'd grown so fond of, was closing rapidly. He needed to fly if he was going to make it in time.

His wings weren't fully grown, but they were strong enough to lift him over the mass of people moving through the airport. Well, for the most part. He swooped dangerously low every few hundred yards until Psyche looped her arm through his and flew alongside him, her gossamer wings shimmering even under the less than favorable man-made lighting.

Eros scanned the crowd, making sure he and Psyche doubled back every once in a while to keep Leo in sight. The man was only human, with feet, not wings.

They'd just passed the Cinnabon kiosk when Psyche jerked him to a halt. "What's up? Why are we stopping?"

When she didn't respond, he followed her gaze to the squirming hive of mortals below.

When he saw what she was gawking at he understood. Hermes stood in an outdated trench coat and his mirrored sunglasses, winged sandals planted firmly on the tiled walkway and holding one arm up like a traffic director. He was invisible to moral eyes, but even though they couldn't see him, they could feel his presence and parted around the space he occupied.

What the . . . ?

It wasn't the tragic lack of fashion sense his best friend seemed to suddenly possess that made his wings flounder. It was who stood next to him, draped in a wispy expanse of fine silk embroidered with dazzling gold thread and beaded with pearls.

"Bonjour, *chéri*." His mother smiled at him and waved. She greeted him as if the goddess of love being down on Earth, standing in the middle of a busy airport with a magical bow and quiver of arrows strapped to her back, was an everyday occurrence.

He glanced at Psyche before offering his mother a tentative wave. Psyche's wings made a rhythmic *swishing* sound as they flapped. His worked overtime to keep him from dipping too low.

Without another word or warning, his mother lifted her massive, glittering bow in one quick, smooth motion. She set her graceful shoulders, shut one eye and took aim. The arrow emitted a melodious whistle as it zipped through the air, and a burst of light pulsated from the point of entry when it struck Psyche's heart.

She gasped, clutching her chest before her head lolled backward. Eros scooped her into his arms, holding true to his promise of catching her should she ever fall.

"Mother! What in Zeus's name are you doing?" Psyche was light as a feather, but his wings were close to giving out.

"Sorry, *chéri*, but somebody had to shoot some sense into her." She leaned on her gilded bow, which was almost as tall as she was. It was her prized possession, he knew, rarely taken out of its glittering display case.

He shifted Psyche into the crook of his arm. "And you decided it needed to happen right now?" A finger on his free hand jabbed downward in a pointing motion, as if the moment was a tangible object in front of him.

"Well, when else was I going to get the chance to rebind your hearts? It's been over four decades!" She placed a hand on her hip before slapping the side of her thigh in frustration. "I had to beg her to meet me for dinner. Someone had to tell her about your predicament. You weren't going to do it with that stubborn pride of yours."

He cradled the back of Psyche's head and nestled her close while they floated above the people hurrying to catch their flights. One arm wrapped around Psyche's waist, his wings burning, Eros glanced down at his mother and sighed. She did have a point.

There was no going back now, only forward. He tried rousing his true love gently. "Psyche? Wake up, butterfly, we've got to go."

Psyche's wings fluttered before opening and closing slow and light. She set a hand on his chest, gazing at him through half-closed lids. "She didn't have to shoot me." A smile broadened her lips. "You do know why, don't you?"

One of his cheeks pulled up, making his grin go lopsided. "I have an idea, but I didn't want to be so bold as to presume. Besides, you know what they say about presuming."

"Smart move, matchmaker." She lifted her head. "But I think you mean *ah*-sume."

"You know me so well." He planted a small kiss on the tip

of her nose. "Say it out loud." His heart thumped with anticipation. It had been too long. "I need to hear you say it."

"I love you. I always have, and I always will." They were both upright now, wrapped in each other's arms, her wings beating slow and strong, his fluttering frantically.

"Turn around, *chéri*." His mother called out, flapping her hand in a circular motion. "I want two strikes for good measure."

"She did go through all the trouble," said Eros. "We probably shouldn't let her down."

Psyche smiled at him, her golden eyes sparkled. "No, we shouldn't. We both know how the goddess of love feels about her baby boy."

They used Psyche's wing power to spin themselves into a more bull's-eye-friendly position. His heart soared as he pulled up his chest and flattened his back. He could hardly wait for impact, and when the arrow sank in, going clean through the center of his heart and out his chest, he marveled at his mother's aim.

When the tip plunged into Psyche's heart, rebinding them anew, he was overcome with passion and lust, romance and tenderness. He let the bubbly cosmic wonder of true love wash over him, its bright light popping and fizzing out of control when Psyche pulled him in for a kiss.

That's when Hermes started yelling.

"Wrap it up, you two. We've got an account to close here, remember?"

Reality came crashing back.

Oh gods, I hope I'm not too late—Shit, my bow!

Panic seized him, and his stomach twisted itself into knots. "I left my bow back at the office . . . Please tell me you grabbed it."

Psyche's eyes widened, and she shook her head.

Eros looked at Hermes, desperate.

"Well, I didn't grab it," Hermes yelled up. "I was too busy helping your mom match-make *your* ass. And I've been a little busy stalling the Fates. You're welcome."

Eros's leaping heart stopped, but only for an instant before the answer came to him. He was the god of love and, dammit, he *wasn't* a joke. It did take strength to be patient and kind. It took real, honest-to-gods courage to bind hearts. Ruling over love was not for the weak. It was a hard job, worthy of respect, and he'd been letting the notion that he wasn't good enough hold him back for far too long. "I'll just use my mom's bow, then."

Without missing a beat, his mother handed her bow over to Hermes. Eros felt a surge of power charge through him as he watched his mother's bow shrink before Hermes stuffed it under the flap of his trench coat.

"Good thinking, matchmaker. Now hurry up, I've bought you some time with the bike messenger and screwing with the airline's computer system, but not much, so get going. I'll meet you there!" Hermes turned on his winged heels and took off.

"Come on." Psyche pulled him by the hand. "We've got to hurry."

"My wings are toast." He nodded at the two shaky appendages on his back.

"I've got you," she replied, dragging him by the hand. Her wings looked delicate, but Eros knew how strong they were. He sighed with relief when he spotted their destination not far ahead.

"My mother was right." He squeezed her hand as they finally approached the gate.

"About what?" Psyche asked over her shoulder.

"I did need you. I mean, I've always needed you, but I would have never made it without you. I should have asked for your help a long time ago."

Psyche reached out and stroked one wing. "Like, four decades ago?"

"More like forever and a day ago." His shoulder blades twitched and tingled, his wings growing another foot.

A knowing grin spread across Psyche's face. She dropped his hand and swung around to face him. Without warning, she pulled him in for a kiss passionate enough to make up for the last four decades.

Warmth flooded the center of his chest, spreading across his back, and he felt his wings shoot up, arching high over his head and lengthening until the tips brushed against his heels. Exhausted intermittent flaps became strong and steady beats.

"How do they look?" He beamed with pride.

Psyche appraised him lovingly. "Glorious."

That's when Hermes clapped his hands.

"Come on, come on, come on! It's show time, matchmaker!" He wrenched open his coat and pulled out the bow and tossed it up to him.

It stretched to an enormous size as it sailed through the air, and even though it was much larger than his, Eros caught his mother's bow with ease. An arrow flew out of the bow's matching quiver and into his other hand.

The bow vibrated with something so ancient and powerful he felt it in every fiber of his being, confirming what he'd known all along. It didn't matter whose bow he used. He was love incarnate. All that mattered now was his aim.

CHAPTER THIRTY-SIX

In the process of surveying the half empty waiting area, Liz discovered an older gentleman trying to hide his nose explorations, mere seats from a toddler blatantly excavating two smaller caverns of her own. Slightly disgusted but unmoved, Liz shifted her gaze toward the center aisle between gates.

Businessmen and women on phones rushed to make their late flights home after a long day of negotiating. Mesmerized teens stared wide-eyed into to their mobile devices. That weird dude in the trench coat, now hanging out by the moving walkway, talking to himself.

No handsome Brits running through the airport trying to stop a girl from getting on a plane.

Exactly, because that true love shit doesn't happen in real life.

Liz sighed and stared at the carpet, the mental image of shoving the attendant out of the way and making a break for it down the gangway so detailed, the commotion several gates down didn't even register. She only looked up when a woman yelled, *"How rude!"* loud enough to wake the dead.

When she did, a wave of disbelief swelled, cresting in her

throat as she watched the sea of passersby part for a man with tousled dark hair. He had gray eyes ringed with the deepest blue and a face she knew like the back of her hand.

The pounding in her chest filled her ears, her ability to breathe diminishing each time her heart threw itself against her ribcage. Was the fairy tale ending coming true?

Leo made his way toward her, disheveled and out of breath, until he stood in front of her. At least she thought it was him. She could barely see through her dimming vision.

Jesus Christ, am I actually going to faint?

"Don't get on that plane." Leo panted as he pulled her from her seat.

She blinked at him, trying to keep the edges of her vision from going any darker. When the cruel image of him kissing Ashley started, making the churning in her stomach worse, she commanded her shaky legs to *move goddamn it* because he didn't get to decide how this ended. Per usual, they refused to listen.

"Liz."

His voice burst through, bringing her back from the brink of darkness, and the world snapped into focus once again. Screw fairy tale endings. Prince Charming fucked up, and she wasn't—and never would be—a princess.

"Please don't go." He took her silence as permission to keep holding her hands. She didn't protest, but she did wish they didn't fit together so perfectly.

Resentment that he could weaken her defenses so easily ground her teeth. And all he'd had to do was run through the airport like they were in some stupid romantic comedy. It made her furious. "Why should I?"

"I don't know . . . Fate?" He shrugged his shoulders. "True love?"

Fate, huh? And did he say True love?

Because that was the last goddamned straw.

She wrenched a hand free and slapped him across the face. "We make our own fate, you asshole."

He winced, leaning back to rub the screaming red imprint of her hand on his cheek. He stared at her, the hard lines of panic softening into pain and regret. Her gut twisted tighter, but as hard as it was, she pulled her other hand free.

"I trusted you." Her voice cracked through the whisper, both arms hanging at her sides, limp and numb now that her anger had found an outlet.

Liz ignored the murmurs rippling through the gathering crowd as she picked up her bag and stepped around Leo to get in line.

"No, no, no. Liz, wait." He trailed behind her, grabbing her by the shoulders and turning her around to face him, just like she'd wanted him to do before. "The truth is, it's because a guy like me finally came to his senses and couldn't let a girl like you get away."

She cringed, wriggling her shoulders free from his grasp. No amount of charm was going to fix this. She held her phone over the scanner. The machine beeped.

Green.

She looked at him one last time, into those eyes she'd fallen in love with from the very first moment she'd seen them. "Goodbye, Leo. It was fun while it lasted, but you're just not my type."

The back of her eyes stung, and she struggled to keep herself from crumpling to the floor. Saying those words felt like the biggest lie of her life, but she forced herself to take a step forward.

"Please don't go. I'm begging you." Leo raked a hand through his hair, panic contorting his handsome features. "We're meant to be. That guy you saw? That wasn't *me*. Well, technically, it was, but . . ."

She hesitated, wanting to believe him.

"Look, I know I messed up—I can see that now—but I don't want to lose you. Hate me forever, never speak to me again, just don't get on that plane."

His words cracked the last of her broken heart in half, the pieces as sharp and jagged as his breath as he stood behind her, waiting. For all the words he did say, he hadn't said the one that counted the most.

Stay.

"I love you, Liz Johnson," would have worked, too.

But he didn't say either of those things. And she wouldn't allow him the satisfaction of knowing that, yes, she loved him, with every square inch of her cold, hard, dysfunctional heart. That she couldn't handle needing someone like water or air or *forever*.

So she kept going.

Liz contemplated whether to put in her drink order immediately or at least wait until she found her seat.

She made her way to the back of the aircraft, hoping she wasn't too close to the lavatory. The guy a few rows ahead was sweating and clutching his lower abdomen like he could barely wait for clearance to destroy innocent lives.

She groaned when she saw a woman already sitting in her assigned row. The woman was slender, bordering on bony, with white-blond hair and purple contacts—because no way on Earth that eye color was real—and of course, sitting in the middle seat.

Liz shoved her carry-on in the overhead bin. Careful not to disturb the ethereal beauty's magazine browsing, she eased into the aisle seat and belted in.

"Can I put in my order for a rum and Coke now?" she asked a flight attendant as he passed her on his way to the back for flight check duty.

"Aaaah, certainly." He blinked down at her, pursing his lips. "Right after I make sure we all know what to do in the event of a fiery plane crash, m'kay?

Liz huffed. Couldn't he see she was desperate? He's lucky she had even shown this much restraint. "If you insist. No ice, even less Coke, okay?"

She pulled her phone out of her pocket, intending to switch to airplane mode, but before she knew what was happening, she was scrolling through pictures of Leo. "True love, my ass," she grumbled, systematically deleting them. "Fate? What a fucking joke. He didn't even ask me to stay."

"It's fine if you don't believe in fate, not many people do," said the woman next to Liz, causing her to nearly drop her phone. Either oblivious she was sticking her nose where it didn't belong or not caring, Blondie McWeird-Eyes continued, "But can I give you a small piece of advice?"

Liz sighed before muttering under her breath. "Sounds like you're going to give it to me anyway."

The woman finally looked up from her *Vogue* and trained her neon eyes directly on Liz. "If there's one thing you should believe in, it's love."

Liz snorted, resuming the deletion of photos. Had she really taken this many? And was the girl in the selfies with Leo really that happy? "Tried that, thanks. Didn't work out, so yeah, love sucks."

"Quite the contrary."

Delete.

"Love may have horrible timing, true, but it's . . ." The woman cocked her head, gaze flicking toward Liz's phone. "Persistent."

Delete.

"Even when it's up against jaded mortals like you."

Delete. Delete. Delete.

Mortals like me? Time to cut back on the prescription drugs, girlfriend.

"And that is what I admire most about love."

Liz paused. Not because she agreed, but because she couldn't bring herself to delete the last photo.

"He didn't ask me to stay." She said it more to herself than the woman.

The woman huffed, turning back to her magazine. "You people and your semantics. He absolutely did too ask you to stay. You were simply so busy looking for an excuse to run you didn't hear it." She flipped a page and went on with her lecture. "Sometimes, Liz, life requires you to listen with your heart, not your ears."

"But I'm terrified he's going to leave." The words tumbled out, uncensored, like she'd drunk an entire vial of truth serum.

"So you're leaving first? Oh, that'll solve all your problems. Sorry to be the one to have to tell you this, but true love exists. It's not perfect, by any means, his timing is usually off, but when you find your soul mate, the one who loves you for you, *scars* and all, you don't walk away from it. Love is hard work, honey. I mean, Cupid can only do so much to get you together, and then *you've* got to do the rest."

Liz's phone chimed. With trembling fingers, she opened her messages.

Leo: please stay

The woman flipped another page. "You have two choices. Stay on this plane and die regretting it, or get off and give love a fair shot. And trust me when I say fate usually isn't this flexible."

The hairs on the back of Liz's neck stood, the realization hitting her like a ton of candy hearts. She didn't know how or why, but she was certain destiny was giving her one last chance. She was broken, yes, but so was Leo. She wasn't her mother and he wasn't her father. Healing together was better than staying in pieces alone.

"Cancel my rum and Coke, will you?" asked Liz, unbuckling her lap restraint. "Against my better judgment . . ." She popped open the overhead bin and pulled her carryon out. "I'm giving love a chance."

The strange woman closed the magazine in her lap. "Excellent choice."

The high-pitch whine of jet engines had Leo spiraling closer and closer to the brink of insanity. He stared at his phone, willing Liz to answer, but none came.

He listened for a voice in his head to tell him what to do. That didn't come either. Where in the bloody hell were these gods when he really needed them?

The last of the passengers had boarded, the waiting area empty except him, the desk attendant and a few overeager travelers waiting for the next flight.

Leo tried his argument again. "Please let me board. I can't live without her."

"That's sweet, but the flight is full. The door has already been secured, and the crew is preparing to taxi. I'm sorry, there's nothing I can do."

Leo slammed a palm down on the counter, her canned responses rubbing the last of his nerves raw. "You don't understand! It's not supposed to happen this way!"

"I do apologize, sir," she continued, unruffled. "I can upgrade you to first-class on our next flight to Chicago if you'd like."

And then there she was, standing in the doorway, white as a five hundred-count Egyptian cotton sheet and looking like she was about to vomit, but still the loveliest thing he'd ever laid eyes on in his entire life.

A gasp, a flood of relief like he'd never known, a weakness that threatened to drive him to his knees, all happened simultaneously. The death grip on his phone loosened, and it dropped out of his hand, tumbling onto the counter. Let it fall. He had his answer.

The look on Leo's face said it all. When he closed the distance between them in four strides, it spoke volumes. But when he reached for her, taking her into his arms and holding onto her like he was never going to let go? There were no words.

He slid his hands into place on either side of her face. She suppressed a sob, blinking back tears. He brushed a thumb over her cheek, and she couldn't help but lean into the tenderness of it. All the strange yet familiar feelings she'd had since the day she met him came rushing at her in the form of a thousand questions.

"Love at first sight?" It was the first one to break free.

He nodded, his smile nearly taking her breath away. Damn if that crazy lady on the plane wasn't on to something. Something bigger and more powerful than either of them was at work here.

"From the first insult you hurled at me."

She couldn't help but laugh, even though there was one major concern still slithering its way from the back of her mind to the front. "So this means you're never seeing Ashley again, right? Because I swear to God, Leo Simmons, I won't go through this again."

He put a finger to her lips. "Gods . . . And you're the only one I want."

Her soul sighed, and she closed her eyes. If someone

would have told her five months ago that she'd be standing in the middle of an airport, convinced by a guy like Leo to give him all of her heart, not just part of it, she would have said it was impossible. But here she was, falling in love.

The holding hands and kissing in the rain kind.

She opened her eyes, and with nothing left to prove, she let go, grasping onto Leo's wrists for support and allowing her tears—and her defenses—to fall.

"Promise me you won't leave," she whispered, twenty-five years of being broken, of secretly hoping someone would be able to fix her, streaming down her face.

"I'm not going anywhere, love. I promise."

"Okay, then I suppose we can try this true love shit." She laughed through her tears. It may have only been the desk attendant Liz heard exhale, but it felt like the entire universe. She tilted her head to get a better view of the onlookers clapping and whistling from a nearby gate. "Great, we're living a movie right now. How cliché."

Leo beamed down at her, his eyes crinkling at the corners. "Admit it, love," he said, turning them in a half circle. She had no idea what he was doing, but she went with it. "Deep down you're a hopeless romantic."

She let her hands drop from their place on his wrists. Threading them through what little space there was between them, she tangled her fingers into the hair behind his ears and closed the remaining distance. "You wish, Don Juan."

He followed her lead, and it felt good, she thought as her lids fell shut, to pull love toward her, not push it away.

The silky feathers of his wings brushed the backs of his legs as Eros circled the clients he'd come to care deeply about. They were more than clients, actually. Liz and Leo, the two mortal souls he'd grown to love.

"Tell him to turn her back toward me," Eros called out to Psyche, keeping his eyes trained on Liz. He wasn't taking any chances. She was known for veering off course at the last possible moment, and his arrow needed to enter her heart first.

Eros waited for Liz and Leo's lips to get closer, keeping his excitement in check as he watched the walls around Liz's heart fade. His magic coursed through him, her walls looking like an X-ray to his immortal eyes. The anticipation of them falling completely away made his wings beat faster.

Wait for it. Wait . . . for . . . it.

Her walls faded a little more, and just before they kissed, neither of them noticed the man wearing awful mirrored sunglasses toss his book aside and leap up into the air next to a woman with butterfly wings and hover alongside her. No mortal did. Nor did they notice that man—god, actually, and the best friend Eros could ever ask for—give him the thumbs up.

"You got this, matchmaker. Do your thing and let's go home. All of us."

Eros inhaled. It tasted stale, smelled musty, and made his heart ache to be back home where he belonged.

Liz and Leo's lips met, and travelers in the gate across from them clapped and whistled. Eros, reminded of the romantic movies he loved so much, let a smile curl one side of his mouth. They were so close to their happily ever after. And he was just as close to his.

There you go . . .

He lifted the bow and nocked the arrow, his magic ramping up, the power of it making him glow.

The walls around Liz's heart were barely visible.

Let those defenses fall.

Winking one eye closed, he aimed.

Walls down, Liz Johnson stood perfectly aligned with Leo

Simmons, their hearts in prime position for optimal results. His own heart thundering, Eros pulled back with all the strength he had and let his golden arrow fly.

It hummed, it sang, it sparkled with dazzling brilliance as it sailed through the air, and even before it sank into Liz's back, he knew in his heart of hearts his aim had been true. The trajectory had been straight as, well, an arrow.

Liz pulled Leo closer as it pierced her heart, bonding her to him forever and always. Eros didn't need the bright flash of light or the rockets of rapidly oxidizing bits of true love shooting out of their chests like sparklers to tell him that, this time around, his arrow had sunk deep into its intended target with zero inefficiency.

It had only taken him 325 gods-damned years, but he'd finally done it.

CHAPTER THIRTY-SEVEN

Eros blew air past his lips in a short burst and tugged down the cuffs of his crimson dress shirt. He glanced at Psyche as they walked down the stone corridor to Zeus's office. She clutched the Johnson/Simmons file in her arms, having no trouble keeping up with his hurried pace. Although she nervously fingered the edges of the papers trapped inside the overstuffed folder, her steps were still as surefooted and graceful as always.

Eros requested that she attend the meeting in the notice he'd sent to Zeus. Liz and Leo were set, taking over Follow Your Heart as their own. It had taken another shirtless meeting of the minds to prove to Liz he was who he said he was, but she eventually came around when Psyche revealed her butterfly wings and Hermes put on the trench coat.

Now there was just one last thing to take care of. One last person Eros needed to convince he was for real.

They came to a stop outside the office door, and Psyche handed the folder to Eros so she could adjust his tie. She ran a hand over the lapel of his jacket, then smoothed down a ruffled feather on one of his wings. "Don't worry. Everything is going to be fine. You closed the account."

"Then why am I so nervous?" Eros raked a hand through his hair.

"You shouldn't be. Hey." She pulled his gaze to her. She took the file back from him and tapped his chest with it. "From here on out, come Hades or high water . . . or Hera . . . we'll always be together."

He gave her a lopsided grin. Then, holding the door open for her, he placed a hand on the small of her back and guided her in. He couldn't wait until she found out why he'd called the meeting.

"Right on time." Zeus nodded his approval. He gestured to a small conference table located in one corner of the room. "Please, have a seat."

After each of them had settled into a chair, Eros wasted no time taking the bull by the horns. "I've asked to meet with you today, sir, because I have a request."

"Oh?" Zeus laced his fingers together, looking at Eros and waiting for him to go on.

Eros squared his shoulders. "I'd like to have my title changed. From here on out, I want to be Co-Coordinator of Hearts, and I'd like Psyche to be my partner." He reached across the table, taking her hand in his. "Love needs heart *and* soul."

"I see." Zeus switched his gaze to Psyche. "Is this what you want?

"Oh my fellow gods, yes," she replied without hesitation. "One hundred percent."

She squeezed Eros's hand so hard he mouthed the word, *"ouch."*

"Sorry." She giggled, loosening her grip but not letting go.

The office door swung open suddenly, and Hera breezed in as if she were invited. "I see you've started without me.

No matter. Let's get this over with, shall we? I haven't got all day."

She marched up to the table and waved her hand over the top. A scene from down on Earth, from the recent past, began to play. With a flicking motion, she sent the image of Eros flying through the airport up onto the wall so they could all see it more clearly. "Eros broke the rules."

Psyche let go of his hand to push the file in Hera's direction. Neat block letters in red Sharpie spelled "CLOSED" across the front. "The account is closed."

"The account may be closed, my dear," laughed Hera, her smugness stinging like venom, "but lover boy, here, used his powers, which was expressly forbidden, and therefore, cause for his position as Chief Coordinator of Hearts to be terminated." Satisfied, Hera folded her arms like a petulant child and waited.

"I didn't use my power." Eros pushed his chair out and stood, ready to fight the ensuing battle of wits head on.

"Zeus said no powers and you used them to fly."

"He said no powers until I was ready to strike. Besides, he said I couldn't use *my* powers. He didn't say anything about Psyche or Hermes using theirs. Psyche carried me, with *her* wings."

Psyche was standing now, too. "He's right, I did. The whole way."

"Oh, you two are pathetic," said Hera through clenched teeth, arms dropping to her sides.

"I believe the correct phrase you're searching for is *in love*," replied Eros.

"Zeus." Hera leaned over and pounded a fist on the conference room table. A network of tiny fissures spider-webbed their way across the top. "I demand an immediate demotion!"

Psyche grabbed Eros's hand and turned toward Zeus. "If he goes, I go."

Zeus's arms were folded over his broad chest, the airport scene playing on a loop. He swiped a finger and fast-forwarded to the near future, revealing Leo handing Liz's mother a bouquet of flowers.

Swipe.

Liz taking a wiggling golden doodle puppy with a Happy Valentine's Day balloon tied to its collar from a beaming Leo.

Swipe.

Leo cradling their newborn baby girl while Liz slept soundly in the bed next to him.

Swipe.

Liz and Leo surrounded by a flurry of blue- and brown-eyed grandchildren.

Eros looked Hera in the eyes, no longer believing he was weak at anything. "The fact of the matter is you didn't win. I beat you at your own game. I closed the account, even though you played dirty."

Hera opened her mouth to reply, but Zeus cleared his throat. "Based on the evidence that has been presented here today, I'm afraid I have no choice but to terminate the position of Chief Coordinator of Hearts."

A wicked smile crept over Hera's face, her green eyes shining with triumph.

"Hence forth," continued Zeus, "and forever without end, until I deem otherwise, Eros, you and Psyche shall each be . . ."

Eros gripped his one true love's hand, pulling her closer to his side. Like she'd said, they would face their fate, whatever it may be, together.

"Co-Coordinator of Hearts."

"No!" Hera stomped a high-heeled foot into the carpeting.

Psyche jumped up and down, her laughter pealing through the office. Her arms flew around Eros, crushing him in a hug.

He returned her embrace, hugging her tightly before facing down Hera. "I'm not going anywhere, so you can direct your jealousy and rage toward someone else."

"Don't get cocky, matchmaker," Hera snarled.

"*Moi*?" Eros spread a hand over his chest. He looked at Psyche and added, "Cocky?"

"Yes, that's exactly what I called you." Hera sneered at him, attempting to keep the fight going. "You're so full of yourself right now, aren't you?"

Eros and Psyche laughed, the low, rumbling chuckle in Zeus's chest making them laugh even harder.

"What's so gods-damned funny?" Hera demanded to know.

"After all this time, after thousands of years trying to figure out how to do me in, you finally got one thing right." He stepped forward and handed Hera the golden apple that had magically appeared in his palm. "I am full of myself."

Stunned, the disgruntled Marriage Manager plucked the apple out of his hand.

"Love," said Eros, bowing his head.

He offered Psyche his elbow and led her toward the door. Putting his hand up top for a high five, he winked as Zeus tapped it. With a spring in his step and love in his heart, Life Industries' famous matchmaker, and newly minted Co-Coordinator of Hearts, ducked out of the office right before a shiny golden apple went sailing through the air in the direction of his boss's head.

ABOUT THE AUTHOR

Kerri lives in Michigan with her husband, son and cat they lovingly but aptly refer to as The Maleficence. Mel for short. When she's not writing, she's probably raking leaves, shoveling snow, or looking into where science is on that human cloning thing. If you've enjoyed book one of the Eros & Co. series, visit kerrikeberly.com to subscribe to her mailing list for news and updates on book two, or connect with her on social media at facebook.com/superkeeky, twitter.com/superkeek, and instagram.com/kerrikeberly.